BASILISSA

THE MACMILLAN COMPANY
NEW YORK · BOSTON · CHICAGO
DALLAS · ATLANTA · SAN FRANCISCO

MACMILLAN AND CO., LIMITED
LONDON · BOMBAY · CALCUTTA
MADRAS · MELBOURNE

THE MACMILLAN COMPANY
OF CANADA, LIMITED
TORONTO

Basilissa

A TALE OF THE EMPRESS THEODORA

By John Masefield

1940

THE MACMILLAN COMPANY · NEW YORK

Copyright, 1940, by
JOHN MASEFIELD.

FIRST PRINTING.

PRINTED IN THE UNITED STATES OF AMERICA
AMERICAN BOOK—STRATFORD PRESS, INC., NEW YORK

BASILISSA

THEODORA, the cast mistress of Hekebolos, the Governor of the Pentapolis, came through the hot September streets of Alexandria, seeking the house of the ex-bishop Timotheus, now one of the persecuted heretics. As a little girl she had been one of his flock, when he had been a parish-priest in Byzantium. Though she had not seen him for seven years, nor been his parishioner for double that, and could not expect to be remembered by him, she longed to see a familiar face, and to have his counsel, even his blame. She was in sore need of someone who would only listen.

She was dressed in black, and wept as she went. She had thought, as she sailed from Ptolemais, that she had lost all things, but on the voyage to Alexandria she had lost her last friend, her trusted, devoted, middle-aged maid Demetria, and now was desolate indeed.

Demetria had told her that Timotheus was in Alexandria, living at a sweet-meat shop "at the sign of the Golden Dragon-Fly". She had said: "Timotheus will tell you what to do." Now Demetria was suddenly dead by

this African death that kills in summer, and here was
Theodora alone and broken-hearted, seeking for the sign
which nobody seemed to know.

The hot streets in which she searched were not respect-
able; they were near the port in what was called Tiger
Bay. Each corner house seemed to be a low inn in which
some man or men made drunken music. From some doors
and windows the frizzed and frowzy heads of ladies who
had been up all the night before and were now painting,
so that they might be up all the next night, peered out
upon her, and sometimes asked, "What the devil is the
little one weeping for?" Theodora was too intent upon
her misery to heed the squalor by which she passed. She
passed through the reek of a nut-roaster, and the lesser
smells of fried-fish shops, cosmetic-mixers and the various stinks of poverty. Presently a Syrian woman, with a
pale, ugly, clever face, came by, bearing parcels from the
market. "The Golden Dragon-Fly?" she said, "the sweet
shop? Why, it is there, just at the end of the street there;
on the left of the road there." Looking in that direction,
Theodora saw it, under its gilded sign of the Dragon-Fly;
it was within fifty yards of her. She thanked the woman
sincerely, dried her eyes, looked at her little mirror and
tidied her face.

She entered the sweet-meat shop and asked for some
small refection of cake and cool syrup. She asked the
waiter if the Holy Father, Timotheus, still lived there.

"Yes," he said, "he lives in the garden." He seemed
surprised at the question, as though it were a fact too
well known to be asked about. Seeing that the lady was
from The City and not likely to know, he added, "Of

course, we, here, think that all know. Will you come here, lady?"

He drew aside a blind and opened a door at the back of the shop. She saw in the glare a space of yard, dusty and whitish, with a small white house under some date-palms at the end.

"That is where the Holy Father lives," the Syrian said. "See; he is there, reading."

Her heart leaped at the thought that he was there. She saw, now, that there was a screened bench against one of the walls of the house, under the date-palms, and that a white thing, which she had thought to be a part of the wall, was a white robe and hood. A man in a white-hooded robe was reading a scroll there.

"Would you very kindly ask him if he would see me?" she asked.

"Go to him," the man said. "Everybody goes to him, unless he's praying."

He held the door for her; with a beating heart she went forward slowly. She was not the innocent little child who had won the prize for repeating children's hymns from this man years before. She saw the saint sit forward, and throw back his hood with a frail hand, so that he might see her. She went forward a few steps, then stood, to drop a curtsey; she remained standing, with drooped eyes, as she had been taught in childhood. The saint rose, searching her face, trying to remember her. He saw that her simple, elegant black dress and jewels were from Byzantium; they were those of a lady. Yet the attitude was that of a girl from his Sunday School in the Old Seventh Ward, which was not the haunt of ladies.

She prayed as she waited, that he would tell her to come forward.

"Yes?" he said. "Do you wish to talk with me? Come into the shade and sit here, then."

She looked up at him, then, and saw the familiar face now much older, thinner and more beautiful than when she had seen it last. It flashed into her mind that all things had been burned out of him that so the divine nature might be burned in. He had been reading a scroll headed in red "The Sayings of Our Lord the Christ." It was held partly open in his hand, so that her drooped eyes could read the title.

"Come, sit," the saint said, showing the stone bench on which he had been sitting.

As she sat, she saw that they were not alone. Two women and a man were kneeling in the dust under the date-palms a few yards away, deep in prayer, with open uplifted eyes and moving lips.

"Never heed those," the saint said quietly. "You are from The City and wish to speak with me? Do I know you? Something in your face is familiar."

He sat beside her; his voice was exquisitely gentle.

"I was one of your flock once," she said. "I am the daughter of Acacios, who kept the bears at the Circus. My elder sister was Comito, the actress. I'm afraid you'll remember her. She sent a lot of her lovers to break up your sermons during all one winter; she did not like your doctrines."

The saint smiled, "You are Theodora, then? What happy times those were. Is your Mother alive still?" She shook her head. "And Comito?"

B A S I L I S S A   5

"She married a wood-merchant; she lives in The City still."

"And you?" the saint said, "are not married, but in mourning, and very sad. I will show you that I remember you. You won a little prize, for repeating hymns without mistake; a little blue locket. Do you come for counsel with me?"

"Yes, Father."

"Tell me everything. These people here know that you come for help."

"I have been a sinner, and am punished and in sorrow and know not what to do."

"You know that you have been punished for sin?" the saint said. "You may mistake the natures of sin and of atonement. You were in the theatre?"

"Yes, Father; after you had left The City. I went to the Imperial Ballet School; Comito got me in; she was a great success, you may remember."

The saint nodded; he knew very well the kind of success Comito had had; it had been outstanding and outrageous.

"I wanted to be a dancer," she went on, "but I wasn't very good. I could have gone into the Imperial Ballet, but Comito took me to do mime in the Old Winter Palace. I didn't care about it, but I was a success in that."

"You had a talent for it," the saint said. "Talents given by God must be used. I support your being a success."

"It wasn't the success I wanted," she said.

"It was what you could do well," the saint said. "It was your natural gift."

"You will know the kind of place the Old Winter Palace was," Theodora said, blushing.

"Most theatres are flower-shows," he said, "displaying youth in flower."

The next point in the story was difficult to begin upon. "Did you ever meet a man named Hekebolos, of Tyre?" she asked.

"Ship-owners and Eastern merchants?" he said. "Yes. I met the old merchant Hekebolos when I was in Antioch. He had a son about whom he was alarmed."

"I was one of the causes of the alarm," she said in a low voice.

"That was not the story told to me," the saint said. "He was a very charming young man and you were lovers, I suppose."

"We were madly in love with each other. Then, when I was going to have a child, he wanted to marry me; but I would not let him. His parents would have cast him off. I have had two children by him."

"Are they dead, then? Is that the cause of your grief?"

"They meant nothing to me, Father. I have no love of that sort. I loved Hekebolos and feared that they would make him hate me. They are now in Tyre, with his parents. In a way, my having the children made his parents less bitter. They saw that I hadn't forced him to marry me. They saw that I wasn't a harpy, out for prey. I loved him, Father, very dearly."

"Love is not yet a sin, child," the saint said. "You had left the theatre, of course, and were living with him in The City?"

"Yes; we were very happy; we were with a lot of

young people, all very gay and wild. Then I thought that
I could get him out of that rather thoughtless set and
make him a success. He is utterly charming, Father. I
thought that he would be wonderful as an administrator,
and that everybody would adore him. He did not want to
leave The City. He was a great horseman and knew a
great deal about horses. In that agitation some years ago
about the improvement of the posts, I met old General
Iakobos, who was trying to get a staff together to reform
the Eastern posts. I asked him to take Hekebolos, which
he did. They got on very well together; we went to
Myra, where we had the happiest time we ever had, buying horses, and arranging the relay-posts. He was only a
junior staff-officer, of course, but everybody loved him.
He really did very well; and Iakobos said at the end, 'Of
course, you may have other plans, but if you wish to
serve you'll be employed again, no doubt of that.' I
thought I would be able to get him away, to some pleasant
place, where we could be happy together, where people
would not look down on me as an actress, outside the
pale, and he could show his talents. When we were back
in The City, I heard that the Governorship of the Pentapolis was vacant. I knew it was the lowest of all the
Governorships, but an old General, who was there when
he was young, said that it was an earthly Paradise. He
kept urging us to apply for the place. 'You young
people, with go in you, are just the Governors the Five
Cities need. The place can be made a heaven on earth.
It's been let down, of course, like everything else in the
Empire, but you'd soon pull it round; it only needs go.
Put in for the Governorship. Iakobos'll back you; no-

one'll go against Iakobos.' So we applied for the post.
I must say, I prayed for the appointment. We used to
talk and plan all day and half the night, what we could
do to make it a success. I used to try to meet builders,
planters and engineers; for I kept thinking about new
aqueducts, harbours, bridges and improved cultivation.
I asked all who had been there to come to talk to us. It
was always easy to me to meet clever men in The City.
Hekebolos was very rich; we entertained a lot.

"There was a great delay in making the appointment;
I was in terror that we had been passed over: but General Iakobos worked it at last. Hekebolos was made Governor for three years, and told to sail as soon as might
be. This was a year ago.

"You may imagine how happy I was, and what fun
it was, selecting things to take and choosing our staff,
for we had the right to take three; all the rest were the
Permanents, who were already there, so we were told."

"You found the reality not what you had dreamed
and hoped," the saint said. "You need not tell me. The
Libyans were raiding and sacking; the planters were all
inside the walls; the farms were ruined, and the northerly gales were worse than had ever been known; no help
could be had from anywhere. Was that not the case?"

"It was worse, Father," she said. "What the Libyans
did was nothing to what the gales did. The Libyans
broke the aqueducts: but the gales ruined the harbours.
All the breakwaters of the ports are down, and the harbours are choked with sand or with mud from the floods.
We found the province ruined and without hope of
proper repair."

"Of course, we heard here that the Pentapolis is ruined," the saint said. "But your lover could not blame you for that."

"He could blame me for bringing him there," she said. "He could do that, for it was my doing. There we were, landed with great difficulty in a city besieged, Governors of a Province we could not explore by land because of the Libyans, nor visit by sea because of the gales; everybody was sick, starved and ruined; everything needed doing at once and there was nothing to do it with. We were at the western port, and the Permanents, who might have helped us, were all at the eastern port. We could not go to them, nor send word to them, and they could not come to us nor send word to us. We had no troops; all the garrisons had gone to Antioch in the war-scare; we had very little food, as all the refugees in the city had plundered the granaries; there were some weapons in the armoury; that was all we had. The ship that brought us had to claw off the coast and get away as soon as we were dropped ashore."

"In fact, the District was looking for a Governor," the saint said. "What did the Governor do?"

"We persuaded the citizens to try to drive the Libyans from the walls; we could see that there were not very many camped against us. So we did that, in a surprise attack, and drove them away. Unfortunately, we could not pursue, we'd so few horses, and those all poor from being shut up. Still, we cleared them from near the walls, and rode guard after that, so that they never came back to shut us up again. Then, as the horses got strength we tried to open up the ways, so that we could relieve the other cities; they were shut up still. It was a dreadful season of gales; we could neither send nor receive any message by sea from September to the end of March. In all that time, we were trying to get booms fixed and caissons sunk where the breakwaters were gone in the harbour. We did not have two days' consecutive work on those booms in all the winter; there was either a raging gale or the appalling swell from a gale, which was worse. We were all very short of food, too, and had to dole out the food. Still, we were new to it, and we had the excitement of it, and some encouragement, too, for all the Libyans disappeared. They were really going south to their oases to plant their crops, but they left our roads clear at last. Then we got the spring plantings done, and patched the Ptolemais breakwater, and when a ship called, going east, we sent word home for what we needed: engineers, troops, horses, food.

"I knew by this time," she went on, "that I had made a great mistake in urging him to this life. I ought not to have gone with him, not being married. My position there was impossible and made his much more difficult. Still, we managed until March; then the spring sickness fell on us, with fever and depression; we were all ill with it, and a good many who were weak from want of proper food and sick from being ruined, died. It was then that my lover began to curse me for bringing him to it, out of his happy life in The City, and condemning him to it for three years. He said that his relatives had always said that I should ruin him, but that for love of me he had defied them. He said that he had always distrusted this going to Africa, but that I had pleaded him into it. He

was ill at the time, of course. Then, when the sickness
was beginning to go and the sun shone again and all
seemed to smile, the locusts came. They are said to come
every seventh year, and had missed the last seventh year.
Perhaps they came in double strength to make up for it.
They came in clouds and ate every green thing in sight.
I sometimes went out into the country to help in fighting
the locusts. I could hear the craunch of their thousands
of jaws on the leaves. The locusts were bad enough, but
I always said that the Libyans would not raid us after
the locusts had been with us; and they did not. But our
crops were ruined; we were even shorter of food than before; and my presence became more and more hateful to
him and to the citizens. They were saying that they were
not going to be dictated to by their Governor's mistress;
he was saying that if he hadn't been a fool he could have
made a wonderful marriage in The City and been Kallimachus' heir; you will have heard of Kallimachus the
horse-racer; he is one of the western lords who owns
about a hundred towns and twenty silver mines. In the
end, Hekebolos told me that he had decided, on his own
loathing of the sight of me, backed by the strong recom-
mendations of the citizens, to fling me out and be done
with me. Before a ship came to take me here, I was a sort
of prisoner, with my maid and dear friend Demetria. He
had left Ptolemais by the time a ship arrived; the Permanent Officials thrust me aboard. By that time, we were
both ill with the Summer Death, as they call it; and Demetria died while we were still on the coast. She knew
that you were here now, and always said, 'He will tell
you what to do.' So I have ventured, Father. Here I am,

a sinner, punished, desolate and in sore need of guidance."

"We are all that," the saint said, "but we do not all
have the wit to know it. You are desolate, you say. How
far are you desolate? You have the look of one not quite
without wealth."

"I have money," she said. "At least I have jewels
which can easily be sold for money, enough to keep me
for three or four years, even if I live extravagantly as I
have lived lately."

"That is much," the saint said, "if you wish to live in
the world; but do I read you aright? You wish that?"

"I long to be out of the world. I hate the world. I am
young, and already every ambition that I have had has
been blasted. I ask only to be helped to some house of Sisters, where I can live in peace, thinking only of God, and
imploring His mercy."

"You are not one to be helped to any house of Sisters,"
the saint said. "We in religion have ways of knowing
those who may help religion and the ways in which that
help may be given. Sisterhood is not your way, believe
me."

"What way is my way?" she asked. "For I have lost
my way and know not what to do."

"You have entered upon your way," the saint said.
"But the entrance to any way is difficult. You entered
yours by the wrong gate, and have been turned back
from it. You did nothing but good to young Hekebolos."

"You do not feel that I ruined him?"

"I knew his father, who told me, that his son was living with a young actress and causing him much anxiety,

but he said, 'I cannot but feel grateful to her for one thing; she has got him out of the horse-racing set; he was going straight to ruin among those racing-men; she has even got him to work a little.' I did not hear your name mentioned. I judge that another woman took sides with him against you at the time of your trouble in the Five Cities?"

"Yes, Father."

"I will not blame love," the saint said. "All love is an image of the divine love. You used your love wholly for a man's great advantage and the right use of his talents; all that I approve."

"All my life has ended," Theodora said. "I know not what to do. I gave Hekebolos all that I had to give of thought and feeling. Now my life is dead in my heart."

"I do not see you as dead," the saint said. "I see you as tested. It is at the outset that candidates are tested. You know the language of the racing-men. You have been run in a trial heat."

"Yes," she said bitterly, "and beaten, and driven out of the Stadium, lame. I ask for some shed where a lame horse can wait for death, or some knacker's yard where such a creature can be knocked on the head."

"There are no such places for living human souls," the saint said. "You have been set in a great stage, and given great gifts, and are now tried and proven fit for great things. You will remain in the world; and the verdict of the world is very much that of the poets, who take the side of the prodigal who loves. You have been tried in a lesser chaos, with a poor helper. You will be tried in a greater chaos, with others of greater strength."

"I have no strength left; no love left. I loathe the very thought of all my life with Hekebolos."

"Yes, perhaps. You said a moment ago that your life is dead in your heart. There are all sorts of lives in the heart; when one dies another springs. In one sense the human heart must die before the divine heart can begin to beat there. You are a part of the Divine Nature which has its hopes and its charity for you. Will you not give it Faith, in return? This City is hateful to you. You are still all shaken from your friend's death. Do not stay here. Go to the bigger stage; go home to The City. But go by way of Antioch, for that is the place now most important to the whole Christian world. You, who will be much in the world, must see that frontier and its problem. Always at this season there are ships sailing to Antioch and thence to The City. In Antioch you must seek out Stephen; I will give you a letter to him. He is a teacher more utterly exiled than myself. He will give you deeper help than I can give. My own gift is seeing what a person amounts to; I see that you amount to much."

"O Father, that you should give me hope and help like this."

"Help and hope are always very near," he said. He looked at her with his clear eyes, in which no guile had ever lurked. "But go to Antioch, for that is where the problem lies, whether the East is to be Christian or not. If we are Christians there, we shall see the East Christian in thirty years. If we are heathen there, alas . . ."

He looked at the three who had been praying; they had now risen to their feet. "Chrysa," he said, "and you,

Artibazan, this lady seeks for a ship to Antioch. What are there, that you know?"

"There are three sailing tomorrow," Chrysa said. "The *Moonbeam*, the *Orontes* and the *Silver Bird*."

Artibazan said, "The *Orontes* will sail at dawn. One going in her would have to go aboard tonight."

"That would be possible," Theodora said.

"Go in her, then," the saint said. "There is a very good text for a setter-forth: 'Commit thy way unto the Lord; trust also in Him; and He shall bring it to pass.' I shall hear of you again; for you 'amount to much', as I said. The prizes you will win will be better than little blue lockets."

The setting sun was glowing on his exquisite old face and the white building. He looked like a transfigured saint sitting in the gate of Paradise; she kept the memory of his beauty in her heart till death. This old man had known all the sciences and arts; he had renounced great wealth and position to become a priest; then, after illumination, he had been driven out as a heretic; now, in exile, more light had come to him; he could give light to those who sat in darkness.

"Father," she said, "you have helped me more than I can say. I have eaten and drunken balm."

"Somewhere you helped me," the old man said. "If you receive something, be sure, you once gave it. Be watchful in the ship. Chrysa, are any of our friends going in the *Orontes?*"

"No, Father."

"I will send a word to the chief steward," he said,

"when I send the letter for you to give to Stephen. That shall be there tonight. Now, my little parishioner, farewell. Be of Hope, Faith and Charity, and nothing in the world will harm you."

She accepted his bidding as the sick man obeys his physician. She sailed at dawn the next morning, having with her the saint's sealed letter to Stephen. She often kissed this note. It was addressed to Stephen at Number Seven, the Water-Gate, at Antioch, in the saint's bold and beautiful hand in dull red ink. It was sealed with his seal of the Cock of Dardanos. It was a precious relic to her throughout her life. Always throughout her life, she cherished the memory of that holy man whom all the churches had persecuted. He had given her hope and faith and charity when all seemed gone into hatred and despair. No day passed, thenceforward, without loving and grateful thoughts of him; he had said that "she amounted to much", when she had felt that she was nothing.

The ship was so crowded with passengers that Theodora had little rest aboard her. Pilgrims going to the tomb of St. Onosius filled all the forward half, the Sisterhood of Saint Zenobitica, going to their Patron's festival, filled the stern, two of them in Theodora's cabin. In the waist, some athletes, going to the Games, and two Greek merchants, one in oil, the other in figs, loitered on deck in the sun, mocked the pilgrims and ogled the women. All day long, the heat below-decks grew, till the Sisters languished. They could not venture on deck, for there the athletes, stripped naked, were at their water-fights and other unseemliness. When the sun was down, in the

cool of the evening, then, veiled, they went on deck in
company. Then, Theodora, who all day long had heard
their moanings, prayers and holy ejaculations, had to
listen to their singing, while, in the bows, the pilgrims,
in different dialects, started their praises of Onosius, including the Life of the Saint, interspersed, at every tenth
line, with his famous utterance concerning the Nature
of God. Betwixt the two parties of the devout, the athletes
mocked and were rude; though they, too, had their de-
votions; they poured oil and cried to St. Elias to give
them the strength and speed of light. When their brief
prayer was done, they sang things less seemly, till the
pilgrims roughly, and the Sisters with dignity, reproved
them. At midnight a pilgrim who was doing penance before visiting the holy tomb always went over the cata-
logue of his sins in a loud voice.

As the passing of the day was tedious, so was the passing of the coast. The winds at that season were the light
land-and-sea-breezes which the seamen knew well how
to take advantage of. In some of the little ports they tied
up for parts of a day, either to take in cargo or to wait
for the wind to spring up. For one night, the ship lay in
the harbour at Tyre. Just ashore there, as she well knew,
in one of those fair houses, were Hekebolos' parents and
her own two children. She was not going to try to see
them. Anything that belonged in any way to Hekebolos
was in all ways loathsome to her at that time.

During her years with Hekebolos she had lived and
travelled like a lady of wealth. On arrival at Antioch,
she went to the famous inn, known as the Daphne House,
where she planned to stay for a few days, while she con-

sulted the wise Stephen, and enquired about the prospects of peace. She had been out of the world for a full
year, almost without news of what was stirring. She
knew that the Persian frontier had been a debatable
land for years. She knew, too, that an unlucky aristocrat,
the nephew of the late Emperor, the young Hypatius,
had been sent to the Persian King, to arrange a lasting
peace just as she set out for the Five Cities. In the last
few days, she had heard that Hypatius had failed in this.
She found at once that Antioch thought of little but the
prospects of war.

"We shall have war in the spring," the hotel manager
said. "The word goes that we have begun to send our
army eastwards. A man was here from Myra last week;
he said we'd a thousand horse there already. 'Our whole
army will be wintering there or near there,' he said. If
the Persian King does not climb down, there'll be war
by Easter."

"And what do you think of that?" she asked.

"Our Emperor couldn't have a better time," he said.
"The Persian King is beset by the robber-tribes all along
his northern province. If we could have the frontier question settled, once for all, then business might return.
That's how Antioch looks at it."

In the cool evening, she walked from the inn to the
Water-Gate, to give the letter to Stephen. Her inn was
in one of the two great streets which crossed in the heart
of the city. Turning away from the city's heart (the
cross-roads), she walked down hill towards the river.
The Water-Gate was at the bridge above the port. The
Gate itself was a noble guard-house and customs office.

No. 7, the Water-Gate, was one of a row of little old houses, once the quarters of the dockyard officers, but now come down in the world. The woman at No. 7 said that Stephen was away.

"He's gone up to the north," she said. "I don't know when he'll be back: not for some days. The roads are so uncertain there now that these robbers are riding. He'll hardly be back this week: but you might look in, in case."

This was a disappointment to her; still, there could be no great hurry. She walked back, admiring the great beauty of the scene in the glow of the sunset. She was full of confidence, that Timotheus had spoken truth, that all was going to be well with her. Her past was over.

She returned to her hotel, meaning to go through an hour or more of the long and hard exercises learned by her in the Imperial Dancing-Schools. She had never neglected them. To be youthful, graceful and elegant always, at all times, was the dancing-girl's duty at the Old Winter Palace, whose management fined any least failure, and sacked at the third offence. As she went through her exercises, she thought that when she returned to The City she would open some gymnasium, for giving grace, new youth and elegance to women who had lost these things. She was young; the world and life were still before her.

When she had finished her exercises and bathed, she leisurely dressed. The fancy came to her, to unpack her choicest dresses and dress in her best with her jewels. These things were in a coffer locked with two keys and lashed with a hide-cord. She undid the knots of the cord, unlocked the coffer, and laid back the thin dark shawl of fine wool which covered the dresses. Under a layer of clothes she had put a soft red leather wallet, containing her treasure of jewels. It was not there. Her pearls, rubies and sapphires were gone. Where had they gone? She had seen them at Alexandria. She had with her own hands packed, locked and lashed them there, just before they were taken to the ship. She had travelled with the coffer to the ship; it had been in her cabin with the two nuns during the voyage, hardly out of her sight. How could she have been robbed? Yet she had been robbed. Someone had very cleverly undone the lashings, opened the locks with a master-key, slipped the bundle away, re-locked, re-lashed and gone, with nine-tenths of her wealth. Or had it been done at the hotel? Had someone come into that locked and bolted room while she had been at the Water-Gate? She would never know; but the fact was, she had lost her wealth. Not all was gone, of course; she had been on the world since childhood and had learned the caution of the hunted. She carried some treasure about her person; now that it was too late, she wished that she had carried it all. Going over the weary days of the voyage, she was certain that the cabin had never been left empty. She or one of the nuns had been there always. The hotel window was bolted and the shutters barred with iron. A trusty guard was on watch always in the corridor, and her door had been locked during her absence. The best hotel in Antioch would be ever on the watch for thieves; besides, she had been away so short a time. She had been warned in childhood that a ship was a most unsafe place and an inn no safer. She remembered a tale of General Cyril's, how some thieves had once robbed him in a ship, by burning, as was thought, a sleep-inducing drug in the deck beneath him, so that he and his companions slept heavily while they were robbed. She and the nuns might have been so drugged, or their food or drink tampered with.

She was dashed by her loss. She had told Timotheus that she had enough to live on, even extravagantly, for three or four years. But now she was a thousand miles from The City and had only enough for three or four months. Like most girls of the theatre, she knew that jewels will ever fetch money; but like all who have been desperately poor, she knew very well how desperately hard a bargain the jewel-buyer drives.

She pulled out her remaining treasures of rings, pendants and necklets. They were very beautiful. They had been given to her by Hekebolos in Byzantium three years before. She knew that he had given a great price for them, and they had been very much admired. They would surely sell for a great price. She would reach The City safely, and be able to start this gymnasium. Still, she remembered bitter days in childhood, when she had gone to the pawn-shop with great hopes, and come home dashed. She had a little terror in her now. Strangers who try to sell jewels are sometimes held by the police. Women who try to sell jewels are often robbed.

In the gay talk of her friends in The City during the last four years, she had heard much of jewels and jewellers. She had heard of the firms of Avarni, in Alexandria, and of the great Mithridates, the Persian, at Antioch. She had seen the sign of Mithridates a little

way up the street from her hotel; she would go there
betimes on the morrow. She went to bed that night in
some anxiety, yet telling herself, that all would be well;
had not the saint said so?

In the morning, she selected the choicest of her pieces
and set out to Mithridates' shop, which was a long, well-
lighted studio, with a counter and show-cases at one end,
and working jewellers at the other. Mithridates, a short,
upright Persian with a face of much goodness and prob-
ity, stood near the door. Her heart was cheered by his
face; she saw that he would not try to cheat her. He
knew at a glance, by the instinct of his craft, that she
had come to sell, not to buy.

"Take a seat, lady," he said. "You have some piece
that you wish me to see?"

"I wish to sell this," she said, handing the piece.

He took it, looked at it; put it on the counter and
touched it in a peculiar way; then lifted it again and examined it with minute attention.

"Were these stones sold to you as genuine?" he asked.

"They were sold as genuine. Surely there is no doubt?"

"No. These are not genuine. They are the very best
make-believe, in a very fine setting. The setting is precious; worth twenty pieces perhaps. The stones are not
worth three. My man John is perhaps better at these
things than I. John, what do you make of these?"

His foreman, a curly, hairy and shaggy man, who
looked a good honest fellow, came limping up. He examined the piece and shook his head.

"It's a rare setting," he said. "If these stones were

sold to you as genuine, you ought to recover in the courts. Did they charge you much for it?"

"It was an expensive piece," she said. "What are the stones, if they are not genuine? They must be jewels."

"I wouldn't say what they are," John said. "Some of these philosophers' stones, as we call them; they make them in the ovens in the East. They are good imitations, and valuable as bits of skill, they must be hard to make; but they're not jewels and have no market value. It is a pity, for being false, they take away the value of the setting, which is good work. It isn't worth anything at present. It is an attempt to deceive." Plainly, he was telling the truth.

"Are these other pieces also false stones?" she asked.

He looked very carefully at each one. "Yes," he said. "They are all false. They are the kind of thing made for what is called 'The Mug's Market', the very rich young man. These have been mostly made by one man, who is a very good designer. Apart from the design, they are nothing."

"How can you tell that they are imitations?" she asked.

"It is our craft and knowledge," Mithridates said. "But feel for yourself. Here are the real stones." He pulled open a drawer and shewed deep wooden compartments half full of gems of different kinds. "All these are real stones," he said. "Lift some of them to your lips and cheek; then lift your own."

She did as she was bid and felt the unmistakable difference. When these gifts had been made to her both she and Hekebolos had been too much in love to have

any thought of fraud. She knew that the jeweller had
been fashionable and the price paid great. She knew that
in some matters, the rich will buy whatever is most expensive.

"You would not care to buy these?" she asked.

Mithridates shook his head.

"We could not sell that kind of thing," he said. "It
would not pay us even to buy the settings. My advice to
you would be to take them to the man who sold them;
he might buy them back."

She thought that the man was a thousand miles away,
and that it was now doubtful, if she could ever get to
him. How was she to pay her passage? How was she even
to pay her hotel bill at Antioch? She had very little
ready money left, and now here she was in an expensive
city, a thousand miles from any friend, with her capital
gone. She knew from the jewellers' looks, that they knew
all about her, that she had been loved by a rich young
man, and was now abandoned in a foreign city with
nothing but his gifts between her and want. Well, if
she were ruined, these men would not see her admit it.

"You have other pieces, perhaps," Mithridates said,
"that you might like me to value?"

She shook her head. "No, I have no others. But it
occurs to me, that you must be visited by many men
from the East, who might care for these things. Would
you care to advance me money on them and dispose of
them when you can?"

He shook his head. "We have merchants from the
East in the spring and early summer; but the season is
long over for this year. And the situation is so grave

with the likelihood of war that we do not expect any Eastern merchants next year."

"Is it so bad as that?" she asked.

"It is as bad as it can be," Mithridates said. "There's a Persian Trade Commission in the city now, staying at The Sun. They told a friend of mine they could not book a single order; everybody expects war by Easter. It is well known that the Emperor has his army stretched along all Karamania ready to concentrate on Antioch in the Spring. Well, what will make the Persian King wait for that?"

"The northern robbers who are raiding," Theodora said.

Mithridates shook his head. "Not so, lady; believe me," he said. "But as to these pieces of yours, I am sorry not to help; that kind of thing is outside our usual custom which is more for what you see. I fear you will have difficulty in disposing of them here at this time. Their maker is more likely than anyone here to buy them, if you would take them to their maker."

"The maker is a thousand miles away," she said. "You can think of no one here who would be likely to buy?"

"The bottom is out of the luxury business," he said. "Everybody is asking jewellers to buy. Of course, there are many jewellers in Antioch, but they will all say the same thing. The certainty of war makes it dangerous to spend money."

She thanked him for his honesty and courtesy. Going out into the street, she had a moment of cruel humiliation; she was now a pauper in a strange land, with a very hard time ahead of her. As she glanced up the street, she saw the shining rayed sign of the big Sun Inn, and remembered that there the Persian Trade Commission had its quarters.

"Surely," she said to herself, "the Persians have ever cared for Greek jewellery. One of them might care to see these settings. It is true, that these men are probably mainly silk merchants, but it is worth trying."

She walked into the Inn, went boldly to the office, and said to the clerk, that she wished to look at the register, at the names of the Persian Trade Commission. She saw, by turning back, that the Persian Trade Commission had been there for ten days, but their names were written in a script which she could not read. A man who was standing near the register, going over the items in a bill, looked up and asked, "Which member of the Commission did you wish to see, Madam?"

She looked at him. He was no doubt a Greek from The City; a well-dressed man of good manners, of the middle-age, for his somewhat curly hair was grizzled, with a well-shaped head, clear-cut, good features, and air of much power and determination; a certain coldness of force about him, she thought, which might become cruel.

"Whichever may be interested in jewellery," she said.

She knew, that the clerk was about to say, that no touting saleswoman could shew her wares there, but this stranger seemed to have a reason for beginning a talk with her. She judged, that she was looking her best, and that most men longed to have such a reason at such a time. However, this man seemed to wish to help her, for he said at once, "Will you come with me? They are in the courtyard here."

He led the way across the hotel to the patio at the back. There, half-a-dozen distinguished-looking young Persians sat upon stools by the basin of the fountain. They were intent upon a game. A seventh young man stood near them also intent. Theodora thought that the half-dozen had been divided into two sides of three apiece. Each of these six held crumbs in their right hands. At the word of command from the seventh each of the six dropped the crumb into the basin to the gold and silver fish which swam there. The seventh noted which side had a crumb first eaten. The game ended as Theodora drew near. The stakes were paid to the winners and the two sides looked to see who was coming with their friend.

Her guide explained in some unknown tongue that the lady wished to learn which of them was interested in jewellery; so much she divined; but he then added something, which made each one of the six look at her in a peculiar way, which she could not quite understand. The look had in it something of hardness, something of suspicion, something of coming suddenly *en garde*. She knew from their look and bearing, that these men were odd merchants. All were less than thirty. Three of them seemed to her to be only about twenty-five. They had an ease and a carelessness which could only come from an ease and carelessness of life; all were men of birth and breeding; they were now very polite and welcomed her. The guide explained again, this time in Greek, that the lady wished to know which of them was interested in jewellery. One of them explained in good Greek that he cared for sapphires, and asked, if she had any. She explained, that she had none, but that she had some per-

sonal decorations, with delicate settings, which she wished
to sell, and had heard that the Trade Commission was in
the hotel, and had thought that perhaps one of the Commission might be a jewel merchant. Alas, two of them
explained, they were not jewel merchants, nor indeed
merchants at all, but officers of the Persian Office of Foreign Commerce. They offered her sweetmeats and sorbet;
she talked with them for a few minutes. Their older
friend, who was certainly a Greek, asked her, if she had
been long in Antioch and had come directly from The
City. He seemed relieved to find, that she had come from
Alexandria and had not been in The City for a little
more than a year.

He added, "As it happens, there is a jeweller near
here, who might be of help to you. He has done little
things for me from time to time. If you would have no
objection, I would show you to his shop; he is close to
this, just off the main road."

Theodora always shrank from the offers of help of unknown men; however, she had no reason to distrust this
man; her need was great; she, therefore, accepted the
offer gladly.

"It is but a step," he said.

The members of the Commission bade her farewell
with much charming politeness; the older man showed
her out, and then into the street, to a lane leading down
the hill.

"This man to whom we're going," he said, "is called
Red Peter; he is a very shrewd jeweller. What he does
not know about stones is not worth knowing. He does a

large business inland with Persians and even into India; some of his clients may care for your things."

With this, they reached the door of a discreet house, with nothing of the shop about it, except the notice 'Peter & Son, Eastern Merchants'. Peter himself opened the door to them, and greeted the elderly man with cringing effusiveness. Theodora concluded that it was the Son, now, not Peter. The man was youngish, red-haired, somewhat bald already, pale-faced and weary-looking, with a thin red beard. He was all oil to the elderly man, but his very astute eye was already on Theodora for what she might be worth to him.

"I will leave you, then," the elderly man said to her. He said to Peter, "This lady has some settings to dispose of. Please see to her for me."

As Theodora thanked him, and saw him bow and turn away, she thought that she did not know his name, and that the words "see to her for me" were odd ones to have chosen. She saw at once that Peter had shrewdly noted every fact about her and about her probable knowledge of her guide.

"A very nice gentleman," he said. "You know him well; hey?"

"No," she said.

"You come from The City; hey?"

"Yes," she said.

"You got settings; hey? No one wants settings. I was with one of my friends last night. He said, 'I got five hundred settings I can't sell.' "

"These are unusual," Theodora said.

"No one wants unusual settings," he said.

He knew that Theodora was in difficulties and wished to raise the wind; he had seen a hundred such; and he knew well that despair and need would bring such a woman down to anything he cared to offer. As she displayed her first piece, he saw that it was of a kind that would please a client of his even then in the city, an elderly Persian with a young friend.

"I look at your settings," he explained, "because my friend brings you. But no one buys second-hand goods. They will not wear what others have worn; that brings bad luck; hey? These things are worthless; hey? The stones are false."

"I only offer them as settings," she said. "They are handsome decorations."

"No one buy them here," he said. "These are western taste; that not go here in the East; hey? This is the East; hey, where they go more for colour; more for the peacock's tail and the butterflies; hey? You got other pieces?"

"Yes," she said.

"How many pieces? You let me see the pieces."

"This is one," she said, shewing the piece she had already shewn. "Do you wish to offer for it?"

"How much you want for it?"

"How much will you give?" she said, knowing that it would (as it did) provoke the reply she had so often heard in the pawn-shops of her infancy: "I can't be buyer and seller, too."

"Nor can I," she said. "If you, who are a possible buyer, cannot make a fair offer, I must go to those who can."

"No one can make an offer," he said. "No one want settings."

"Very well, then," she said, "I will take them to their maker. Good morning."

"Come, come," he said, as soon as he saw that she was going, "that was not what I meant. I say, this is a bad season; nobody got any money, what? No one buy. I cannot sell these things, even suppose I buy, see, not till spring-time, when the Barbarians come. Suppose the robbers are on the road, so that the caravans cannot come; suppose there come war, as everyone believe; I lose my money again, see."

"I do not see," she answered. "These are not decorations for Barbarians, but for ladies of fashion, who will pay handsomely for them."

"These kind are not the fashion," he said. "The fashion is all for these small pins; these big set pieces are for Barbarians."

"What will you offer for this one?" she asked.

"I will give fifteen for the one you show, and expect a little one thrown in."

"I will go to my friend," she said. "You do not know your business."

He let her reach the door and pass into the sun, and then came after her, with the words, "Now, lady; no need to run away like that. See, now. I would not do this for anyone but you, now. But you are a friend of the Silpi, as we call him. I like to oblige any friend of the Silpi. I offer you something a little better. You I dare-say want a little money; now I maybe want a little jewel to show to one of my clients. He just got a girl, see; he want to make present, not too expensive. Very likely, he not like the false stones. I do not know. I think I give you twenty for the big setting."

"You will not," she said. "I had rather take it back to Byzantium and sell it to the maker."

The remark was one of a kind usual in bargainings; he said, "You live in The City, hey? Where you live in Antioch, now?"

"I do not see that that concerns you," she said. "Are you going to give me forty for the big setting?"

"I am not. Twenty was what I said. It is not worth it, but you are a friend of Silpi, and besides I like you. I like the way you do business, see."

"We are not doing business," she said.

"See, now. You a lady," he answered. "Ladies they not understand about business. They think it all done for they got bright eyes, see? It not so. Trade go from bad to shocking, nothing to do with eyes at all. You like to leave this setting with me a day or two, maybe I see my client who got the girl, see."

"No," she said. "I shall not leave any of them with anyone. If you care to pay me forty pieces for this big one, I will let it go."

"You ask forty. I tell you honestly no man pay twenty for a thing like this. I take back twenty, see. I give seventeen, see? You not know your business. The stones worthless, the setting all old."

"In that case, of course, you cannot want it," she said. She gathered the piece with a swift sure hand and passed out of the shop.

"See, now," he pleaded. "You not take things so."

However, she was out of the place; he followed, saying, "You wait a little, see. I perhaps have another look."

She knew that this sort of dealer would gladly spend a day bargaining over anything offered for sale. She knew that indifference was her best policy. She had no doubt that he had scented a bargain, and would not readily let it go. She remembered a phrase of Hekebolos, for a dealer in The City—"One of these second-rate hyaenas, always after a second-hand bone"; well, this was such an one.

"See here," he said, at her elbow. "You come back, see; we go on with our talk, see. Perhaps my client who got the girl, I go see him, he perhaps offer a lot of money, more than its worth, see."

"Go to him, if you wish," she said. "I will perhaps call again in a few days, to ask. Good morning."

She went swiftly out and away, but heard him follow her calling to her to come back. She knew that he followed her into the main street, where she supposed he gave up the chase. She returned to her hotel, and reckoned up all her money. It was little enough, when all was told. She would have enough to pay her hotel bill. But would she? She was not sure that she had enough even for that. Then, for some unknown period of time, she would have to stay in Antioch till she could find a ship going to The City. She would have to sail during the next two or three weeks, for the sailing season was almost at an end. In The City, her sisters would help her to find work. She would have to get back to The City as soon as she possibly could. But how was she to pay for her passage of a thousand miles by sea? She would have

to go by sea; she could not possibly afford the land route.
If she delayed for only a few days, she might lose the
last ship of the season and be stranded at Antioch till
April. She had a very unpleasant twenty minutes, thinking of these things.

Then she wondered who this man was whom the
dealer called Silpi. What was he? What was he doing
with this Trade Commission? And what was the Trade
Commission? It certainly had nothing to do with Trade.
"Officers of the Office of Foreign Commerce," she reflected. The men were well-born, well-bred Persians, no
doubt, but they had nothing to do with commerce. They
were cavalry officers doing a little spying for the Persian
King, no doubt. They had been along the coast no doubt,
westward to Myra and beyond, southward to Tyre and
beyond, to learn the truth of this reported gathering of
the Empire's troops for war in the Spring. If that was
what they were, who was this Silpi? Was he an Imperial
officer with an eye upon them? Was he an Imperial
Secret Service man? What little jobs had Peter & Son
done for him? The man had been courteous and kind to
her, but she had not taken to his face. There was something secret and sinister about the face. Silpi. She could
think of no man nicknamed Silpi. In her set, which spoke
of most men and women famous in The City by some
nickname or other, the name of Silpi was unknown. He
must have been out of The City for some years certainly.
However, her main concern was to find a cheap lodging
at once.

Here the thought of the saint was helpful again. She
felt sure that the woman at No. 7, the Water-Gate,

would find a room for her. She would go there at once,
to ask.

On her way, she thought she had better visit one of
the state pawn-shops, to pawn one or more pieces of her
jewellery, so that she might have money enough to pay
her hotel bill beyond all doubt. The state pawn-shops
were known to her from childhood. They were run by
very shrewd men, who knew to a nicety the lowest market sale value of every article offered and then would
advance up to one-tenth of that sum. Still, she wished
to be able to pay her hotel bill without any trouble when
it was handed to her; if the pawn-shop would lend her
a few pieces on her small jewels she would surely be able
to do this. If Peter later on bought the bigger jewels, she
could either retrieve the pledges or sell the tickets to
Peter. She had not been into a pawn-shop for a good
many years, but found them unchanged; they gave her
a shrewd tenth of what seemed to be the sale value. She
pledged two small jewels, with the knowledge, that the
trade knew very well what to offer for her kind of ware,
and that now she knew what to expect. If Peter or some
other did not buy her goods, she would find it hard
enough to reach The City before sailings ceased for the
winter.

However, she was much cheered at this time by the
thought of the saint in Alexandria. He was her friend;
he had urged her to come to Antioch; he had helped her
profoundly; and had said that Stephen would help her
even more. Stephen would be back from the frontiers
soon, within the week, she hoped. She knew that saints
like Timotheus and Stephen could always work miracles,

even against want of money, so that possibly they would
contrive to help her to a passage, if not by sea, then,
perhaps, as companion to some wealthy woman going
overland. These thoughts came flitting gaily in the sur-
face of her mind, but behind them was always the dark
doubt and fear of being stranded in that far town; she
was grimly alone there; ah, if Demetria were with her
still.

At the Water-Gate, she found that the woman who
tended No. 7 had a little room to let at her own house
next door at No. 9. She saw that the room was clean and
light; she therefore took it for a week. Finding the
woman thoughtful and good she asked her why everybody talked so surely of war coming in the spring. The
woman said that it was generally believed to be due to
some misunderstanding. The Emperor Justinus had sent
Hypatius to make peace with the Persian King, who, as
she said, was eager for peace. At the frontier, there was
some unhappy chance. Hypatius, some said, insisted that
the King should come to him, he being the representative
of the Emperor. King Chosroes, the Persian, being eager
for peace, might have done this, but someone, so it was
reported, persuaded him that the request was a deliberate
insult. He had, therefore, refused to see Hypatius at all.
After that, there had come some harsh words from
Justinus, and the report that the Imperial army had
moved eastward. She added, that the whole matter was
so cloaked in lies carefully spread abroad by one side or
the other that it was hard to know where the truth and
the right lay; both sides had done grievous ill to the
other. She thought that the Emperor could settle the

matter in five minutes, if he would come to see the King, "but pride lies in the way, now; and they say, too, that he is not strong enough for the journey."

This led to enquiry, what ships were likely to be sailing for The City. The woman said that there were two, but she rather thought that they had sailed that morning. "But if you will come to the end of the lane you will look right down the wharf and see if they are there." Thirty yards of walking showed the wharf to be empty, the ships had gone. "It's late in the season now," the woman said. "I'm not sure there'll be another ship sailing now. Is it so important that you should go to The City?" Theodora told the woman frankly something of her present situation, and knew that she had won her sympathy. "But don't be distressed," the woman said. "Master Stephen will be back in a few hours at most now; he is the one who'll be able to advise. And now, if I might say a word, I'd have your things moved out of the big hotel, before they charge you for another day, as they will if you leave it until noon. And I'll send the boy Ajax up for your things with the hand-cart."

Theodora went back to the hotel to pay and leave. As she went in, the hotel men looked at her somewhat strangely, not as they had looked on her arrival the day before. She was very quick to notice the effects she had produced; she had been on the stage long enough for that. She felt sure that in some way word had gone about that she had been trying to sell jewels and had been to the pawn-shop. She went across to the office and asked for her bill. The Manager said that her bill had been taken to her room but that she had been found to have gone

out; here it was. Unfortunately, he said, the hotel was very
full at that season and he had had to make other arrangements for the room in which she had slept. Her things
had been packed in her absence and were ready in the
hall for her. In fact, as she glanced over the bill, she saw
them there. Word of her poverty had spread; she was being got rid of. She was thankful that she had pawned her
little jewels; without that extra money she would have
been lost. She kept a steady face, and paid the bill. She
wondered how it was that they had guessed that she was
poor. No doubt they had guessed or been told that she
was trying to raise money on her jewellery. Had Silpi
told them, or one of the Trade Commission? Had Peter
followed her to the hotel, and spread the news, so that
she might be pressed for her bill, and perhaps be made
glad to take less for her jewels? Or had one of the hotel
staff followed her and seen her enter the pawn-shop? Or
had the police, who doubtless had some eye on strangers
in Antioch now that the Persian question was so acute,
seen her in the hotel and again in the pawn-shop, and
sent word to the hotel to be careful? Could it be that
Silpi was one of the police, perhaps a Chief of Police or
head of an Intelligence Department? With some difficulty, she persuaded the hotel staff to load her goods on
Ajax's barrow, and so took leave of wealthy life, as she
supposed, forever. She was going back to poverty, anxiety
and hard work. Well, she was used to all three from
childhood.

On her way down to the Water-Gate, she asked Ajax,
who was an African, what the two ships were, which

were just coming up the river under oars. They were painted white, and carried blue streamers.

"Him despatch boats," Ajax said. "Him go between here and Smyrna."

She knew that there was such a service, carrying officials, mails and messengers. "But why two?" she asked.

"Him bring some weapons for de war," Ajax said. "In de spring we fight de Persians; we cut deir troats, I tink."

The ships drew in to the wharf as she reached the Water-Gate. She was met by the landlady, with the news, that a gentleman had come to see her, and was waiting at the end of the road. For an instant, she thought that Silpi had been attracted, and had followed her out; she then saw that it was Peter, still intent on a bargain.

"See," he said, coming up to her. "I your friend, see? I see my friend, see, about them things. He give perhaps twenty piece for that one. You give me them settings, see. I give you twenty piece, see, and chance he give me twenty. I run the risk, see, because I like you. I not do it for anyone. You give me the piece, see, and I give you twenty piece. Why you turn away? I go all over the city to see my friend and try to sell your thing. I your friend, see? I go up and down, and wear out my shoes, to get you a good price. I give twenty piece. You let me take all you have, maybe I give you something handsome thrown in."

She got rid of him by going indoors. He hung about outside, walking up and down and sometimes calling out from the street, that he would give twenty, though he

would lose money by it, but didn't mind doing that for a
friend. He stayed there for more than two hours.

When he had gone Theodora walked along the wharf.
The two white despatch ships now lay alongside; both
were crowded with labourers discharging cargo of some
sort by sling, tackle or hand. The nature of the cargo
could not be told: it was all boxed and baled. She walked
past them, going westwards along the wharf, and presently sat upon a bench, not far from the ships, to watch
the river and all the work going forward among clatter
and cries. Presently, two carriages came down from the
city to the wharf. She saw that they contained Silpi and
some of the Persian Trade Commission. All went aboard
one of the despatch ships and were there for some time.
She thought idly, that that was the first sign that she had
seen, that the young men were mixed up with trade.
Then she thought, that if the ships were carrying arms
and these men were soldiers engaged in spying, their
presence on board might teach them a good deal. She
thought of going to the wharf-keeper in the office at the
entry, to tell him to have an eye on these men; and yet,
what had she to go upon? At that moment, Silpi and the
Persians all left the ship together, with an official whom
all upon the wharf saluted. She judged that this man was
the ship's captain: probably the visit was harmless. At
the blast of a whistle, the men discharging cargo knocked
off their work to eat and drink. She strolled towards the
ships, admiring their neatness. An elderly seaman who
had been in a post of authority, tallying the cargo as it
went ashore, asked her to step aboard and see the ship.
She thanked him and did so.

"Are you just from The City?" she asked.

"No, lady, only from Smyrna," he said.

"Are you going back there?" she asked.

"Yes, lady, as soon as ever we can get this stuff out and the new stuff in. It's nearly the end of the sailing season; we daren't wait."

"Would you take me there?"

"Why, lady," he said, "we're a Government ship, and only take passengers on Government warrant. You'd have to get a warrant from the Praefect for that. And as a matter of fact, I hear we're full up from the Praefect's warrant already; he's sending all Sosthenes' people back with us. They're theatre people I understand."

She did not know the name Sosthenes; she had heard that the Government sometimes sent theatrical companies to perform in these eastern cities. She judged that this would be a Smyrniote company now going home. She determined that she would see Sosthenes at once, to find if she could be included in the company.

"What cargo will you take back?" she asked.

"Why," he said, "the passengers'll have a lot of stuff, I hear; and as for the rest, the autumn caravans are late. They say the robbers are on the roads this year. We may not get much in that way. Anyhow, we don't carry general cargo, only Government stores, or gold and jewels and that. If the robbers are on the roads, there'll be very little for us to take, but we'll wait till the last minute, of course."

"What would be your last minute?" she asked.

"The day after tomorrow," he said. "I'd say tonight,

if it was me, for the little white birds are all gone; it's time ships were off the seas."

"Do you know the man who was on board here just now with the young Persians? The man whom they call Silpi?" she asked.

"The fine-looking fellow, who went ashore with the Captain? Yes, that's Nicanor. He's been out here for years. Nicanor of the Bays, they call him."

"Why?"

"God knows. He's a rich man and trades with Persia I judge."

However, at this moment an officer called him to his meal; he could talk no more. She thanked him and went ashore.

She knew that the theatre lay beyond the great cross-ways near which the Sun Hotel stood. She did not know the name Sosthenes; she had been out of the theatre world for some years, and knew none of that world from Smyrna. Still, there was a bond between the members of that world; there was a bare chance that she might be squeezed in upon the warrant, and so get to Smyrna before sailing ceased. From Smyrna, she could easily reach The City by the usual post roads and Government diligences. At Smyrna she would feel that she was in one of The City's suburbs. In the company there might be one who would remember her sister Comito. Vulgarity like Comito's could not be forgotten in a few years; it blazed a trail and left a reek of the pit. Generals and premiers might be forgotten in a few months, but not one like Comito.

She had not gone far from the wharf when the man Peter beset her again.

"See, now," he said, "why you not give me those pieces? I your friend. I give you now only eighteen piece for that big one, see? You ask me tomorrow, you only get fifteen. No one else give you so much. You give me the piece. I give you eighteen piece for it. You trust all the other piece to me. I show them to my friend, see?"

"Nothing doing," she said.

She walked on, followed by him. She knew that her only chance of a fair price was to seem indifferent. All the time, her mind was doing sums, first, the amount she could expect from her jewels, next, the cost of the journey home, next, the probable cost of having to winter in Antioch before she could sail; next, the cost of getting, say, to Myra, or other Karamanian port, and wintering there, which might be cheaper than Antioch; next, the prospects of earning her living in Antioch, if she had to winter there. Trade was bad, everybody said; nothing was doing; the threat of war had upset everything. She might get nothing to do throughout the winter. Whenever she paused at a crossing, Peter, with his dank wet red hair and weary face was there.

"Why you not give me that piece, see? I give you seventeen piece. Not one man in Antioch give you so much. I send word to all de trade, see; they all know me. You not get more than that. You be stranded here. You won't get to no City; de ships stop now for de winter. You better make friends with me, see? You soon be in the gutter, with no friend here. You got out of de hotel for no money already."

She turned on him fiercely. "Get out," she said, "or I'll hand you to the civil guard."

He slunk back at the threat, and she went on, sick at heart, to think that he was probably right; she would not get more; she would be in Antioch for the next seven months. She prayed to God that somehow she might find a friend with Sosthenes who would get her included in the warrant. Without that, her future looked black enough. She had told herself that she would never mind going back into poverty. Now that she had gone, she knew that she did mind. She did not like the thought of that little room at the Water-Gate; even after the ship, it seemed grim to her. The good Stephanos might be back in a few days, and might find her some job, in church-cleaning or mending vestments, at which she could work till sailing began again. Antioch seemed like a prison which had chained her by both ankles for an unknown sentence.

At that instant, she had clearly and suddenly a mental picture of the noble, sweet head of old Timotheus against his white shelter; all would be well, he had said. Since he had said that she ought to be at Antioch, she must not doubt it; for somehow the thought of him was like truth and wisdom. He had learned all knowledge and renounced all joy and endured all persecution; yet somehow he had all things of knowledge, joy and safety flowing in upon him from a beauty undying.

She had at that moment reached the great cross-roads in the city centre. At that point there was a sudden checking of the flowing of the people upon the sidewalks, and as suddenly an exquisite great burst of flute music.

Coming up from the bridge were men in blue and silver riding white horses; behind them came others, supporting between them a banner of blue on which letters of silver proclaimed

Last Two Days
SOSTHENES BALLETS

After this banner came more white horses, drawing three floats of flute-players playing a haunting music which struck right into her heart. As these passed, lo, following on them came charming little boys, also dressed in blue and silver, each saying to the passers and spectators, "Come to the Ballet this afternoon. Please come to the Ballet." They went on, following the melting music amid much applause and general delight. She heard enough from the people near her to know that the Ballet had been at Antioch for some weeks, that a man called Perdiccas was the chief male dancer and that they had done well. She knew from the beauty of the procession and the quality of the music that this Sosthenes Ballet must be something hitherto unknown. "He must be a man with style and wealth," she thought. "Those costumes cost fifty pieces each, and the little boys' costumes probably twenty. But who designed them? They are lovely."

After the procession and its followers had all gone on, she slowly followed towards the theatre. Most of the people were on the south or shady side of the road; she preferred to cross over into the sun, because from that side she saw the crags, with their battlements and towers. She had always loved the sun; besides, she wanted to get a good view of the theatre from a little distance. She had always heard that it was the one theatre in the world which could compare with the theatre at Athens. She saw it now amidst some old ilex and olive, a white column or so, with the gleam of gold and many flag-poles flying blue and white banners. Behind it, as a sort of crown to it, was the rock with the towers against the intense sky. She had the pavement to herself there; she stood still to look; certainly, it was one of the fairest sights she had ever seen. Athens had been beautiful and holy to her; this place was the world, the flesh and the devil, if compared with Athens, but it was splendid.

To her left as she stood to gaze was a little pretty lane of white houses sloping up somewhat from the main street. The houses were in little gardens; creepers had been led along their walls; these creepers had now changed into vivid scarlets and yellows. She half noted, that someone came from one of these houses. She did not turn her head, but stared once more at the ilex trees at the theatre entrance. "They go in there," she said to herself, "then along the gardens to the seats. There are some in already." Indeed, she could see the upper tiers of the house, with people seated or moving. "There will be twenty thousand there this afternoon," she thought. "I will go, now, and try to find Sosthenes or his manager."

She was crossing the little lane, upon her way, when she noticed that the person who had come from the house was standing on the pavement looking at her. The person was a young, graceful and very elegant woman, staring at her, as though she recognized her.

"Theodora," she cried. "Do tell me, aren't you Theodora?"

"Yes," Theodora said, "I am Theodora. But who in Antioch knows me?"

The young woman caught her hands and gazed at her fixedly. "Theodora," she cried. "O, dear, I am so happy to see you again. Dear, let me kiss you." Impulsively, she kissed her cheek. "And you don't remember me," she said, "I see you don't. Well, why should you? But I remember you. I've thought of meeting you for years and O, I've hoped I might. Do you remember a little girl who called herself Plutomaria, at the Old Winter Palace?"

"Plutomaria?" Theodora said. "I ought to remember such a name; but I'm afraid I don't. Wait, though. Was there not some little wild dance from beyond the Danube?"

"O, she does remember," the lovely creature cried. "O, darling, darling Theodora, don't think that I will ever forget you. Don't you remember how I used to do high-jump-dances to the pan-pipes. Do you remember coming on me in tears once?"

It was difficult to think of that radiant, happy face in tears; Theodora could not remember this.

"We were all in tears, often enough, at the Old Winter Palace," she said. "But one looks back on it with a kind of affection."

"O, it was a heaven to me, after you saved me," the woman said.

"I saved you? What do you mean?" Theodora asked.

"You remember that old beast with the thin face

whom we called Anthrax? He was always badgering me
to go to his flat or I should never get another engage-
ment. He was a beast to some of the girls. Well, one day
he was final. Then, just as I was in tears and absolute
despair, you came in. You were out of the theatre, then;
you'd left the stage; but you'd come in to see your sister,
Comito, the great comedian. You saw what Anthrax had
been saying, so you went for him and told him to leave
the poor girl alone. You said, 'You leave that poor little
child. If I hear of your bullying her in any least way
again, I'll turn Comito onto you, and we'll hound you
out of every theatre in the Empire.' Do you mean to say
you don't remember that?"

"I do seem to remember something of you being in
tears."

"Don't you remember saying that Comito's young
men would tar and feather him at just one word, so let
him remember? You won't deny that you said that? Your
sister Comito. You admit that you've a sister Comito?"

"O yes, indeed," Theodora said. "But I had forgotten
all this."

"I suppose you do kind things like that every day of
your life and can't remember a tenth of them. But I remember. Anthrax was like a whipped dog, and never said
another word. To think that you forget. And I never
thanked you then and haven't since; but O, I've prayed
God to thank you. I was lost but for you then: done for.
I hung about the stage doors for days hoping to see you
again, but you didn't come again. And your sister said
that you had taken to political life. But come, now that I
have found you, I'm not going to let you go. You must

come with me, and come at once. What are you doing in Antioch? Where are you staying? You are living here?"

It is ever sweet to be remembered and thanked. To be appreciated by the radiantly and exquisitely beautiful is a rare experience. Theodora marvelled at the extraordinary fairy beauty of this young woman and at her affection.

"What am I to call you?" she asked. "Are you Plutomaria still?"

"No, no. I'm Macedonia. I'm ballerina with Sosthenes here. There's my name going up on the banner. Macedonia. You see I come from the wilds and called myself that, when I began to dance in the new fashion. Come along to the theatre now. I've got to dress almost at once. I'm dancing Psyche and Andromeda. Do you mean to say you've never seen Macedonia; but of course, you've been in political life, so, of course, you've not."

"I know nothing about Macedonia," Theodora said, "except what I see, which is altogether enchanting."

"Ah, you wait till you see me in Andromeda," the dancer said. "I call her that but it is St. George and the virgin really. You haven't seen the new fashion of the dance. Sosthenes made it. It's done on the toes; it is purely elegant; it has nothing of the flat foot dance of the country festivals and so forth. O, my dear, I am so happy to see you again. Come on, now; we'll cross the road above the theatre, if you don't mind. I'm rather a success, and people waylay me. We'll go in by the back way there is. Now tell me, as we go, what you are doing? Are you living here?"

"I only came here yesterday."

"And are you alone? Are you going to live here?"

"I'm alone. I'm trying to get away."

"Where to?"

"The City."

By this time, they were past the entrance to the garden which surrounded the theatre. Theodora saw that the entrance was beset by groups eagerly peering down the street.

"There they are," Macedonia said. "The men are there to mob me, the women are there to mob Perdiccas. A little further, then we'll bolt for the secret door. Our watchdog George will be there to let me in. Come on, now; we can see from here. Yes, there is George; we'll cross here then and bolt in."

Theodora saw across the street a mass of outbuildings attached to the theatre. She saw a small crowd of men there near a small door guarded by two men in blue and silver. The two women moved swiftly across the street to this door, the two big guards made way for them among the waiting crowd who spoke like worshippers beseeching. They called her "Queen" and "Star"; they begged for relics, a withered flower, an old glove. She moved swiftly through them, with a few swift words. "Thank you. Thank you. You are too charming. But I've no relic left; not a leaf, not a petal." Some of them begged her to take notes and packages. "Give them to George," she said. "Take them, George." The door opened for them and as swiftly shut behind them. Macedonia took Theodora's arm in the half darkness of the cool passage. In a minute she was in a beautiful room, facing north, cool, quiet, filled with flowers, and one corner heaped with baskets of fruit, boxes of sweetmeats, lengths of silk and other tributes from adorers.

"Now here I have my heart's wish," Macedonia said, "the thing I've longed for for years." She flung her arms round Theodora's neck and kissed her, saying, "Thank you, thank you, thank you for all you did for me, saving me."

Theodora held her and looked at her. She was much touched and said, "And that little wild thing has become the delight of the world, then?"

"No, no, no," she said. "But listen; you are going home to The City?"

"I'm afraid I can't until the Spring," Theodora said. "I fear there will be no ship."

"Do you want to go back?"

"Indeed I do."

"You must come with me," Macedonia said. "Sosthenes has worked it. The Governor is sending us all in his despatch-ships, the day after tomorrow."

"To Smyrna," Theodora said.

"Not a bit of it, all the way home; we shall call at Smyrna, of course. Dear, you will come with me? You will? You really will?"

"Do you really mean that you can take me?"

"But of course I do. I need you. I'm never going to part from you again, if you can bear with me so long. Where are your things? You must come to live with me."

"I'm in a little room down at the Water-Gate, No. 9," Theodora said. "I've very little money, to tell the truth."

"You've got all my money and all my heart and all

my skill," Macedonia said. "So, listen. I've got to dress. Perhaps you'll stay with me, as in the Old Winter Palace. You write a note to your landlady, and I'll send George and my packer down to bring your things to my house. I live in a little house near where we met. And, O, what fun it is to have you here. I am so glad."

She was plainly very glad. Such gladness is a communicable joy; it made Theodora glad. To be welcome, to be loved, after such loneliness and anxiety is deep joy to the soul. But apart from that the sweetness and the charm of Macedonia would have won anybody; she was young, radiant and vigorous; she had a look of vivid happy life about her altogether charming and good.

"Now write, write, to your mistress Tryphosa," Macedonia said. "That's the way. Now I'll send George and my packer down to bring your things. My home is your home, and I'm your slave. Why don't you beat me, mistress? I play this virgin in the St. George; it has made me famous, they say, but I know that it was not St. George but Theodora who saved me."

When the messengers had been despatched, Macedonia said, "I'm going to ask you a very great favour. I see that you have kept in practice. Will you put on practice dress and work with me while I warm up?"

"Why, indeed I will," Theodora said. "And another thing you must let me do. I was taught massage by my mother, so as to massage Comito when she did acrobatic things. I'm a very good masseuse, in the old Greek way. If you are dancing hard on a hard floor you'll find me very restful after a performance."

"The very thought of you near by is inspiration to me," Macedonia said. "Now come on to my dressing-room."

The theatre had a big practice and rehearsal room, already busy with parties of dancers who were warming-up at the barres or in the centre. Theodora knew already from what she had seen of it, that the Sosthenes management had a style and a distinction unlike anything in her experience. The costumes in the practice rooms were plainly the work of genius. When she saw Macedonia's costumes, she said,

"Who is Sosthenes, who does these things?"

"A dancer from Athens, who became a painter; he is a musician, too, and a sort of demi-god. I don't think he's quite human, but he made the Sosthenes Ballet and nothing like it has been seen. He made it in Smyrna. We've been at it for three years, and have made all Karamania and Syria and Egypt our abject slaves. Now Sosthenes is taking us to a theatre in The City. You will see what we are. We're something new. Here are some practice dresses, if you really will warm up with me. But this is my Dresser, Eurycleia; Eurycleia, you must meet my great, great friend Theodora. Can you tell us, if Sosthenes is in his office? He is? Come on, then, Theodora. You must see him; he isn't human, but he won't bite."

She led the way to another big room facing to the north. Here she found Sosthenes, and introduced him to her friend. Theodora saw before her a rather tall, heavy man, with a grave, keen scrutiny. He was pale, middle-aged and industrious, Theodora thought. He was working with a young man at the effects of some coloured stuffs upon wicker models. His face lit up at the sight of Macedonia.

"Ha," he said. "Come in; we've got the effect now. Is this your friend?"

"I should think she is," Macedonia said. "This is Theodora, my sparring partner and manageress. She is going to look after me, she says, but not so much as I'm going to look after her. She is coming with us to The City in my cabin; that is easy to arrange, isn't it?"

"Of course, if you wish it. Lady Theodora, may I introduce my young friend Sotion, who is doing the dresses for a new ballet we're planning?"

"I met you years ago," Theodora said to the painter. "You knew my sister Comito."

"Ha," Sosthenes said, "you are Comito's sister. What a mime. Marvellous."

Sotion at the coming-in of Theodora had watched her eagerly; he had sighed for that dark-eyed beauty years before, when he had been an art student following the theatre.

"I remember you," Sosthenes said. "You used to do a marvellous little dance between the verses of a song. The song was nothing, but the dance was something to remember. Where did you get the dance?"

"O, there were many dances," Theodora said. "Comito was always finding someone to teach me a novelty."

"The song was called 'Tiddley-om-pom-pom,'" Sotion said.

" 'High, boys, ho, boys,
Tiddley-om-pom-pom.'

I've got a drawing of you doing it."

"The song could be bettered," Sosthenes said, "but the dance was adorable."

"Nothing that she ever did could be bettered," Macedonia said. "Come, now; we must change and warm up; time's passing."

Sosthenes called out: "I'll come round in half-an-hour to take you in front. You mustn't miss this show; we shan't be doing the *Psyche* tomorrow, when we close."

After the warming-up, Theodora borrowed a very beautiful wrap, so that she might sit in front, during the performance. The coming-back to the theatre had been strangely delightful. She had not liked the theatre world when she had been of it; yet now the easy comradeship of people who, besides being good artists, were what the slang called "Good troupe-ers", and the charm and sweetness of Macedonia, were welcome. It was so different being under a remarkable man, good at three of the arts, and able to fuse them into a fourth, from being under old Garbage and pestered by Anthrax. Now Sosthenes called for her, and led her out of Macedonia's room.

"Watch my entrances and exits," Macedonia cried. "Watch everything I do, and bludgeon me for it."

"I shall watch everything you do," Theodora said.

"You will," Sosthenes said. "She is the wonder of her time. You've not seen her lately."

"Not since the Old Winter Palace."

"She's as far changed from that," Sosthenes said, "as the Bird of Paradise is from its egg."

He led her through the manager's door into the vast auditorium, which rose up tier upon tier in a blur of faces and bright colours. He led her past the side of the great white marble orchestra, and by a gangway through the massed music, all in the blue and white of the Sosthenes company. The conductor was tapping his chin with his baton as he waited for the signal.

"Let us sit here, now," Sosthenes said, shewing her to one of the marble seats usually kept for the chief City Magistrates.

The conductor saw his signal, stepped to his box, tapped, and at once the overture began.

Ever since she had entered the theatre, Theodora had known, that the direction was something both new and splendid. It was not only beautiful to every eye, it was ruled, ordered, cleanly cut, and in all things exquisite. She noted that before the music began all people were in their seats. Now she saw that the gangways were gated; late-comers were shut out. The illusion which Sosthenes had tried to create was now to have its hour; those who had come to experience the illusion were not to be disturbed while the illusion was created. But she was at once held by the music. She was fond of music; she had some little skill with zither, harp and two kinds of pipe; she had played these for a living. Now she heard a remarkable company playing under the best conductor in that civilisation. She did not know him; she had noticed his charming young face, with its rather noticeable strong chin; now there it was transfigured and aflame in the box lifting the eighty musicians into the Paradise to which he had found the key. "What a conductor," she thought; "and then, what musicians, and what an overture." She looked at Sosthenes beside her. He was not in Paradise, like the conductor. He had a block of thin wood

upon his knee. To this block some twenty vellum sheets
had been pinned. He was now staring at the conductor,
the musicians, and various parts of the house, and making little notes in shorthand in crayon. He had an eye
for everything, and the crayon was busy. Once, when
two musicians who had a momentary rest, passed a joke
under their breaths and smiled, the crayon made a black
mark and Sosthenes looked murder. Near the end of the
overture, she glanced to her left. A few seats away, in the
row behind her, was this man Silpi, whom the old seaman
had called Nicanor of the Bays. He was with two members of the Persian Trade Commission. Nicanor (or Silpi)
was rapt with the music; the Persians were looking at the
women, of whom there were many and very lovely, all
set out (so Theodora thought) with more lavish colour
and sparkle than was admitted in The City, and all staring, so Theodora judged, at the divine young athlete
who was conducting the music. The overture climbed and
crashed to its close, and at once passed into the *Psyche*
music with a little dance of little unearthly figures whose
exquisiteness made the entire audience of twenty thousand people spell-bound. She heard no cough, no movement from the vast crowd, nothing but the light foot-fall,
the unearthly music, and Sosthenes' crayon on the vellum. Macedonia had told her and had sung to her the
flute motif which preceded her entrance; she sat waiting
for this, entranced by what she saw, and finding little
odd memories of her friend coming out of their hiding-
places. She had been a little shy, skinny girl from the
wilds, able to jump and do hand-springs. What would

the stage show? There came the drum music, with the effects of distant thunder; she had been told to get ready at this point. She looked to her right, for the moment was near now.

"Watch, now," Sosthenes whispered; she was already watching. The flutes took up their haunting cry, and in an instant Psyche was floating on, and the men and women were weeping unashamed in ecstasy; and Theodora understood what had happened. That little wild, skinny, shy girl had become the exquisite creature of her century, supreme for lightness, charm and grace. No wonder that this creature was beset. It was plain, now, why Antioch was wild with joy in her. Such a thing was not seen more than once in a hundred years; and those who saw her now, saw the genius set forth with a blending and fusing of all that was noblest in all the arts. Genius was appearing in such a splendour as had never before been seen upon the stages of the world. Macedonia had told her to watch everything she did and then to bludgeon her for it. Watch everything. How could she help watching? But how criticise or help this wonderful thing? Theodora had danced; she had been through the schools and learned the métier; and only now saw what dancing ought to be or could be. It would be days, she thought, before she could understand this wonder. But that she would adore it and help it with all the power of love in her, she had no doubt. She watched the man who danced the god with some jealousy. Like everybody among the twenty thousand, she had begun to love Macedonia. She was only some three or four years older but how much older in wisdom of the world. Yet here was

Macedonia moving in a glory of success which seemed to put her in another planet.

When the ballet ended, Sosthenes drew his crayon across his seventh page of notes and said, "Like to come round?"

She said that she would love to speak to Macedonia. "But first," she said, "I would like to say that I think all this is marvellous. Nothing like it has been seen. You are wonderful."

"You see what I'm trying to do?" Sosthenes said. "Did you see any change in Macedonia?"

"Change?" she said.

"She was always this," he said. "The butterfly was there, only waiting for a little sun. The Old Winter Palace was more Winter than Palace, perhaps."

"I cannot tell you what I think," Theodora said to Macedonia. "It was the most exquisite thing I ever saw."

"I'm glad you like it," Macedonia said. "But, oh, do watch me and tell me where I'm wrong. Watch me in this virgin thing."

"I'll just knead your ankles," Theodora said. "If you have much to do in the next ballet you'll find a little work on them very refreshing. Lie down, now, and I'll have your shoes off. You were liker a spirit from Heaven than anything I'd believed possible. I don't marvel at your room being piled with flowers and all sorts of joys. You are the most exquisite of living artists," she said. "I have never praised anyone like that before. I did not think that anyone like you, or at all like you, could exist. I think you are too lovely to describe. I shall always say that."

"My dear," Macedonia said, "if you had not passed when that Anthrax beast was attacking me, I should have been broken, and never been anything at all. I cannot tell you what a joy it is to think that my dream has come true, and that I have found you again and really danced for you and heard that you have liked me a little. I have always looked on you as a sort of a queen, and prayed that I might some day have the glory of dancing in your presence. You see, my dear, there is something very queenly about you. I used to notice you a lot at the Palace. In your last two seasons I had to be in the wings ready to begin while you were doing your songs and all those mimes with Comito: O, you were good in them. I used to wonder, if you would ever teach me miming, but never dared ask you. I saw you play the Queen more than once. Do you remember that absurd play of the Rival Queens, which you and your sister were so wonderful in? I think your head as it is, is adorable, and very beautiful; it is so exquisitely put on its neck; but it does lack one thing, and that is a golden crown, with a lovely blue amethyst or sapphire in the front here, set off by your hair. That is the one thing lacking in a very lovely creature."

"My dear," Theodora said, "you are the one Queen here, and how anyone can keep from crowning you on the spot at each performance I cannot understand. But, of course, they do crown you, with laurels and bays and myrtle and flowers and poems and adoration."

"That is nothing, dear," she said. "It is all due to Sosthenes; he made me, as he made everything in this company, but he does not care twopence for any one of us, nor does he care for success. One success only lights up something new to be done; something that one of us might do; then he sets-to to do it for us. We all know very well that it is all due to him. He pulls the talent out of us. When the people crown us, and drag us home and so forth, it is not we who deserve it, but he."

Theodora went back to her place for the St. George, wondering what would happen at the end. They had been in ecstasy over the Cupid and Psyche, a charming pagan tale. What would they be after St. George? The tale and its setting belonged to that district; everybody there had a pride and a possession in the legend. What would happen when the fable was presented? She was soon to know. It went in a long rapture of cheering, which grew and grew until all present were almost in a frantic frenzy of joy. Men and women wept, and were not ashamed; they leaped upon their seats to cheer and wave their scarves and sob and sing. As before, they flung jewels, flowers and other presents upon the stage; the attendants, in their blue and white cloaks, came with baskets, filled them with these things and then bore them to the divine Macedonia and the godlike lad who had danced St. George with her. Long after the play had ended, the applause lasted, and showers of gifts succeeded; time and time again the entire company had to form or defile before the back of the scene while the principals came forward to be cheered and cheered. It did not occur to the audience, that the maker of the illusion, who had used the marvel of Macedonia, the heroical youthful strength of the St. George, the genius of the musicians and of the painters, and the youth and grace of the dancers to an end clearly per-

ceived, deserved something of the glory. Sosthenes was
at the back somewhere, saying polite things to some of
the dancers and cold things to others. He was unmoved
by this success. He had watched the piece from in front,
as ever, and now had his notes to read to the company.
So-and-so had a jewel two inches astray in her hair; the
other must change his wig; what had caused that delay
on the right in the slow movement? another had crossed
on hops instead of *en glissade;* why had she worn that
red scarf, where was her blue one? one culprit had come
out of line, another had looked vacant, another had
seemed bored. They must all go over that scene later and
get the ensemble better. "Get it *right,*" Sosthenes said.
"It will NOT DO. It looked frightful;" and the culprits
went off cowed. He kept repeating at intervals: "Everybody is to be in the rehearsal room after the comedy."
The performance was to end with a farcical ballet.

Theodora noticed that no one not of the theatre was
allowed behind the scene. This was indeed a change from
the Old Winter Palace, where the friends, admirers and
lovers of the company made merry every day behind the
scene. She liked the change; it gave the makers of illusion a distinction.

She waited till Sosthenes had finished his notes; then
she went to him and said, "Sosthenes, you must be sick
of praise, and I am not used to giving it, but I must say
to you that you have made a new thing and a divine
thing. I had not thought it possible to be so shaken in a
theatre. I thought the theatre was all earth and you have
brought out of it this miracle of a flower, all colour and
fragrance and mystery."

He seemed pleased, and was so, for this was Comito's sister.

"It does for fable what the churches do for faith," he said, "only, we keep joy, which churches tend to kill with fear. Macedonia has just urged me again, to urge you to come home with us. I gladly do that, saying, that you will do me and Macedonia, too, a very very great service, if you will and can. Only, I fear it may be difficult; we have to sail tomorrow."

"I thought it was to be the day after."

"Well; we're late as it is; we have stopped on for an imprudent week; the seamen are anxious; and the man Nicanor, who is coming with us, has decided not to stay beyond tomorrow."

"Is he of the company?" she asked.

"No, but he worked the Praefect to send us home in the despatch-ships, so, of course, we must a little meet his wishes."

"I would love to come with the company, if you really could take me," she said. "I could be ready tonight. I thank you very much for the thought."

"I thank you," he said. "It is a great thing for Macedonia, a really great thing."

"Tell me," she said, "is this man Nicanor of the Bays?"

"Yes," he said.

"Why is he called 'of the Bays'?"

Sosthenes looked at her, with some wonder. "I am growing old," he said. "I was afraid I was."

He had to go then, to speak to someone of the theatre; she returned to the front, to watch the farcical ballet. Macedonia came with her, and sat in Sosthenes' place.

Theodora wondered again who this Nicanor was, who
was not of the company, yet was coming with it, and
had, by some extraordinary political influence persuaded
the Praefect to send them all home in a Government
ship, or ships. Well, she knew something of what political influence could do; she had touched the fringe of that
world. There was a proverb, "The nearer the bone, the
sweeter the meat"; the Praefect of an important district
had more power than the Emperor. She glanced at Nicanor, who sat there with his Persians, sometimes starting
a merry theme, then enjoying the chase of it with them.
A few minutes before the trumpets blew for the beginning of the farce, he left his seat, came to Macedonia,
and said,

"May I congratulate you once again on your performance? I have seen you dance Psyche twenty-three times
and the Virgin thirty-one times and each time as though
I had been translated to a new kind of Paradise. And
may I say to the Lady Theodora that I hope Peter was
able to be of service?"

"Oh, we set out the board," she said. "We are now
debating the gambit; serious play may begin in a day
or two."

"I am sorry that I did not know that you are a friend
of Macedonia," he said. "It would have been easy to
have taken you to one who does not debate the gambit
quite so earnestly."

As the trumpeters came out at that moment, he bowed
and slipped away to his seat.

Theodora thought, "No, you did not know that I am
a friend of Macedonia; but you were perplexed by my

coming in to your supposed Trade Commission, and put your pertinacious spy upon me, to find out who and what I am."

She was both pleased and puzzled by him. He had a look of power, he had real charm, he had, no doubt of it, taken trouble for her; he must have been someone of distinction, for the older people all knew him by a nickname; he must have wealth and position; he looked as if he had a grievance and as if he might be very cruel. All these things passed through her mind, while she reflected about the nickname.

"Are the Bays a cavalry Regiment?" she asked.

"They may be," Macedonia whispered.

At that moment the conductor tapped with his baton and the farce began.

It was not in her nature to be one of a company without being of service. During the farcical ballet she reflected how she might be of service to Sosthenes in marshalling the company and its belongings down to the ships. They were to perform that next afternoon, and to be on board, and if possible away from the wharves within an hour of the end of the last ballet. She knew that the sudden putting forward of the sailing time must have added much to his anxieties. She saw much that she could do. She could mark the baggage for the particular ship in which it was to go; she could overlook the sea-store, and be certain, that each ship was properly equipped, with food, drink and bedding; she could spend the night on board the ships, marking out the berthings; labelling and listing them, so that each man or woman would be able to go at once to his or her quarters; she could arrange for the wagons to have the properties and baggage at the ships at dawn, so that everything would be stowed except what was needed for the last performance; all these suggestions seemed to her to be useful; yet she knew, that Sosthenes might already have men arranging all these very things, and she knew, too, that she might easily make an enemy of someone by offering to take over the work. A few words with Macedonia told her what would be and had been done, and what might with great advantage be offered. Sosthenes was pleased with her offer and gave her two jobs, that of checking certain sea-stores in each ship at dawn, and, later, the task of driving all those allotted to her particular ship out of the theatre and down to the wharf. The two ships were called the *Queen of the Seas* and the *Royal Fortune*. Those sailing in the *Queen* were called the Reds, and had themselves and their belongings marked with red; those sailing in the *Fortune* were called Blues, and were marked with blue. Theodora was to be in charge of the Blues, of whom there were sixty-eight.

"What the seamen want," Sosthenes said, "is for there to be no delay, so that they can drop down the river and be well out to sea, really well out, before the wind dies. We've been here a month; half these girls have got adorers who will want to say 'good-bye'. You must tell them that if they're late they'll lose their passage."

Word had passed through Antioch that the company would sail upon the morrow. Macedonia said to Theodora, "There will be no leaving by the stage-doors now; we shall be beset. We shall have to hood ourselves, mix with the audience in the garden, and get away that way. The performance tomorrow will be an hour earlier than usual, but even so, we shall have a struggle to get away. The Praefect is coming, and all the magistrates; they'll all make speeches. We have had an extraordinary success here; but, oh, I shall be glad to be away. I feel that war is so near here."

They hooded themselves in black wraps, and ran out into the tail-ends of the audience now loitering out of the gardens. They crossed the street, and were almost at the charming little house, when a familiar figure came up to Theodora.

"I your friend, see. I say I give you twenty pieces for the thing you show me, see? No one else give it; but I like you, see? You got beautiful eyes, hey; like gazelle's eyes. I give it for your eyes, see?"

"Here; run away, run away," Macedonia said, as the door opened to them.

They went in and closed the door; but for some time, they saw the figure of Peter staring up at the windows. Whenever he caught their eyes, he made supplicating gestures and opened and shut and then re-opened his hands, to shew that there was no mistake about the twenty. There could be no doubt, that he might be a useful spy; he took plenty of pains over a case.

"He found out somehow, that my things have been brought here," she said. "I hope you won't mind."

"I don't mind," Macedonia said. "But do tell me, what does he offer twenty pieces for?"

"Some settings I want to sell."

"But, my dear, wait till we reach home. My father is

in business; he knows all the jewellers and everybody else; he'll sell your things for you and get you three times what you could get; these people are all in a ring together."

It set in to rain presently, and rained hard, so that when they next looked out, Peter had gone. The two friends worked at packing, and then talked their hearts out to each other, before an early going to rest.

The night filled the valley with sweeping cloud and made the torrents from the rock to roar through Antioch. The morning broke with surpassing beauty upon a revived world all sparkling. Cataracts were whitening into mist down the crags, and all the tired fountains were now spouting. Theodora was aboard the Blue ship by sunrise to check the sea-stores. Her old friend, the seaman, saw her and said, "A nice freshet to deepen the bar for us; and a good job, for we'll be sailing heavy; however light some of these dancing dames may be."

The stores were not enough for what the voyage might become. She judged it wise to order more of a good many things for each ship; any surplusage could readily be sold along the water-front in The City. She was not without knowledge of the ways of purveyors of sea-stores; she took the old seaman with her to the dealers and had the casks unheaded, searched, and loaded into her waggon before she paid money for them. Going back aboard with her last wagon-load of stores, she found the Praefect of the District on board, making sure that the ships were ready to receive the company.

"You are in charge of the arrangements?" he said.

"Tell me what you want, and I'll try to see it put aboard."

"Sea-beds and straw-mats," Theodora said, "and a lot of military blankets."

"I can give you lots of those," he said. "Anything else?"

"Yes," Theodora said. "There'll be a huge crowd at the theatre this afternoon; we shall have to fight to get through. Could you possibly send javelin-men or some mounted police to clear the ways for us, so that we really can get on board?"

"I'll have the streets lined," he said. "You dancers have been the one bright thing in this summer, and all you want is ease in getting away. Damnable, I call it. How we're to live without the ballet henceforth, I do not see."

"Perhaps we can come again, next summer," she said.

"There'll be a lot of dancing here, next summer," he said. "You say you'd like some blankets. Come this way." He led the way across the wharf to the warehouses which walled-in their landward side. In the great open shed were piles of bales and boxes. "Those bales are blankets," he said; "fifty to a bale. How many d'you want?"

"Three for each ship," she said.

He called to the wharfee to put three bales of blankets in each ship, with proportionate mats and beds.

"You can turn-in all these to the stores man in The City when you get there," he said.

"You seem to have plenty," she said.

"Getting ready for war," he said. "Now is there anything else I can do for you?"

"If you could very kindly suggest to the magistrates not to speak at length when they bid us farewell this afternoon, it would perhaps give us a chance to get away."

He looked at her with approval. "That will be easier said than made effective," he said. "Some of them love to talk. But what you had better insist on, is that all your company, man and woman, shall leave the theatre by the little side postern kept for the magistrates. They can slip out there and down the lane by the side of the torrent, and reach the wharf that way. The theatre gates will be so mobbed, that you'll never get out that way."

"I'll leave word about it," she said.

She went to No. 9, the Water-Gate, which was only a hundred yards away, to ask if Stephanos had returned yet. He had not come, but might be in any day, the woman said. Theodora felt that now he would never come in time for her to see him; in a way she was glad, for now she would always have Timotheus' letter, to be by her always.

She had to go aboard the Red ship after this, to make sure that the costume baskets for five of the ballets had been brought safely below. She was down below making sure that they were properly tarpaulined, when she heard the voices of the Governor and Nicanor on deck above her. The Governor was saying,

"You know all these Ballet people; who is the little dark woman, with big black eyes?"

"Theodora, do you mean?"

"I don't know her name; she was on board here just now arranging things."

"She's a new arrival," Nicanor said, "but seems an old friend of theirs. She asked Sisamnes and Pacorus if they would buy some jewels. I thought she might be one of the other stable, so I put Peter onto her. She came in from Alexandria, as a wealthy woman, but was very hard up next day. There's something odd about her."

"Do you think she is one of the other stable?"

"I shouldn't think so," Nicanor said.

"I've taken the liberty of putting aboard that wine you liked," the Governor said. "You ought to have a fair journey. I suppose you'll put into Smyrna to hear the news."

"Yes," Nicanor said. "And I rather think that we shall find Tino there, on his way out overland: Commander Tino, of The Emperor's Chestnuts."

"I should think it certain," the Governor said. "Now I want to show you your cabin and all your precious belongings."

They moved away forward, while Theodora, having finished her task, went on deck and then ashore. "Why might I be 'one of the other stable'?" she asked herself. "So Peter *was* put on to spy upon me; I was sure of it. Why should I be spied on? What was the little plot which I might be supposed to be enquiring into?" Tino, as she knew, was the nickname for Justinian, the Emperor's nephew; he was to be in Smyrna, on his way to Antioch. That shewed, that there was to be war with Persia in the spring. Justinian was coming east to command, then, so much was certain. At once, it leaped into her mind that Nicanor was an elderly cavalry general. The Persian Trade Commission was, of course, his secret service of

brave young men who could speak Persian. They were in
Antioch to report to their chief and, of course, he was
now going home to report to the Government. He had
suspected that she, Theodora, was a woman in the pay
of Persia, trying to find out what his secret service had
found out; so that was why Peter had been such a pest.
She was delighted with these thoughts as she walked to
the theatre. She was glad that Nicanor was not to be in
the Blue ship with her; somehow, she wanted to be in the
other stable.

That afternoon, the audience outnumbered any ever
known in Antioch; every seat was filled; every approach
was blocked. The hills behind the theatre, and the ram-
parts along the crags were all black with people longing
for some glimpse, however distant, of their adored dancers. Hundreds, who knew that they could not approach
the theatre, came down to the wharves and took place
there. When the performance ended, the orchestra would
have been mobbed, but for the Praefect's guard. There
was some ceremony to be observed. The Praefect said
that no Governor could be a servant of the Empire, if he
did not reward such talents as had delighted all his Province. He gave a gold box, containing the citizenship of
Antioch, to Sosthenes, a fillet of gold to Perdiccas, and to
Macedonia a robe of the finest Persian silk and a string
of the choicest Arabian pearls. Then one of the magistrates spoke of the aesthetic value of education, and another talked of the educational value of aesthetics; then
another said that aesthetics were marvellous correctives
to materialism; another said that if materialism were
corrected by aesthetics, and where a Macedonia was it

always would be, why, surely that was the happy mean
spoken of by the philosophers. Another said that he was
sure that all Antioch would join him in singing "Farewell to the Fair".

The bands struck up and thirty thousand people took
up the song.

"Cut away now, by the little door," the Praefect said
to the company. "In five minutes it'll be too late."

They went at speed, out by the little, unknown door,
and down the lane, which was partly a stairway, along
the gushing Silpian torrent. At every turn, they dreaded
an inrush of admirers, who might sweep them away.
Theodora had one arm of Macedonia, Sosthenes had the
other; they ran the whole way, and never dreaded a run
more. All the way, the roaring crowd was following, by
the main streets. At the wharves, the horse and javelin-
men made a passage for them. They ran through it besieged by heaving multitudes. Bands were playing and
people shouting three different songs: "Farewell to the
Fair", "Macedonia, my darling", and "O Golden Sweets
of the Dance". The captains of the ships were at the
gangways. "On board; on board," they shouted. "All on
board and call your rolls. If once the crowd gets down
here we'll never get away tonight."

Lancers of the Praefect's guard convoyed down the
wagons which contained the costumes worn that afternoon. The seamen hove the baskets aboard, while those
responsible for the company checked and counter-checked
the rolls, to make sure that all hands were there. The
ships were in contest, which would get away first. Theodora saw the crowd surging against the wharf-approaches,

but unable to get past the guards and the rope-fencing. Among the agitating arms were two which seemed to signal to her. They belonged to Peter, who was now shewing her that he was still her friend and would go to twenty-five. Many of the girls near her were weeping; there were frenzied signals from the crowd to them. The press at the approaches grew visibly greater, there were cries of pain and fear, but the guards still pushed them back. Then, there came a clatter of hoofs. The Praefect and his staff came onto the wharf at a fast trot and reined up opposite the Blue ship. Nicanor and another, who had ridden down with the Praefect, hurried along the wharf and into the Red ship. The Praefect cried that he was proud that under his governorship such artists had come to Antioch. Antioch's loss would be The City's gain; he wished them God-speed, and a happy voyage. "Come soon again to Antioch." The speech was meant for both ships. All were now aboard, who were coming. All the bands which had silenced for the Praefect struck up "Farewell to the Fair"; the gangways were run down; the towing boats in the river gave way and plucked taut the towropes; all the hold-fasts were cast off, and with a roaring of cheering the voyage began. At that instant, just as the ships began to sidle and loiter clear of the wharf, a club of young men, all wearing blue and white, in honour of Sosthenes, came with a rush past the guards to the wharf's edge, flinging bouquets of flowers to Macedonia. Every bell near the wharf was banged and beaten; and so to all this noise, tumult, frenzy, music, cheering, tears and craziness the ships drew into the stream. In a moment, the crowd seemed tiny and unreal. Both ships

were now out in the stream with boats ahead, colours flying, and rowers ready. Their trumpeters blew their
"Loath to depart", and at this, the oars dipped, and the
two ships began a race to the river-bar. The shouters and
wavers became little specks and tendrils and then not
even that.

Theodora watched the crowd of towers recede; she
blessed Antioch, and gave her grateful thanks to the old
saint who had sent her there. He had meant her to see
an old persecuted saint; instead of that she had met this
exquisite young dancer, who had done all that the old
saint could have done in giving her new life and hope.
She was still somewhat bewildered at the suddenness of
the change. Only the day before, she had been at her
wits' ends, friendless and with not much chance of reach-
ing The City. Now, here she was, surrounded by love,
trusted and of use, with the certainty of work if she
wished for it, and homeward-bound, beyond all hope,
homeward-bound.

They lost sight of the Red ship during the next day.
The fair weather held for them; they made a good passage. On the voyage, Theodora learned that Sosthenes
had been building a theatre in The City and hoped to
open there with his new ballets as soon as possible. He
planned to have a season until Lent, then to visit the
cities of the Aegean, to try out other ballets, and then to
play through the later spring and summer in The City.
His theatre would be something very new to The City.
She came to know him a little in the voyage. He had
been much in the Persian Court as a very young man;
his father had been ambassador there. He had been much

impressed by the Persian King's Royal Ballet, and had
known very well two Greek dancers, Photios and Battos,
who had been Masters of the Ballet there. He had danced
in their school at Athens a year or two later. To the
methods of the Greeks and the Persians he had brought a
genius for refining the vigorous dancing talent everywhere in the Greek world south of the Danube, and a
most unusual musical knowledge. With two friends, a
musician and a painter, he had displayed some trial
pieces before King Chosroes and the Persian Court, with
much success; but Greek matters had been falling out of
favour there for years; he had returned to The City, and
had passed several springs and summers trying his methods here and there. He had then inherited great wealth,
and had determined to build his theatre, while trying a
large company in the great theatres of the Karamanian
and Syrian cities. He had succeeded beyond all expectation.

Some of his dancers had been recruited from the dancing companies of Athens, Alexandria, and Antioch; some
were from The City; many from the Heptapolis. He had
gone here and there, picking talent where he saw it, and
using it in a new way. He had with him fable-makers,
musicians, designers and composers, as well as dancers.
He had welcomed Theodora from the first, because he
saw how greatly Macedonia loved her, and how much
she would benefit Macedonia. He saw, too, that she had
a head upon her shoulders, could undertake and do effec-
tively responsible work like the checking of stores and the
equipment of a sleeping deck. He soon came to see that
she had a certain eye for a stage-effect; she was "of the

theatre", but not as he had expected the sister of Comito to be. This one had an elegance and a style; she could be of use to him fifty times in a day. He asked her to join the company for the time as directress of the women. She was to be in charge of *"le livre rouge, les remplaçants, et le rouleau"*.

As for Macedonia, she had never been so happy. She had urged Theodora from the first to come to live with her. Her parents, the merchants, were now very rich, and would be so glad, if their daughter's friend would live with them. All through the voyage home this offer was repeated. Theodora thanked her for her love and tenderness and said, that she would love to stay for a few days, if she might, till she could sell her jewels and make a little home for herself. She meant to make a life for herself. She would see Macedonia often and love her always, but wanted not to be dependent upon anyone ever again.

In failing weather, the Blue ship beat up to The City, and then with song hove to the wharf and made fast. Soon Macedonia and Theodore were driving side by side through the wet streets in the first of the lamp-light. It was good to be back in The City in those familiar streets.

"O, it is good to be here," she said.

"Welcome home, dear Queen," Macedonia said, lifting her over the threshold of her home. "Here are my mother and father. This is Theodora, my great friend, who was so good to me in the old days at the Winter Palace."

The two plump, black-eyed, sleek and exceedingly as-

tute parents knew all about Theodora's kindness to their
child: they welcomed her with an effusion of joy and
gratitude. They were people of much natural kindness
and goodness, very astute at anything like a bargain, but
generosity itself where affections were concerned. They
had a house full of beautiful things, chosen with an eye
to their value fifty years hence. Theodora judged it to
be a house full of shrewdly and even hardly-driven bar-
gains. However, she was welcome there, and it was quiet
and luxurious. After the long days on the seas in a shared
cabin, the great baths and the cool, stable, spacious rooms
were delightful. Theodora asked for nothing more delightful than to bathe and be made trim, to change into
her loveliest things, and then fall asleep in a comfortable
bed. Outside, as she drowsily heard, a gale blew with fury
to take off the last of the leaves: it was good to be
ashore out of all that.

In the morning, a new life began for her. Macedonia's
father gladly undertook the sale of her jewels, and told
her at once that they would fetch a good sum, enough
for her to live upon in a simple style, for two years. As
the Red ship had not yet arrived, there could be no set
rehearsal. Like the rest of the company, she went to the
new theatre, to see the company's new home and to go
through the practice. It was in the hands of the deco-
rators, who were making it beautiful with much lively
painting of life of the theatre. It was said at rehearsal,
that the Red ship, being behind them, had not reached
the sheltered waters before the storm and would, therefore, have made for the lee of some land, or for a harbour. When the practice was over, she drove with

Macedonia to see Demetria's mother, to tell her of her
daughter's death. She had known the family for some
years. Another of its girls, somewhat younger than
Demetria, one Kallianassa, like her sister for honesty and
goodness, asked if she might take her sister's place. Theodora said that she should, when she had made a little
home.

After this, Theodora drove alone to see her elder sister
Comito, once the idol of the music-hall, now married to
a timber-merchant, who had made large sums in Government contracts. She lived in a big house on Middle
Hill, with superb views north, south and east. She was a
good deal older than Theodora, though still young. Indo-
lence and easy living had begun to shew upon her figure;
she was plump and would soon be plumper. Easy good
nature was in every line of her. She was fond of Theodora and glad to see her; their ways were very different,
but they had been through a good deal together and
knew each other's good points.

"John's out," she said (John was the timber-
merchant), "so we can talk. I see that you are through
with that man Hekebolos. I was sure he was no good,
that bird; but when a girl's as much in love as you were
what is to be done? You're well out of it, whatever you
may feel at the moment. So you mean to work with
Sosthenes. I've not seen his show. I don't go to shows
now. How are you off for money, dear? Got any? That
bird Hekebolos was a bit on the wee side, if you ask me.
It's all very well in business, but in love a fellow ought
to be a bit possessed by the god, I always say, for love in
those birds doesn't often last, and then what has the girl

got to fall back on? You were robbed in the ship? My dear, that's another sign you felt it. When a girl's got the K.O. from a bloke, she can't keep an eye on things. You can sell the other things? You're lucky to know a man in the trade. John says, 'There's no such thing as trade; there are just a few conspiracies.' But talking of money, dear, I've got some for you, seven hundred and fifty pieces; I have. It's a legacy. Uncle Paulos, Mother's elder brother. He wasn't any use to us when we needed it; he never saw us; I dare say you never saw him. Well, he wasn't exactly the King of Sheba; he ran a wine-bar and fried-fish shop at the far side of the Hippo. It was a little place, no cop. He died last Easter and left it all to his three nieces. John felt it wasn't worth keeping on, so Anna and I said 'sell it', so he did; he'll pay you your share. Would you like to live here, dear? All I've got is yours, as you well know, and John would love you; I don't mean physically."

"Ah, no, dear," Theodora said. "It's dear of you to suggest it, but I feel that I'd better be alone till I've made my life again. What I want to do is to take a little house. Do you know of any charming little house that won't take all my money?"

"I do," Comito said. "John's got two, semi-detached, just at the back of this, between his timber-yard and the children's playground, if you know that beauty-spot. Come up to the next storey; you can see it from there."

They went up, and looked over John's well-stacked timber-yards. One patch of the yard was bare of plank, beyond it was a space and then a little green garden surrounding a small double white house. A road ran past the property to the north, another bounded it to the west. To the south was a small playing-field, fitted with swings, giant strides and climbing-ropes.

"That's the playground," Comito said. "You can see the school to the south there. The children yell a bit in the afternoons, otherwise it's quiet. There are lots of shops and neighbours just over the rise; you can't see them from here; it isn't dangerously lonely; and there's a civic guard-house quite close. John's men make a bit of a noise with the planks, of course, when they're loading or unloading. It's the near side of the house that is to let; the far side's let to two of John's aunts; they're great on horse-racing; they bet a lot. They get tips from the stables, they say, but John told them straight out, that they'd have to keep to the silver-ring or go under; he wasn't going to keep them, no, nor yet their bookies. They're at all the races, but they won't bother you at all; they're quiet enough. Phenie and Phosie their names are. We'll have some food; then you might like to see the house. It's in very good order; we had it painted in the summer, and it's always kept aired. The rent's a hundred and sixty-five pieces a year; the roof's good and there's a bit of garden."

During the meal, Theodora asked after her younger sister Anastasia.

"I was wondering when we'd come to her," Comito said. "Well, she's got a little boy, and she's made a name for herself. She's in with a pretty sickening set at The Three Crazy Shepherds in Meridian Street. They're very clever and all that, but I do like the sexes kept distinct, I must say. They do mime and that; she's what they call 'their mis-leading lady'. John hears all sorts of things; he says the Patriarch's police are having the place watched. She'll get a red ticket if she's not careful. She's not our style of clever, but she's got a style of her own, believe me. She's got a flat in what we call Paphian Court."

They looked at the house; Theodora took it at once.

"Now about furniture," Comito said. "I've got a lot of Uncle Paulos' furniture in store, for it is good, solid work, and John was for holding it. Anna won't look at it; but it will about fit you out. You've got solid sense and know how good work holds its own. I can let you have a lot of linen and things cheap. I know you, my dear; I'm not going to offer charity; we'll bargain about it. Pots and pans will be all you'll really need to get. There's a man from Samothrace down at the wharf who has a lot of this blue and white striped ware. It's very good, strong stuff; it doesn't chip; it's well baked, and it looks well. Marcos is the man's name; we'll go down there, shall we? I'll drive you down. Do let us. I love the wharves, and these island-shops, and, my dear, I love you and long to talk and talk. God, I'm glad you're quit of that would-be-thought; he was nothing but a suit of clothes. Come on, now. The girl'll fetch a chaise for us."

They drove to the wharves, to look at Marcos' pottery. As they turned into the open space on the water-front, Theodora saw the Red ship heaving in to the naval pier below them.

"There's the Red ship," she said. "I must go to welcome them, and see that the blankets and mats are turned-in to the Stores Intendant."

"He'll see to that, if you tell him," Comito said.

"I must do it," Theodora said, "or there won't be a blanket or a mat put back. Besides, there may be a ton of stores of different kinds belonging to Sosthenes. If I'm not there these fellows will pillage the lot."

"That's God's truth," Comito said. "Come on, then; we'll get aboard."

They drove on to the naval pier to see the ship come alongside. On the pier was a little company of patricians, with waiting carriages. A little knot of half a dozen men stood together, with another half-dozen, plainly less important, a few yards from them. They all wore small green badges on their left shoulders.

"We seem to have run into a Green Rally," Comito said. "That's Hypatius. What brings them all down to meet your ship?"

"Not love of the arts, I should say," Theodora said.

One of the less important group left his friends and came up to the two women as they left their chaise.

"You may not remember me," he said. "Theophanes? I lodged at your mother's once, in the old days." He was a big man, of about forty, with a lame left leg, and a voice, which even in quiet conversation was remarkable for its quality. "You're Mistress Comito, and you should be Mistress Theodora. I couldn't keep from saying a word. Your mother was very, very kind to me."

Theodora had no clear memory of him; Comito shrank from him as though he bit: she bridled, and said,

"What brings you down to the wharf?"

"O, we've just come down to welcome some friends,"

he said. "There they are, on deck. I must go now. I'm Theophanes, at The Roost, in Philemon Street, if you're ever passing that way."

He saluted them and went limping after his party, who were now at the gangway, to welcome Nicanor and one of his Persian friends, who were the first persons permitted to land. Nicanor came up the gangway, smiling and stern, to greet all there. After he had embraced the patricians formally he was deliberate with the others, giving to two or three a tempered handshake, and to the rest a smile or a nod. Hypatius led him to the waiting carriage and drove off.

Theodora spent the next two hours securing the naval stores for the Government and the other goods for Sosthenes. The stewards on board had not expected any interruption of the sort; she left them routed, humbled and angry.

"We must leave Marcos for tomorrow," Comito said. "You must come home, now, for some food; then I'll drive you to your Macedonia. It was like that dog's insolence to speak to us, that Theophanes. You wouldn't remember him much. Before your day. He was at the Palace, as a young man; he sang imitations of famous singers, and did some acrobatics; he had an awful fall from one of his tricks, and wrecked his left leg. Mother nursed him. Mother was awful good to artists in trouble. God, dear, she was a lesson to us. He went out of the profession then, into politics; he was a labour agitator and came near a quick end. He was out of The City for a long time; he'd got something to do with the silverminers. John knows all about him. He's a ward-politician

now, runs all the Sixth Ward for the Green Party. I've
crossed his lines a lot in these last months. You ask John
about him. But make no mistake : he's becoming a real
figure now; he's such an orator. He's a shady dog and as
tricky as they make them, but he's got all the Even
Wards right under his thumb. The Roost, in Philemon
Street is a bar."

"It was nice of him to remember Mother," Theodora
said.

"He's got all the talents of a clever politician," Comito
said. "He won't forget a face, nor the kind of trick that'll
take you. Next time he meets you he'll know you like to
hear Mother praised. I know his little ways. A lot of
John's men live in the Even Wards, and for the last year
he's been urging them to strike and so forth. He believes
in getting all associated trades, like builders, brick-makers,
timber-merchants, plumbers and glaziers to mass together and hold The City up to ransom. As he runs the
Even Wards he has the Ward-rates as a money-box."

She plainly had other quarrels with Theophanes, which
she kept to herself. Theodora did not ask more of him.
Instead, she asked,

"Who was the man who landed first, with the Persian;
the man they'd all come to meet?"

"I don't know," Comito said.

"I met him at Antioch. His nickname is Silpi. He's a
friend of the Praefect there, and I suppose is in secret service of some sort finding out about the Persians. His real
name is Nicanor. They called him Nicanor of the Bays."

"Was that Nicanor of the Bays?" Comito said. "Well,
I can tell you about him. You never cared for horse-

racing; I don't myself; but when you were a kid and I was going round with the boys I used to go to the races a lot; some of my boys put money on for me when they knew of something. But long before all that, I was taken to the races by Kumothoe's party. I played little servant to her, same as you did to me, when you began. It was the first time I ever went, and as it happened, I saw Nicanor's win. I was a kid, but I'll tell you about it, for it impressed me a lot, and it's still talked of sometimes, by these old race-goers."

"You never told me about it," Theodora said.

"No, very likely not. I was keeping my going to the races very dark; Mother didn't exactly approve of Kumothoe's gentleman friends. Of course, I don't know anything of horse-racing, but you know it's exciting the first time, all the crowd and the dresses, and the way the cars come round the bend, and go crash. I was hoping a team of grays would win. They came up the straight, dead level with another team; everybody thought they'd do it. Then this Nicanor came round the bend on the far side. He looked tremendous. He just lifted his team along, just as though he were picking them up and flinging them. He was screaming at them and all splashed with foam from them. I'll never forget it. How he made up the lead, I can't think. He must have reckoned he could do it and then made them do it. He did it by a short head; the Axion Bays, they called them; they were no good afterwards, but those fellows wouldn't mind that. It was a very famous win. That's why they called him Nicanor of the Bays. It was talked of all over the world."

Theodora asked Macedonia's father, if he knew any-

hing about Nicanor of the Bays. The little sharp black
yes of Menodotos gleamed.

"Yes, I do," he said. "I hear he came back today, with
our Ballet people."

"Yes, I saw him land. Do tell me about him. Is he in
he secret service?"

"I imagine that all that he does is very secret service."

"I saw him in Antioch, with some Persians, or pos-
ibly they were Syrians," she said. "I know that he won
a famous chariot race."

"Yes; the Imperial Gold Cup. I saw him win it. He
and a few friends won enormous sums of money by it.
They were his brother's horses. His brother was Theokritos: does that mean anything to you?"

"No."

"He was a Green. He had very great estates in the
west. When the last Emperor was failing, Theokritos
hoped to become Emperor after him. He gave his agent
an enormous sum of money, over a million pieces, a good
deal more, to bribe the Imperial Guard to bring this
about. Now the head of the Guard, Justinus, thought that
he would prefer to be Emperor himself. So he took the
money, bribed the Guard to choose himself as Emperor,
and, as soon as he was chosen, he put Theokritos and his
agent to death."

"Good Heaven."

"You didn't know that? Not many do. It isn't wise to
talk about it. I tell you, for you are as a daughter here.
Things are done in politics which aren't done in civil
life, nor even in business."

"But Nicanor is in the Emperor's service," Theodora

said. "He was with the Praefect at Antioch. He came home in the Government's ship."

"So did you," he said, "but you aren't in the Emperor's service. How can he be in the Emperor's service when the Emperor killed his brother? They were together in all things. Nicanor would no more serve Justinus than he would eat with a lackey. He's in blood-feud with Justinus. Do you know what a blood-feud is to those fellows? It is the one thought by day and the one dream by night. He was in Antioch for the blood-feud and has come back here for the blood-feud. He was met by the Green Faction leaders. You look out, then, for blood-feud from the Green Faction."

"I've been out of things for a long time," she said. "My first impression has been that things are very quiet and contented here."

"I hear lots of tales," he said. "I have a finger in many businesses. I meet people, and I go up along the coast a lot. I am in the salt-and-dried-fish business, which takes me north once or twice a month. All those fellows were in the last rebellion. They're in blood-feud with the Emperor. They make no secret of it, they're coming down on The City when the word comes, to avenge those whom they lost when they rebelled."

"They were disarmed, after that rebellion," Theodora said.

"Certainly; now they are re-armed. They make no secret of it. They show me the arms; all very good; and they know how to use them. There are seven battalions of picked spearmen drilling morning and evening within thirty miles of our North Gate. What have we got to

oppose them? Our army is all on its way to the East; it
is strung along the Karamanian Coast. Besides, for political reasons, they sent a Green man to be Praefect in the
North. You'll never find a Green Praefect very active
for men of the other side."

"That makes the north a danger point," Theodora
said. "The east is another. Everybody at Antioch was
certain of war in the spring. The south has its own problems. What about the west? Is that another danger
point?"

"There's rather a cry for a change," he said.

"A change must only make things worse," Theodora
said.

"Men have more will than wisdom," he said. "A
change will make things different."

"What is the trouble in the west?"

"Just the Green Faction again. All the great land-
owners and feudal lords are there with their slaves and
privilege. They do not call them slaves, but what else
are they? All of them are of the Green Faction, and all
of them under the last Emperor just shared out the great
appointments among themselves. How can they sit still
under an Emperor who was a private soldier under at
least a dozen of them? He was batman to Lord Kallimachus's father. Then the Empress, born a slave and
afterwards a camp-follower. These great ladies from the
west come to do their waiting-service at the Palace, and
the old Empress asks them how they do fish-patties. They
say she asked the Lady Kallinike out to have a pern'orth
of whelks off the barrow. They loathe her. Then there's
the young Prince, Justinian."

"One minute," Theodora said. "They said in the east, that he is coming to command the army there. Has he gone yet?"

"No. He was to have gone, but the old Emperor, his uncle, has been ill with his wound again. That wound is the cause of half the trouble, really; he can't get about and look after things. Every now and again in the autumn the wound breaks out. It did so some weeks ago, and the nephew had to postpone his going. The nephew's another cause of the trouble. The Emperor is training him to succeed him as Emperor. The Emperor Justinian, eh? Well, all the Most Illustrious and the sons and daughters of the great they writhe at the thought; they loathe Justinian."

"He's not a private soldier or a camp-follower. Does he ask the ladies out to pern'orths of whelks?"

"They'd like him better if he did. No, he's a scholar. He's always with old priests and old lawyers, reading old Gospels and old Law. He's a new-comer here, and no one so far has a good name for him. Of course, you wouldn't expect those feudal people to like a scholar; they'd prefer a charioteer, or a pugilist, or a man who trains performing dogs. But even the Church people dislike him; they like a good Orthodox chap who will persecute a heretic. They say he always sees both sides of the question. Then, of course, he's new here. He is a provincial, just come to town. He does not know how he offends. To give you an instance. A certain lord to whom I'd been of service asked me to the Autumn Races. I don't belong to that world, thank God, but I went, I always do. I was near some great people who were running teams, and they were watching the Prince who was in the royal box. The Prince never once looked at the races. He looked down once or twice as the cars went to the parade, then he went through state reports all the time. These lords who were watching said, 'Look at the fellow. Look at him there. Insulting the whole nobility.' It is one little thing, but it shows you. He did not know that he was giving offence to some hundreds of landlords from all over the west, how could he know? But he was, all the time that he was thinking that he was serving the State, he was infuriating Greens and Blues alike. They call him the Sardican Sage, and Tino and all sorts of worse names. Then he will not marry the girls that are brought up for him to see. Twenty or thirty fathers and mothers would like their daughter to be Empress; they bring out their girls, and he asks them if they have read Zozimus on Babylas, or Chrysostom on Isaiah. They don't find that much fun, of course, but one would have thought they'd put up with it, to be Empress and have three new frocks a day."

"I've come back to a new world," Theodora said. "If the Prince, Justinian, is to command an army, I suppose he knows something of war."

"Every Sardican knows something of war. But you cannot believe what fury his appointment has roused. All the Greens expected that Hypatius would get the command."

Now Hypatius, the last Emperor's nephew, was a by-word for military incompetence. Theodora knew something of war, having lately had to organize and fire a campaign of her own. She had heard much of Hypatius' uselessness. Her face showed her feelings.

Mendotos said, "You must have the aristocracy in supreme command; otherwise the army contracts get into the wrong hands, and the war will be fought by soldiers. But I am talking Rumour. You may begin to fear that you have come to a troubled City, and a threatened Empire, and a doomed dynasty. I go about, and have many fingers in little pies, and hear all sorts of things from different quarters. I have to decide on what I hear; so I say to myself, 'I must use caution.' There are signs, my dear, that it may come on to blow."

"Blow hard?" she asked.

"Maybe; enough," he said.

She had leave of absence from the theatre for a few days, while she moved into the Number One, Arbutus Terrace, as it was called, with Uncle Paulos's handsome, well-made things, some nice linen and other properties from Comito, and a new set of pots and wares from Marcos. Kallianassa helped in the arrangement. The house was spacious enough, though it had only four living-rooms. From the northern windows she could see a gleam of blue water and the Asian shore; from the eastern window the white walls and red roofs of Sycae across the water; from the southern upper windows she looked over towards the Palace and the marvellous harbour. She loved the little house; it was a queen of a little house, with beauty on three sides of it and useful shops on the fourth. Being ever scrupulously neat, and industrious in neatness, she soon had the simple house arranged.

She went to see her young sister Anastasia at her flat in Paphian Court. She had not seen her for some years; Anastasia had been touring and she had been with Hekebolos. She was smaller and even more delicately made than Theodora; she was the queen of the tiny theatre of the Three Crazy Shepherds, where the wits enjoyed elegant and pointed social satire, and the small, masked mimes in which she excelled. Her flat was like herself, small and elegant. Her white walls had but one decoration, a drawing in black chalk of herself. Knowing that the wits would certainly have plied her with epigrams about events and persons, Theodora hoped for instruction.

"You will know everybody," she said. "I've heard disquieting talk since I landed. How dangerous is the situation?"

"The Greens never admit that Justo is Emperor by right; they think he got the purple by fraud; so he did. He's lately had his nephew Tino here, planning to make him co-Emperor, with right of succession. The Greens don't like that, naturally. And they don't like Tino, either. I've not met Tino; I daresay he's all right; but he's always reading Theology, what we call 'The sour milk of the Word'."

"There must be something more than that stirring, surely?"

"O, yes, plenty. The Greens are raging because of Hypatius. You see, Patie was the old Emperor's nephew, and did expect to be Emperor after him, on the grounds, that as there were no brains in his head, the crown couldn't hurt him. Justo simply put him aside and took

the throne. But Justo did try to placate Patie; he sent
him to Persia, to make peace with the Persians. Well,
now Justo thinks that he never tried to make peace, but
insulted the Persians so that the negotiations would stop.
They did stop, as you know. Justo's a very suspicious old
man, and he thinks Patie did stop them. Anyhow, he has
recalled Patie, deprived him of all his offices and orders,
and has simply wrung the lives out of his staff, trying
to get something against him. I hear he's got nothing;
but all the staff were younger sons of these great Green
landlords in the west, and they are all wild with fury.
Then, the last rebellion left some blood-feuds to be settled. It's an unsettled time for your new theatre to be
opening in. Here's my friend, Brusanian. Come in,
Brusie darling. This is my sister, who wants to know all
about Tino."

Brusie came in; he was an elegant young man, with
finger-nails painted green to shew his political leanings.

"Tino?" he said. "I've just heard Tino's latest. Lord
and Lady Olympia, you will know the pseudonyms, have
a daughter Phemonoe. They own a hundred square miles
or so, and Phemonoe had expressed willingness to be
Basilissa. You know the sort of thing: 'I bring birth,
breeding, and the support of all the cousins you'll find
places for, and in return I am content to share your
power.' Good. They come to arrange the matter. Lord
Olympia with one ambition, to win the Imperial Gold
Cup; Lady Olympia with one madness, against the waste
of public money in pampering the poor. In the midst of
them Phemonoe, not indisposed to love, if the purple bed
be ready. They come. They see. Do they conquer? Tino

begins. He wants their support on the Council for doubling The City's water-supply. Lady Olympia falls foaming, biting the mats. He continues. He wants their support in stopping the damnable cruelty of the Races. Lord Olympia bursts three blood vessels and is carried out senseless. Tino turns to the seeker for love. What manuscript gospels has she in the family library? She, with biting coldness: 'Really, I think you had better ask the librarian who is paid to look after such things.' They went away mad with rage, and, of course, Tino didn't even know that he had made a mess of things."

Theodora came away soon after that, but not before hearing some of the other gems of Brusie's mind: "My father is bringing down my black hair in anguish to the bankruptcy court": "Love takes two to make, and too too much trouble": also a fragment of poetry:

"Friend, what is left for youth beneath the sun?
  Who does not feel too old at twenty-one?
  What can be left, to suffer or to do,
  Ere the decrepitude of twenty-two?"

She gathered also that he was the son of Philip the Pisidian, the sub-Praefect of the Imperial Household, and that, therefore, his tale of Justinian might have some slight foundation in fact. On her way home, she was surprised by a crowd across her way. All the western road was blocked by people waiting for an approaching procession which was marching across the Fourth Ward with a military band and singing. The tune and the words were to become very familiar to her. The Fourth

Ward was a stronghold of the Greens. The windows were hung with Green banners, and most of the crowd wore Green rosettes. As the band drew near, the crowd took up the refrain:

"Up with the Green Flag and down with the Blue." It was a political procession, she supposed. Possibly some ward-election was in progress. She stayed to watch it, for the band was at point to pass. It came past in style, with kettle drummers on greys, followed by banners bearing the words "Vote Green for Liberty": "Hypatius asks your vote": "Vote for Hypatius". After the band, came men in columns of five, each man wearing a Green sash; after these came horsed floats, bearing allegorical figures, Peace, Plenty and the like, all comely women, attended by nymphs who flung little Green favours at the passers-by. "Hypatius for Liberty," they cried; so they passed on and left the way clear for her.

She wondered what Hypatius had to do with Liberty, and how and why people were to vote for him; other matters put him soon out of her mind.

Early the next morning had been appointed by Sosthenes for the opening of rehearsals at the new theatre. The company had to gather there, betimes, in the street, before the traffic of the day had begun. A priest was to bless the house, Sosthenes was to speak, and Macedonia was to unveil the design over the entrance and give the theatre its name. All the dancers, being superstitious, had dreaded stormy weather for the rite. However, Nature was kind; the sun shone and the air was still. All the company mustered, without one absentee. They stood there in the empty great street, staring at the newly-cut stone with the mason's dust still white on the pavement. The priest was there; he prayed that the theatre might be for the joy of Christian men and women for many years to come, and that those working in it might be blessed with inspiration and the happiness of giving happiness. Sosthenes said that he had been loyally helped by all there, and now had something to tell them: the Emperor, their Ruler, had heard of them, and had asked that they would perform for him. "The Emperor has commanded a week of Ballet, for his Court and friends, partly to celebrate his recovery from a bout of pain, partly to celebrate the coming departure of the Prince Justinian to command the Eastern Army. This is a great honour," Sosthenes said. "It is wonderful to begin here in the presence of our Ruler. I now hand the key to our chief star, the Lady Macedonia. I ask her to unveil our emblem, to name the theatre, to open the door, to be the first to enter, and to declare the house open. After that, we shall all hurry in, the door will be locked, and we shall begin rehearsal of the Antioch programmes, as soon as you have put on practice dress. Lady Macedonia, will you display the emblem?"

The dainty, exquisite, radiant woman took the white line and plucked the curtain along its rod. Behind the linen, along fifty feet of the façade was a marvellous coloured high relief of white swans in flight across a blue background, done by Phalanthos the Lycian. Nothing more beautiful had been seen in The City for years. "I name this theatre THE SWAN MAIDENS," Macedonia cried. She stepped lightly, opened the door, stepped across the threshold and called aloud, "I declare the house open."

After this, all the company flooded in, and after wandering over the house, admiring all its beauties, and chattering with joy at being attached to it, having a sort of possession in it, they scattered to the dressing-rooms.

It was a small theatre with a big stage. It seated some five hundred people in great comfort, so that all had good sight of the entire acting area, and freedom of movement in their places. The lighting of the house and stage was mainly daylight, cleverly admitted and reflected. The artificial light was most skilfully multiplied by reflectors. In that most beautiful City of clear light, the daylight, so helped, sufficed for the effects desired, which were those of the orchestra, or dancing-floor, as well as those of a framed picture.

Theodora had come to the theatre in a black practice dress, covered by a robe. She had only to cast aside the robe and tie her dancing shoes, to be ready to help Macedonia in the warming-up. They were going to work not in the practice-room but on the stage itself. She came up onto the stage, and there found Sosthenes with Iophon, the painter, who was doing new costumes for them.

She said to Sosthenes, "What a very beautiful frieze you have made for the entrance. And what a happy augury, to open to the Emperor."

"Yes," Sosthenes said. "The ships which brought us, brought news of our success at Antioch and mentioned Macedonia. Well, Macedonia, the province, is a sort of Paradise to the Emperor; his people come from there. He is really coming to see her. If he likes her, he'll probably kiss her and call her his niece; do, please, warn her. Of course, he isn't very well, and may change his mind about coming, or the Empress may change it for him. This City's full of sycophants. Word has passed that the Court is coming, and everybody everywhere is pulling strings to try to be in for the opening. I wonder, if you'll look at these costumes of Iophon's, if you have a moment."

She went into the wings and tried the costumes; she chatted with Iophon about them. Something in a ray of light made her say, "What a charming effect you could have in a Danae ballet, instead of a fall of gold, a rush of little loves in cloth of gold."

Macedonia called her at that instant, and she joined her friend for the warming-up. Iophon went back to Sosthenes.

"She can mime and pose, that one," he said. "You ought to let her dress a show some time: she has the feel. She might ruin you, but it might be quite pretty."

"I don't care enough for women to let one ruin me," Sosthenes said. "I serve them up as a dish to the public, it is true; but I prefer men cooks, like you, thank you; with them I know where I am."

The rehearsal began almost immediately; they ran through the first ballet, took the second half of it a second time; ran through the second ballet, and then broke off for twenty minutes. Theodora took Macedonia to her room and deftly massaged her feet and ankles in the subtle way of the Old Winter Palace. She had just finished, when a messenger knocked at the dressing-room door and asked her to go to the practice-room about some costumes. She was in her practice dress, still. She came out of the room and trotted along the corridor. Being new to the building, she took the turn which led to the stage. She saw someone loitering about there, seemingly lost. She turned and presently reached the big practice-room, which was heavy with the smells of new-sawn wood and white paint. No one was there. Some baskets of costumes were ranged near the wall. Someone had taken some costumes from these and arranged them, perhaps to air, on lines stretched from the barres. A woman with a duster looked in from the opposite door, and said, "He's gone away, Miss, the painter gentleman." She supposed that Iophon wanted her for something, for these were his costumes for the ballet of The Golden Apple.

She was examining them, when she heard a step and turned. She saw a strange man advancing towards her. He was unlike anyone she had ever seen; this, in itself, told her that he was an unusual being. He was of the middle height, rather handsome, with the long brown moustaches then worn by the Most Illustrious. He had an odd look in his eyes, as though he couldn't find what he wanted, but meant to go on looking (so she summed it up to herself). He wore the white and gold of Praefectual rank, with the special, broad banding of the almost scarlet purple of the Imperial Palace. He wore three small embroidered blue crosses, one at the throat, one at each shoulder. She thrilled through with the thought, that this was Prince Justinian, the "Tino" of Brusanian's story; no other man could look like that or wear those marks of rank. What on earth brought the Prince here? She knew that "ceremony and respect" called upon her to curtsey; and that not even Macedonia could curtsey with more grace than she. She curtseyed, and her curtsey was a very beautiful thing, well worth going a mile to see.

He bowed and said, "Do forgive me. I followed you here. I'm afraid I'm lost in this building. I'm Justinian; I came to see Sosthenes, if he is anywhere here."

"He is in the theatre," she said. "I'll find him, Prince."

"No, no," he said. "Please, one minute. Are you the Lady Macedonia?"

"No," she said, "only her friend."

"Do you dance with the company, may I ask?"

"I have been a dancer, but not with this company. I am a helper here."

"How very beautifully you curtsey." She blushed. She liked being appreciated, yet she felt just a little queer about this. "I suppose you were at Antioch with the company?"

"Just at the end of its stay, Prince. I came home with them."

"A friend in Antioch writes that your Ballets are the most amazing things ever seen. Is that all this dancer Macedonia, or is it Sosthenes?"

"Macedonia is marvellous for lightness, grace and radiance," she said, "but Sosthenes makes the Ballets what they are."

"It's a new synthesis, I suppose," he said. "That is the marvel everywhere: a thing is dead, and without meaning; a genius turns it into its constituents and mixes them anew; then there is life again."

"I hope you will think so," she said.

"I wish some Sosthenes-Patriarch would do as much by the services," he said. "The chants are all threadbare and the ritual is like the mule turning the applepress, 'half asleep half the time and dead asleep the rest'."

"If you will be seated, Prince," she said, turning down one of the hinged seats on the wall, "I will find Sosthenes for you."

He moved towards the seat. "That's very kind of you, but I will find him. Tell me, while you were in Antioch was old Stephanos preaching?"

"Alas, Prince, no. He was away in the north somewhere; he had been preaching outside the city, and had not returned."

"You say, 'Alas'. Are you one of his flock, then?"

"No, Prince, I never saw him, nor heard him preach. I had a letter for him, but was never able to present it."

He looked at her with quick interest. "Did you go to Antioch from Alexandria, by any chance?"

"Yes, Prince."

The answer seemed to excite him. "Tell me, will you," he said, "if you can forgive the question, tell me, was your letter to Stephanos from Timotheus?"

"Yes, Prince," she answered.

She had not expected such an effect from such a question; his face became radiant.

"You saw Timotheus, then? Tell me, are they persecuting him? Are they half killing him? How is he? You actually talked with him, only a few weeks ago."

"Indeed, Prince, I did. They are not molesting him at the moment. Some of his friends there told me that the Orthodox were cruel to him when he first came there; but not lately."

"Even the Orthodox will recognize a saint," he said, "if they let him live long enough. Did you hear him preach?"

"No, Prince. He talked to me and advised me."

"Tell me; did he speak of being kept from preaching?"

"He cannot preach in any church. He can preach at the sweetmeat-seller's. The little boys are sometimes paid to shout outside when he does so. But then he goes out and talks to them, and they all become his friends. But since the beginning of the year even the shouting has been stopped."

"Ah," he said, "Philotas has done something then. I heard Timotheus preach before he was driven out of The City. He was the greatest light that ever shone on me. His word was like light, the darkness went before it. Unfortunately, I was only in The City for a week, then. You heard him often, perhaps?"

"Yes, Prince, when I was little. I was his parishioner. I feel that I owe everything to him. He is the greatest living soul."

"You are lucky," he said, "to have heard Timotheus often. I only have his writings, but I carry those with me wherever I go. Which do you like of the writings?"

"I only know the *Evening Hymn*, the *Prayer in Affliction*, and the little piece, *My Father's House*."

"You have the kernel of the matter in those. But don't

you know *The Journey to The East,* and *Why Thomas Went?"*

"No, Prince. I have heard that they are for theologians."

"They are for Timotheans," he cried. "They are two golden keys for unlocking the entire universe. Will you, please, tell me your name?"

"I am Theodora."

She was beginning to wonder, if she were. She was now talking with the heir to the Empire about a deprived priest in exile on the count of heresy. The Ballet, Sosthenes and everything else seemed gone into air. Here the pair of them stood, linked with an admiration for Timotheus.

"Lady Theodora," he said, "will you tell me where you live? I want to ask you to let me send you those two short books of Timotheus. You ought to know them."

"That is very, very kind of you," she said. "I cannot tell you what Timotheus means to me. I am not Lady Theodora; simply Theodora. I live at One, Arbutus Terrace."

"O, up there on the hill, beyond the timber-yard?"

She was astounded. How did this heir to the Empire know two houses in an out-of-the-way quarter?

"Yes, Prince," she said; "near the playground."

"I know it," he said. "The master of the School there is the writer on St. John, a man called Pammenes. I often go to see him on texts and so forth. But if you will let me, I will send you those two books; and others later, perhaps. You will know that the two I mentioned are the heretical books. By heretical, I mean illumined by God; a horrible shock to tallow candles."

She laughed; she had a very winning laugh. He looked at her with admiration. She knew that he had liked her laughter and her curtsey. She saw Sosthenes in the doorway, perplexed at the Prince's coming, and wondering what he was finding to talk about with Theodora.

"Here is Sosthenes, Prince," she said.

"Ah, thank you," he said. He moved over to Sosthenes and shook him by the hand. "Let me welcome you to The City," he said, "and congratulate you on this most beautiful theatre. I come now with a shocking proposal, and as I know it to be shocking, I felt that I must come myself to make it in person. You must tell me if it be quite impossible."

"Nothing should be impossible," Sosthenes said.

"We know that some things are inexpedient," Justinian said. "I come to ask, if your first performance might be tomorrow? The Emperor asked, first, for three days from now, but he wants the plan to be advanced. I have to start to the East not later than a week from tomorrow. That would give six full performances for the Court and friends before going."

Sosthenes had an impassive pale face, and kept his countenance. Theodora knew what he was feeling.

"Three different programmes, each given twice," he said.

"That would be perfect," Justinian said.

"I'm afraid not," Sosthenes said. "It will be old work, and it will not be perfect. But it shall be done. Tomorrow, then, at the time appointed for two days later. We will be as ready as we can be. We will not fail you, Prince, be sure."

Justinian said, "I know you will not. And believe me, I well know what I have asked of you and of the Company."

"No, no," Sosthenes said, "we know that it was you who asked. We are very sensible of that. All shall be well."

"I'll go, then. My Uncle, I know, will be delighted, that you can do this. He asked me to express to you his sense of your kindness, if you could undertake to do it."

Sosthenes went with him to the door and shewed him out of the theatre. He came back at once and called all the company to the stage.

"We have to open tomorrow," he said. "The Emperor and Court will be here. We open with the Swan Maidens, The Merry Men, and St. George. Get dressed. We must try all the costumes at once."

Theodora had expected an outburst from him, for he was a man of quick temper, prone to fly out against any slighting of the arts or any want of understanding of what an artist needs. He did not fly out. He said, "We shall have little sleep this week. A new theatre and the company just landed. Still, the Prince came in person to ask it as a favour. The last Emperor would have sent his butler with an order, and wouldn't have got. Justinian knows about art and thought. He knows a lot about most things. What was he talking to you about? Law?"

"No. Heresy," Theodora said.

"Had you met him before?" Sosthenes asked.

"No; never. I didn't know who he was, but guessed by his purple."

"I suppose he knows more about heresy than the Bench of Bishops."

"He does, he was illuminating. But I must get to these costumes for Macedonia."

The work that day was taxing and tiring. From time to time, about once in every four hours, Theodora and Macedonia crept out of the theatre for a breath of air. When they came out, for the first breath that day, they were conscious of a noise like barking from two or three different points. Macedonia asked what it was.

"O, it's only public speaking," Theodora said. "A preacher, or men trying to sell things, or a ward-election."

"Do let's go along to hear one," Macedonia said. "One can always see a good crowd effect, which may come in useful."

"No one wants a crowd effect when you're on the stage," Theodora said. "But come on; it will only take a minute."

They went up the slope towards the nearest of the barkers. He was standing on a small two-horsed waggon in the square of St. Eudokia. He wore Green favours; his horses had attendants and trappings all spanged with Green rosettes. The speaker was a big, burly man with a mouth of much stretch and a bellow of a voice.

"Yes," he was saying, "I asked you that to find out, and you give me the answer I wanted. You say Hypatius lost his army."

"So he did," a man at the edge of the crowd said.

"Yes. Perhaps you were there to help him lose it?

Why did he lose it? Because the Blues gave him no chance
to save it. Because the Blues starved the army, so that it
had neither weapons nor transport, so that it had neither
full ranks nor trained officers, nor food, nor information,
and then sent Hypatius up to fight the enemy who had
all things. Did he hesitate? Did he risk the disgrace of
refusing the command? No, he took the command, and
made such an attack on the enemy as Leonidas made on
the Persians at Thermopylae. That's the man Hypatius
is, a hero. And now he is coming to your help again. He
and the Green Party are coming to save you citizens
from the evils that beset you."

"That's the style," a young man cried. "Good old
Green Party."

At this some musicians who had been among the
crowd, waiting a cue, struck up a tune. Their fugleman
cried, "Now come join in everyone. I'll sing the chorus
first; then you'll all know it." He struck into the chorus:

"Yes, we'll lift aloft our glorious Green Banner
Above the Blue that fain would drag us in the dust."

It was a rousing tune, and he was a persuasive singer,
who knew how to win all there into taking part. For two
minutes the little crowd was very happy. At the end of
the song, the singer cried: "I thank you all for joining in
the song. Be ready to greet Hypatius with it, when he
comes to save your liberty." The musicians then climbed
aboard the wagon, and struck up the march "Up with
the Green Flag, etc." The men with the Green rosettes

led the horses, and off they went with music, to another pitch. Away to the westward another band was playing that march. Down below on the Fish-Quays, another speaker or barker was yapping; very soon, he ceased to yap and another band began there, with another very good voice to sing to it, and an even better tune. From further north, on wafts of wind, came other yaps and singings.

"They are everywhere," Theodora said. "Now we must go back. Why is Hypatius coming to save us? How is he going to do it?"

"It is only the usual autumn Ward election," Macedonia said.

"O, no; it is more than that," Theodora answered. "The Ward elections must be over. It is some magisterial election. The Greens are taking a great deal of trouble over it, to have all those musicians."

"They always spend a lot of money on elections," Macedonia said.

"I liked that tune," Theodora said. "Comito would have made that tune go all over the world, if she had had it at the Palace."

"She would indeed," Macedonia said. "But you would have made it go into one person's heart, which is a great deal further. There never was anyone like you."

"Now come along," Theodora said. "We've got to work."

While waiting in the wings with Perdiccas, watching Macedonia on the stage, she said,

"The Greens are very busy everywhere."

"Yes," he said, "with musicians and wagons. They have some in every Ward. They are said to be going to run Hypatius for something."

"What for, some Praefectship?"

"I don't know, something important. It might be the army. Justinian's being sent to command the army. They resent that, of course; he'll command so many important Greens. They always think that the army belongs to them."

She pondered this, at intervals, during the day. She reflected that Perdiccas had probably guessed rightly. That would be the answer; the Greens wanted the army to be commanded by a Green. Hypatius was the most important Green in the army or out of it. The Party was now stirring, to cause Justinian to be recalled and Hypatius put in his place. Yet she remembered what had been told of recent happenings. The old, distrustful soldier in the purple was not likely to consent to Hypatius taking his nephew's place. Indeed, was it not plain, that he had appointed his nephew to the command to spite the Green Party, and disgrace Hypatius still further, to show him and his friends that the Greens were distrusted and despised. No doubt that was the Emperor's purpose. This was the reply or counter-blow, or the preparation for it.

Twice, when she left the theatre for a two minute walk with Macedonia that afternoon and evening, she heard the strains of the Green bands, playing either the march or the song. Both had now caught the minds of the crowds, little boys were singing the words, and men and women sang snatches of them at work. They were rehearsing late that night. When she slipped out with

Macedonia to a little fish-eating-house down the hill for
some bread and anchovies in a brief rest, she came upon
a bigger effort. Some hundreds of lads and young women
were in procession along the wharves, to the massed
Green bands. They marched with torches, which were
made of some oily rags mounted upon sticks, and gave
out more smoke than light. With rapt faces these young
people went by singing that they would lift aloft the
glorious Green banner. They were lifting it aloft, some
of them, and finding it unruly in the gathering wind.
At the end of each chorus, the leader of each company,
probably some fine young athlete from the University,
would shout, "Ready," pause an instant, and then shout,
with all his followers:

> "One
> Two.
> Three.
> Hy . . . patius."

After this, they went on with the marching song about
the banner.

"They're having great fun," Macedonia said.

"Stupid of them to use rag," Theodora said. "It always smokes. They ought to get those resiny Easter
candles, you know the sort, which are all bright light."

"I like that smoky effect," Macedonia said. Indeed,
after the crowd had passed it looked something like Sa-
tan's army slouching back into Hell after a defeat.

"What a day the Greens are having," Theodora said.
"First the speakers, now the students. It is all designed
to insult the Emperor, don't you think?"

"Oh, no; not insult. These are students; they are only enjoying themselves."

"Somehow, I don't feel that this is enjoyment or playfulness. It may be all froth, but the tide that lifts it is a powerful thing and stretches far."

"My father's been talking to you," Macedonia said. "Everybody with a gloomy view of the world tells Father the very worst that he can imagine. Then Father, who believes it all, is more than usually cautious, and makes a lot of money. He is always hearing of men who are going to seize power, or burn the navy or some other wild thing. Then Father says, 'Money is going to be tight', and refuses a loan, or offers only half what the seller wants."

"Well; come back now to the work. I don't know what money is going to be. I know that all The City will be mad with joy about you this time tomorrow."

"Ah, dear," Macedonia said. "At Antioch and Alexandria and Athens, I had a mixed audience. The mixed audience so far has always been enchanted. But any special audience is difficult, as you know. It'll be the Court tomorrow, with the officials. The Purple, as you know, is not very elegant at present, and the permanent officials are always jaded and superior. Perdiccas calls them the 'Permanent Sniffs'. The next day we shall have the left-overs, for whom there was not room the first time, then the Court again, then the left-overs. I shake in my shoes when I think of what it will be."

"I will eat your shoes without salt if you do not lay them all prostrate with joy," Theodora said. "The Purple, as you call it, or them, may not be elegant; but it

does know how to dance. The Emperor was famous for
it. He is looking forward to it intensely, and when he
sees the reality he will probably make you dishonourable
proposals. You will enchant him as you enchant everybody."

They rehearsed very late and far into the morning.
Theodora did not reach her little house till the bells
were ringing for the three o'clock service in the monas-
teries. On the table under the lamp was a little package
tied in rough blue linen. It was from Justinian, with a
note written by him, in the dull red indelible ink which
looked so well upon parchment. It said briefly that he
begged that she would accept the little scrolls by Timotheus, and that he looked forward to the Ballet. The
scrolls were copies made by some skilled scribe, who had
added capitals of simple flowers, the toad-flax, the wild
strawberry, the speedwell and little white clover; they
had been often opened, for the strings were somewhat
worn. She knew that they were his own special copies
which had been made for him and carried about by him.
Tired as she was, she was thrilled by the gift, and by the
knowledge that Timotheus was near her. She would be
able to commune with him daily. She would be able to
find other books by him and come to know his mind. Ah,
but would she? He had been persecuted; his books had
been sought out and burned. These two copies might well
be the only writings by him in the whole City. The
Prince of the Empire had given them to her. It was a
princely gift more precious to her than much fine gold.
She kissed the scrolls and sat for a time blessing Demetria, who had caused her to go to Timotheus, and pray-

ing for the joy of that old man who had given her such comfort, and led her back to a life which held friends and interest for her.

She could not sleep for a little. She thought of things to tell Macedonia, and to see to directly she reached the theatre. Many, many little things had to be done; she imprinted these on her memory, and settled the order of their doing. She thought, then, of the giver of the gifts, the Prince. She had met and talked with the Prince. He was not by any means the indifferent person of gossip. She compared that gracious, earnest, very simple, active man with the tactless boor of Brusanian's ill-natured tale, and the gossip of the others. "He is always going about with old priests and lawyers, reading old Gospels and obsolete laws." Well, the old often had wisdom. Old Gospels and laws preserved what was true and just. Whatever has been true and just will have something of truth and justice always. She thought it possible, that if the Emperor and the Court liked the Ballet, the Green Faction might contrive to trouble the next performances. With this thought, she fell asleep.

It was a busy day at the theatre. At an early hour people had begun to gather at the entrance and in the street, either to admire the design of the Swan Maidens or to take positions from which to watch the Imperial procession. Theodora was busy throughout the morning. From time to time, when she could get out for a gulp of air in the intervals between the runs-through, she heard here and there the strains of the Green bands and the barkings of the Green orators. When the doors at last opened, the audience entered. The officials of the Court

and the families of the Praefects came to their seats; the
house glittered and was fragrant. Theodora, who had
contrived to come to the front of the house for a moment,
recognized some of the faces and remembered some of
the gossip about them. As she waited near the little door
which led to the stage, she heard the distant cheering of
the crowds in the road and then, plainly, the beat of the
kettle-drums of the cavalry guard. At this sound, she
beckoned to those within. The four trumpeters whom
Sosthenes had made famous throughout the East, came
out with their silver trumpets, and passed to the entrance.
Sosthenes had prepared a surprise for the old Emperor.
As he dismounted from his coach, these trumpeters blew
the marvellous cavalry-call of his old regiment. Sosthenes, who was waiting there to receive him, had the satisfaction of seeing him gleam with pleasure as he stiffened
up to attention at the sound. Both he and Euphemia, the
old Empress, were profoundly touched by that old call,
which had roused them in many a rough fortune when
they had been of the regiment. As the call ceased, Theodora slipped into the wings to cheer Macedonia, who was
now shaking like a leaf at the thought of going on. They
heard the house rise and cheer, as the music played the
Imperial Welcome. There was no going back now. The
plunge had been taken, the swimmers had to enter the
water. In an instant the ballet would start; what would
happen then? Theodora heard the house settle to their
seats, amid a buzz of talk which lulled as the overture
began. Theodora prayed, as she held Macedonia there,
"O God, let this be a success. Dear child, don't fear.
You'll win this house to be your slaves. O God, let Sos-

thenes triumph. Macedonia darling, now get ready; the curtain's going up. O God, help us."

The curtain rose on the Swan Maidens, and at once the chattering, idle, empty audience ceased to chatter, to be idle and to be empty. Theodora still held Macedonia to her, for that frightened fawn was whispering that she couldn't do it. "You can do it," Theodora whispered back; in the slang of the Old Winter Palace, she added, "You know you can do it. You can knock these gajoes silly and get every hand and every foot." At that instant, the music reached the warning bars; she released her friend and thrust her from her. Macedonia gulped, gave a wan glance at her friend, slid two steps nearer the stage, gulped again, and on the beat floated on, like a bird of enchantment. Theodora held her breath with joy, for from that instant the house in front of her froze to a tensity of stillness. She was old to the ways of the stage; she knew the degrees of attention to be won by the art. She had known outrageous, riotous support, in the old days of Comito, when the house would be helpless with laughter; she well knew how to win that kind of support; but this was a very different thing. This was the thing which she could never dream of doing; this was holding the audience breathless with joy by sheer beauty. Macedonia had taken all those worldlings in one instant into the heart of romance.

She watched her friend in each step; she had known her to be exquisite in this part, but had not expected that the audience would make such a difference to her. With this audience, and on this new stage, she surpassed anything that Theodora had ever seen or imagined. It was

as though the excitement in the house all focussed as it
was in a small space had given her the perception of new
beauties that might be added to each gesture and each
step. It was as though this added beauty lifted her at last
into another way of being, in which every mortal and
perishing thing in her fell away, and she became a spirit
whirling in an exaltation. The act ended in a movement
of inimitable grace; and then the tumult began.

Theodora saw Iophon beside her suddenly; he nodded
to her, that the thing had gone well; but indeed it had
gone better than well; all the house was in frantic joy,
shouting, crying, waving and flinging. As at Alexandria
and at Antioch the rain of flowers, jewels and trinkets
came down upon the stage. There could be no doubt of
Macedonia's triumph; nothing like it had been known
in The City ever; not even at a chariot race. Five minutes passed, and still the tumult rang; ten minutes passed;
they were still cheering. The dancers were all on the
stage bowing and bowing again and again. Whenever it
flagged for two seconds, the officers of the Guard, sitting
back near the entrance, shouted: "Macedonia". Theodora
stood with the stage hands in the wings. "I never saw
anything like this," one said. She saw the excited, happy
dancers laughing and crying on the stage, or going down
into the orchestra to bow; then suddenly the shouting
of the audience rose to a roar, not wholly of applause,
partly of indignation. What was causing this change in
the mood? Theodora turned to the hands near her; the
noise in the house hushed suddenly. In the hush she
heard plainly the blare of an approaching brass band
outside the theatre, playing "Up with the Green Flag

and down with the Blue". She heard and could just see
some of the Court leaving the house to deal with the disturbers. By a happy hint from Sosthenes, the musicians
in the theatre struck up the Imperial Welcome. The audience rose and cheered the Imperial couple. In the midst
of the cheering, the dancers made a swift chain which
glid round the dancing-floor, made obeisance to the Imperial pair, and so slipped away to change for the second
ballet.

The second ballet went like the April flowers, which
lead on the flowers in May. Again, in the interval, the
Green bands attempted to march past the theatre. One of
the stage hands went out to see what happened. He told
Theodora that it was only just these young Green lads,
with the songs; nothing serious; the Civil Guards were
there, now, he said, and had taken three of them to the
cells and smashed a drum.

Then came the third ballet, with Macedonia's great
solo dance. Sosthenes sent word before it began that at
the end, all the company would remain on the stage till
the Emperor dismissed them. The third ballet went with
superb effect from the beginning. At the end of it, Theodora stood in the wings with a cloak for Macedonia. She
watched the adorable grace of her friend, and knew the
rapture of the audience. The ballet ended in a roaring
storm of cheering. In the interval, many of the Court
had sent out for flowers, baskets of fruit, and rosettes of
blue. These now were laid in heaps along the dancing-
floor. A stage hand beside Theodora said, "The old Emp
is said to be just off his head with delight." In a moment,
the Imperial welcome was played, and as the audience

rose and cheered, the 'old Emp' appeared upon the stage, limping pitifully. Theodora had a good view of him now; he turned to the left towards her. Sosthenes, who was backing before him, said, "Forgive me, your Majesty, will you beware of those flowers?"

"I can see. I can see for myself," the old man said testily, and on the instant tripped in the flowers, stumbled, and rapped out a barrack oath. No doubt, he gave his wounded groin a twinge, for he turned and called, "Mind this garden stuff, Pheemy. If you break your knees, it's fifty pieces off your value." He spoke with the broad Sardican accent which was the delight of all the mockers of the Court. It was as though, shall we say, Louis Quatorze had spoken in public with a Breton dialect and the oaths of the barracks.

"I'll not break any knees," the old Empress said. "Hearts are what ladies break."

With this, the royal couple reached the left of the stage, close to Theodora, who curtseyed and took note. He was an old, rude, sturdy figure, with extraordinarily shrewd eyes, gleaming; she was older, and had a weary, flabby, flagging face of much kindness and placid good humour. She said to herself, "They are old, and childless; they love to be near youth." Justinus looked at the dancers, then looked hard at Theodora.

"Wait, now," he said. "You're not she, are you?"

"No, your Majesty," Theodora said. "She's on the stage."

"Who are you, then?" the Empress said.

Before she could reply, Justinus was peering along the ranks of dancers, and crying aloud: "Where's this

girl what danced the girl, then? Where is she, what? Eh?
I don't see her. Ah, there she is." Macedonia came forward and curtseyed. "Dammy, girl," the Emperor cried,
"I'm not going to eat ye. Come here, will ye? See,
Pheemy, this is the little baggage. Dammy, child, you
made us feel we were at home again. How you did it in
those little slippers I can't think. See, Pheemy, this is the
little baggage did the part. Dammy, if I won't have another kiss from you." And at this, the Emperor of the
world caught her very friendlily by the shoulders, and
did, though with great delicacy, just touch her cheeks
with his lips. "You kiss her, too, Pheemy," he said. "She
smells just as sweet as my old father's little brown cow.
Child, you may dance till the end of the world yet never
give such pleasure as you give to us. We know all those
dances, don't we, Pheemy, eh, 'Candle-light' and 'Maids
a-Milking' and 'Hey go the Reapers'?" Something made
him aware of Theodora: he turned to her. "And who's
this?" he asked. "Eh, she's a fine black-eyed girl. Is this
one a friend of yours?" He was by this time pawing
Theodora as though to make sure that she were not a
stage-property.

"Yes, sir," Macedonia said, "my great friend."

"You've got a very fine-looking friend, what; eh,
Pheemy? And she's your very great friend. I like that:
'my great friend'. I like folk what stick up for friends.
But, dammy, girl, you'll take cold, after dancing; run
and put on your cloak. See, your friend's brought your
cloak. Put it on. What do you call yourself, hey? Macedonia? A fine name. The finest name. No name to touch
it and no place. Hear that, Pheemy, she's called Mace-

donia. I knew she'd have some name like that. And you
come from there, darling?"

"My people do, sir, from Dirke."

"Dirke of the Dove-nests; ah, child, my old grand-
dam was from near Dirke. Well, run away, child, and
put on your warm things after dancing, you and your
friend, and you'll hear from us, be sure. We're all Macedonian at the Palace, all the lot of us; and you've taken
us all home today. Now, away with you or you'll take
cold."

He dismissed them, and then with good humour and
much genuine shrewd criticism went to each member of
the company with praise and chaff and encouragement;
and then, to the astonishment of everybody, said,
"Where's the man who planned it all? What's his
name?" Sosthenes came forward and named himself.
"Well, sir," the Emperor said, "you gave us my old
home again. The finest show what ever come to Byzantium. These silly fellows are all for wild beasts and
horse-racing; but we in Sardica have more sense. I know
about dancing. I danced like the best of you in my young
days. I'll not keep you all now; but I thank you on my
Empress' account and my own. Dammy, I've not enjoyed anything so much in all my days." He then
seemed to remember something, and said, "But where's
my nephew? O, are you there, nephew? You wished to
speak with this Macedonia girl. I've sent her away, so
you can't. These girls are like a blood-horse; they get
hot in a gallop and they have to rug up or take cold.
You'll have to send word to her later. Come on; we must
be getting back. I've got those Syrian fellows coming to

supper and have to tog up, parade dress number one, for
them. Lead off, leaders. Other squads in succession; trot.''

The leaders led off, and the others in succession trotted. Theodora, who had seen Macedonia to her room,
and had then returned to the stage for last details, found
the house almost empty, and the stage upon which such
an elaborate world of illusion had been built, now a bare
dancing-floor, on the edges of which the sweepers stood
with brooms and pails waiting to get the place swept.

The Emperor and his Court had gone; it was all as
though it had not been at all. Far away, somewhere in
Sixth or Eighth Ward, a band was playing "Up with the
Green Flag". Sosthenes appeared from nowhere as was
his way.

"A bigger success than Antioch," he said. "I've got a
carriage for you and Macedonia at the side-door, in the
alley; otherwise she'll be mobbed. There are three hundred waiting. We must shorten the third ballet, if it's to
be like this; cut out the slow movement altogether. We
start rehearsals in exactly two hours from now, as soon
as the theatre is swept and aired. See that Macedonia
has some food."

She said that it had gone beautifully. He spread his
hands in despair. "O that Second Flute," he said. "He
killed the act."

He passed on his way to scalp the Second Flute; Theodora hurried to take Macedonia home, for food and fresh
air. As they passed the waiting-room, on their way to
the side-door, two men came out. One was the Prince
Justinian, the other a much older, handsome and very
elegant man, dark-eyed and smiling. Justinian said,

"Forgive me, if I stop you to say one word. My Uncle cannot thank you enough for the beauty of your performance today. He was famous in the sword-dances when he was young. My Aunt, too, danced the torch-dances. They both asked me to praise you and to thank you. May I say for myself, too, how wonderful I thought you? I cannot speak as a dancer, only as a lover of beauty. But my friend, Philip, here, who has watched dancing for a long time, would like both to thank you and to praise you."

Philip, whom Theodora knew to be Brusanian's father, and one of the Chamberlains of the Court, said, "Indeed, I long to do both. I am like Nestor, in some ways, for I remember many generations of dancers, taking their generation as ten years or a little less. I remember the great dancer, the Swift Sea-Wave, Kumothoe; you can tell from that how like Nestor I am. But I am unlike Nestor in other ways, for I do not count those times as better. The Swift Sea-Wave, lovely as she was, was not fit to tie your dancing shoe-strings." Macedonia was thrilled by this, for Kumothoe was a legend among dancers. "And I know how dancing shoe-strings should be tied," he added. "The inside satin crosses the instep *over* the outside satin; then it never comes undone. Is that not so?"

"We always hope so," Macedonia said.

"Come, then," Philip said, "let me show you to your carriage."

Theodora summoned her courage and thanked Justinian for his most precious gift. She felt that Philip pricked up his ears, and looked fixedly at her, as though asking, "Who is this ballet-girl, who has precious gifts from Tino?"

"Ah," Justinian said, "I only grieve that this week will give you little time to enjoy them."

By this time, they were at the carriage; they were handed-in, and rapidly driven home. It is much to delight your ruler and be handed to a carriage by the ruler's heir.

It was a hard week for the company; they performed daily to the Court and the guests of the Emperor, and gave three programmes in the six days. Each programme was given twice; each spare minute was given to rehearsal. The Imperial couple came to each performance, which was a thing unheard of in Byzantium. More than that, the Patriarch came to three performances, and publicly went upon the dancing-floor to tell Macedonia that no man could watch her without having a more exalted thought of womankind. He said to Sosthenes that he had done much to restore the ancient sacredness of the stage; and to Perdiccas, that his St. George ought to be seen by every school-boy in the Empire. "The old boy means well," the stage-hands commented.

It was a week of intense work, but great delight; it was a week of victory. In the intensity of the work, Theodora knew little of what was happening outside the theatre. She heard that the Greens still sent their wagons and bands about The City, with speakers praising the Greens and singers leading the crowd to sing the Green war-songs. Whenever she left the theatre for a moment, the bark or the song of these people came to her from somewhere not far away. It even seemed to her, as the week went on, that the Greens were stretching down more from their usual haunts to Three, Five and Seven Wards along the water-front, which were strongholds of the Blues. She was told that people going to work in these wards would be joined by single men, who would begin talk with them upon indifferent subjects for a while, then lead the talk to politics and the great beauty of Green policies both for home and abroad. Always, too, the dinner-houses, the taverns and little eating-houses were beset with such speakers, who spoke of the importance of peace in the East, and of the loss of liberty at home. As the week went on, she heard that the name Hypatius was always being mentioned. Hypatius for Liberty: Hypatius for Peace in the East: Hypatius to defend your Freedom. Plainly, a great deal of money was being spent by the Greens. It was generally felt that it was all designed as a protest against Justinian's appointment to the command and the policy which was leading to war with Persia. On the fifth day, she heard one violent speaker making these very points. There was in The City a good deal of feeling against both matters, but Theodora could not believe that any citizen would urge that Hypatius should command the army. Why was Hypatius being mentioned?

She mentioned the matter to Iophon, as they worked together over some costume. Iophon had been with some friends the night before. He said,

"They are going to run Hypatius for Consul."

"Surely, they could do that without all this pother," she said. "The Consulship is never contested. No-one wants to be Consul."

"Well, it's a sort of an honour," Iophon said, "and Hypatius' stock is pretty low at the moment. It would give him a leg-up."

"But it is nothing but an enormous expense," she said. "The Consul has to entertain and give displays and so forth."

"No; it's a little more than that," Iophon said. "It is a distinction. The Consul is in a way the Chief Magistrate, and has the presidency of some committees. His wings are clipped, I grant, but it sounds well. 'Make way for the Consul of the Year'. If you haven't any distinction at all, it is jolly to have one added to you. He is rich enough, and as he is under a cloud he is going to buy the distinction."

"I don't think anyone'll vote for him," she said.

"There won't be anyone else to vote for," Iophon said. "He'll be Consul. He'll probably ask Sosthenes to give a gala performance in the Hippodrome."

She did not think much of the case at the moment; she had much to do. In bed that night, she thought of it again, and now reflected, that with the Emperor ill or ailing, through his wound, and the heir to the throne far from The City engaged in an unpopular war, the Consul, the chief magistrate in The City, might have a great deal of power, or might snatch some from the opportunity. She knew that Hypatius would not have much luck in snatching, or get much support in his snatch; but people near him or behind him might get a good deal. Certainly Hypatius had not thought out and arranged all this clever appeal to the citizens. He had not caused those men to the north to be armed and drilled.

Someone had done that for him, or for political ends which he might serve. One of the great western lords might have done that; or might not Nicanor of the Bays have done it? He was in blood-feud with the Emperor; he might well be the mover. But with so many possible causes of trouble, there might be many movers, each working alone, yet all tending to disruption. Many little ferments here and there might throw the body politic into raging fever.

They came to the last day of the performances. On this day, as Theodora passed to the theatre, she saw that Iophon was right. The waggons of musicians and speakers now bore Green banners on which, in white letters, were the legends,

Hypatius for Consul.

———

Vote for Hypatius and Liberty.

She thought to herself, that he was taking a most costly way to ensure himself a vast expense; however, that was his business. At the theatre, she found to her amazement and delight, a note from Philip, the acting Chamberlain of the Palace, saying that their Imperial Majesties commanded her presence at the Palace to supper that evening; black would be worn. She found that Sosthenes and Macedonia had also been commanded. She knew at once that she was only bidden as Macedonia's friend . . . or was that true? Had she been bidden because Justinian would be there? Had Justinian asked that she might be of the party? She had a quivering hope that that might be so. He was a friend and a disciple of

Timotheus, and thereby linked to all things of hope and promise. Macedonia was in ecstasies of expectation and of terror. Sosthenes said he had always feared that the performances would lead to this. "All the same," he said, "he does show us that he appreciates us. Even if he clears us off with fifty others in the Big Hall, it will be more than his predecessor ever did. I wish he'd asked Iophon and the Music."

Macedonia said, "Perhaps he has"; but it was not so.

Theodora did not cavil at the invitation. It was the first time that she had been bidden to the Palace, and would certainly be the last. She knew very well that all three of them were members of the theatre, and, therefore, excluded by rigorous law from marriage with anyone of even the lowest of the ranks. She, herself, was the cast mistress of Hekebolos, who was by this time probably the discredited and perhaps cashiered Governor in the meanest of the Appointments. Still, for this one evening, if this were known, and it almost certainly would be known, for the Palace Secret Police enquired into the past of every guest, it was being overlooked, and she would be the guest of Empire. Black would be worn, and a carriage would be sent. All the rest of the day was an excitement. Her one good dress was black; she well knew that she looked her best in black. Still, it was such an occasion as had never been in her life. "I will remember every least thing of it, forever," she said.

When she had dressed to her satisfaction, she heard the carriage, and so set forth upon her quest. Presently, she had the joy of seeing the sentries cross spears to bar the way at the gate and salute with spears when they

knew that she was an imperial guest. She knew nothing
of the Palace; she had never been in its Precincts before.
Hekebolos had never been within, even to kiss hands before taking ship to the Five Cities. He had never been
to the Emperor, even then, only to the Praefect, who had
kept him waiting an hour before seeing him. Now she
was driving within the Palace Precincts to what the sentry had said was the Quarters, the small, private dwell-
ing of the Emperors at the side of the great castle, where
Empire received only private friends.

The carriage stopped at a lighted door by which stood
two giant Sardicans, with blue cloaks tossed over their
shoulders, white kilts spanged with silver, and the terrible, three-headed Sardican darts in their right hands. A
blue matting with gold edges lay stretched for Theodora's feet; two officers of the stirrup, as they were
called, opened the carriage and helped her to alight. Her
entrance was awaited by maids, who led her to the tiring-
rooms, which were furnished in the manner of a hundred years before, with hard black chairs; on the walls
were pictures of saints with hard black eyes. She was
then led to a waiting-room, where she found Sosthenes
talking to a very sweet, benign old chaplain, who came
to greet her, saying, "I am Father Serapion, the Chaplain here. I have to tell you the few simple things you do
on entering and leaving the presence." When he had
told these, he said, "The other guests here will be Her
Highness, the Mother of Prince Justinian, the Prince
himself, your friend the great dancer, and a Count Atorios, if I have the name correctly, who has come on a
mission to the Emperor. You will sit at the end of the

table on the Emperor's right, with Sosthenes on your right hand. The Count will be on your left."

Justinian came in an instant later; he was friendly and merry. He spoke charmingly to her and to Sosthenes about the beauty of the performances, and the intense pleasure they had given to all their guests. Father Serapion said that three of his flock in the Palace had asked if they couldn't have something like it at Christmas, in the Great Church. The Count Atorios came in; Theodora bowed and smiled. Macedonia came in at that instant. She had hardly learned the procedures, when doors at the end of the waiting-room were opened by two swordsmen in blue. As they opened, a gigantic Sardican trumpeter, in a blue tunic and white kilt, strode through them and cried, "The Rulers of the Most Holy Empire await their guests." They followed Father Serapion into the room. At a table set for eight, the Emperor sat opposite Euphemia. Beside the Emperor, a tall woman, plainly Justinian's Mother, stood. The greetings and obeisances were all easier than they had feared they might be. The Chaplain intoned a grace and at once left the room.

They sat to table, two to each side of the table. Theodora noted that the wall decoration was a frieze of the Funeral Games of Patroklos. Sosthenes was on her right, talking to Justinian's Mother, who seemed good and sweet, but had upon her certain marks, which Theodora had seen in her own Mother, and knew to be the marks of Death. On her left was Count Atorios, whom now she could observe. He came from some outlandish part; she had found him difficult to understand in the waiting-room. Now that she saw him in better light, she was deeply impressed by his face. He was pale, as though he had been through much suffering; but she had a sudden instinct that an extraordinary spirit was burning there. What he was and where he came from were unknown to her; his accent was the strangest she had heard, but she knew that she was beside a most unusual man, in whom courage and beauty balanced and made something divine.

"I am so sorry," she said, "if you find my speech difficult."

"I don't," he said. "When I can see a face, I know what the speaker says."

It was strange, but certainly, she found now, that she could understand him.

"Do tell me," she said, "from what country you come."

"I come from Britain," he said. "Perhaps you have not heard of it?"

"O, yes, I have," she said. "It used to be in the Empire, and then the pagans got it. Have the pagans got it still?"

"No," he said, "I've got it at the moment, more or less. I am here to try to persuade people here to secure it. We want some ships and shipwrights; and then some horses, and some men trained in your cavalry tactics. Is that too much to ask?"

She reflected that the entire Empire, upon all its marine coasts and frontiers, cried for just those things.

"So many are asking for those things," she said. "I was in the Pentapolis and at Antioch a few months or weeks ago. All there were crying out for ships and cavalry. How did you get here, though? Was it not a frightful journey?"

"No," he said simply. "I hoped to get the things, and saw no other way. I've got to this point."

"And with the things, you could turn out the pagans and secure the land back to the Empire?"

"Yes, and to Christianity. I believe I could."

She saw that the old Empress was busily talking to Justinian; she longed to talk more with this man; she had never before seen a man from Britain.

"You speak with faith," she said; "that is nine-tenths of every battle."

"It is all that I bring," he said. "We have nothing else; we have no money; a little wheat, wool and corn; and a breathing space, as it happens, which may last a year or two; I hope it may. I want not to lose the breathing space, but to get ready for what will follow, when the pagans begin again."

"What are the pagans?" she asked.

"Pirates of different races," he said, "with varying customs. For a little while they will or may leave us alone."

"I think," she said, "Her Imperial Majesty wishes you to speak to her."

He turned to the old Empress, who wore the strange triple head-dress of a Sardican lady of high birth. This had been a jest for years throughout the Empire, being the head-gear which the poor soul had longed to wear in her native village seventy years before, and had not then been allowed. Sosthenes was saying something to Justinian's Mother. The Emperor in a loud voice said to

Macedonia, who may have hoped that his wound was not troubling him, "It's troubling all the time. An old wound's like an unhappy marriage: night and day the devil. But by my way of it, an old man's legs are like an old horse's legs, always needing rubbing and not worth the trouble."

Something about legs reached the ears of the Empress, who called out, "What's that you're saying about legs?"

"I was saying that yours are the best in the Empire," Justo said. "And they ought to be on all the coins."

"They were good legs," the Empress said, "but I defy any woman to keep good legs after seventy-nine or eighty. And what would be the use? Who would want to see?"

"All the world, surely," her husband said.

"No, no," the Empress said, "no such luck. Some of the flesh and the devil might, but not even much of them; not the world. The world knows better."

"But every woman can keep good legs till ninety," Macedonia said. "My old teacher's teacher is eighty-four; she dances still, and does her practices. She stands on her head for twenty minutes every day, to let the blood run into her brain."

"There's something in that," the Empress said. "A lot too many women keep their genius in their legs. It's best to let some of it into the head."

As this seemed to sum up and end the topic of legs, whose main purpose must ever be to support the head, the Emperor started something fresh. He turned to Theodora and asked:

"Are you a countrywoman, hey?"

"No," she said, "I was born in The City here."

She had been born within a quarter-of-a-mile of that dinner-table, but she was not going to allude to that.

"I don't mean that," Justo said. "I mean, do you come from the good old Sardican landscape?"

"The Emperor means, do you come from Dacia," Macedonia said.

"No," Theodora said, "no, Excellency; 'but my great ability might warrant the supposition.' "

The Emperor banged the table. "Hear that, Pheemy?" he called. "Hear what this little woman says? She says, she isn't a Dacian, but her great ability might lead one to think she was. She's got some sense, Pheemy. The boy said she had. I must remember that. I must tell that to the Patriarch. 'No, I'm not a Dacian, but my . . .' what was it now . . . 'great ability might lead you to think I am one.' I like you for saying that. Pheemy always used to say things like that. Well, you're as like a dark Dacian as can be; that's the next best thing to being one. This Macedonia here; she's the flower of the land; I never saw anyone dance those Dacian dances like her, since the day I left my village and came to be a soldier. Ah, well. I could dance, too, in my young days. 'If you can't dance, you can't do,' we always said. It's true, too. No man could be head-man in the village, nor sergeant to a troop unless he could dance. I'd like to make it a rule in life," he said. "Don't you think we ought to make Patriarchs dance, before we raise them to the Patriarchate?"

"Sir," Sosthenes said, "it might not do to have Patriarchs under thirty."

"Still," Justinian said, "you would admit dancing into ritual?"

"Indeed I would; why not? You have David, and the universal testimony of the past. God must be worshipped with rhythms."

"They do it in the East," the Emperor said. "I've seen 'em dancing to their gods. It's very pagan."

"We could find something Christian," Sosthenes said.

However, the Emperor was off on another topic now.

"You've all just come from Antioch," he said. "Now, my dark young Dacian," he said, turning to Theodora, "what are the Persians up to? What was said in the bazaars, hey?"

"I was not in the bazaars," Theodora said. "I was only two days there."

"I go a lot by what is said in bazaars," the Emperor said. "I get these reports a yard long which I can't read; a word from the bazaar's worth ten of them. What's said in Antioch Bazaar is what Chosroes does next spring."

"I am sure that you heard two things," Justinian said; "an expectation of war and a longing for peace."

"Yes," Theodora said. "What I did hear was, that the Persian King does most truly want peace with you; he has troubles enough on his own borders to the north. He only wants a real assurance that you won't attack him on one side while he is fighting on the other. In the theatre, I overheard a man saying, that you could make friends with him for the next ten years if you wrote to him and sent him some ivory."

"I'm not much of a hand at writing," Justo said.

"They bring me these charters and laws and things, and I put some red paint on 'em to make 'em law."

The Empress who had been paying close attention said, "Tino or Philip, or someone, could write a letter. The Eastern Praefect could deliver it."

"And ivory, you said? I hate to think of ivory going to a pagan."

"No," Euphemia said, "no ivory to a sun-worshipper. Ivory's gone up and up since the Persians started buying it. The Patriarch was saying he can't get enough even for the reliquaries."

"It sounds to me too much like trying to buy him off," Justo went on.

"Not in the least," Theodora said. "Could you not simply say, that you hear he is beset by savages on his borders, and that as a brother ruler you sympathise and assure him that you will not try to snatch an advantage? In the meantime, perhaps he might care to have this ivory? He is building an ivory room, like the King of Samaria."

She had never before been called upon to speak her mind before Empire; nor had she expected that Empire could be like this.

"I could dictate a letter," the Emperor mused, "and Philip or the boy there, or the Praefect could put the moonlight on it. But Pheemy's right about the ivory. I'm not going to send any ivory to a pagan. Bone is what he'll have to use, or this old wood the sap's died in; that's like enough to ivory for a pagan. But I believe this young woman's right about the Persian King; he may want peace. But he's a vain man, and he does stick

out for form. He wants me to humble myself to him.
Will I? He can ask till he turns blue. Let him crawl to
me, if he wants peace. I'm the Emperor."

"You are here," Theodora said, greatly daring, "but
he is Emperor in Persia. Every Persian King reflects that
once all the world in sight from here was his, or tribu-
tary to him. You are both great princes. Say that you
recognize that; and that no great prince shall disturb
another in his trouble. He has thought that you have
been trying to snatch advantage; he has resented that.
Show him that you aren't thinking of any such thing;
and he'll be grateful; not perhaps as grateful as any or-
dinary man, but more grateful than a king usually is.
There is no need for you to send any Embassy. Send a
letter by the Praefect, with some gifts. If ivory is scarce,
send some other treasure; white mules are what he longs
for."

"I don't doubt," the Emperor said, "other people like
white mules, too; they're not so easy come by, since Vitalian sacked the breeding-station."

"A thousand white mules would be cheaper than a
war," Theodora said.

"I'll see him stewed in hell before he gets a white
mule from me," the Emperor said.

"Well," Theodora said, "why not white peacocks? He
longs for white peacocks and silver pheasants."

"How the devil do you know that?" the Emperor
asked.

"I met a Persian lady in the ship going to Antioch,
who told me. He longs for any white creature because he

thinks it is to some extent released from the need of action and turned to thought."

"If he'd turn a little whiter himself," the Emperor said, "it might save some trouble. There's a man just across the water with white peacocks, any number. I'll have to ask about pheasants. But what's he going to give me? I'm not going to do all the giving, I hope. What do you suppose he'll give me?"

"If he gave you peace, he would give you a safe frontier, wouldn't he?" Theodora said.

"Yes, and for how long? You can't trust a word these fellows say."

"That was what the Persian lady said to me, of your Ministers," Theodora said, "that the Persian King couldn't trust a word they said."

"By God, I'm not surprised," the Emperor said. "That's my own view of 'em, if you ask me, but nothing's been proved against 'em, so far."

Theodora was wondering now if she would be sent to be beheaded at the end of the meal; she was not used to talking to Emperors; still, she was aware that the old man was friendly, and liked the truth.

"It seems to me," the old man said, "that all your advice is just nothing but Christianity, which is dangerous advice in politics. I'd say, that now's the time to fall on Persia, now that her border's all beset."

"That wasn't the view in Antioch," Theodora said.

"Well; you were there," he said. "What was the view?"

"The view was, that all the tribes of the east are moving west, and the one thing people hoped was that Persia might be free to stop them. If Persia doesn't stop them, they'll come west, right into your Empire, and stop all your trade caravans. They're doing that now. Half the trade caravans are stopped already."

"These tribes . . . they're the lads with the ponies," the Emperor said. "They'll only come as far as there's pasture. Nations aren't like men, young lady, they are a great deal worse. You can give help to your next-door neighbour, but not to your next-door nation; that's the way to death."

"Well, he that loseth his life . . ." Theodora said. "Suppose that you fall upon Persia now; what amount of life will you get from that? The raiders will raid her and get a lot of spoil. You will, with great difficulty and vast expense, send an army to the Persian frontier and fight one or two inconclusive battles. By the time you have lost your first army by disease and desertion and sent out a second, not half so good, the raiders will have turned on you: they'll be over all your frontiers, pillaging your cities. Then you will have to make peace with Persia on Persia's terms, not yours, and turn to defend your property. I am only repeating what the people in Antioch were saying. They have to live beside Persia, and want her prosperous and friendly."

"I hate the Persians," the Emperor said. "Every damned bargain I've tried to make with 'em, they've tried to get the better of me."

"Uncle," Justinian said, "this young lady has said the very things I have been feeling, yet unable to formulate. I do feel sure that she's right. I'd better go to King Chosroes and see what I can do. In addition to the pheasants and the peacocks, I would suggest some of John's white ponies. That would save the white mules for your kettle-drummers. I would start next week and I don't doubt we could come to some friendly arrangement."

"I doubt you'll get much good from King Chosroes," the Empress said. "Get him to be a Christian first, I say. If he'll become a Christian, then we may believe him."

"Everything has to have a beginning," Justinian said. "If he'll give me a friendly welcome, I don't doubt that I'll be able to win him."

"Well, I always believed in a personal talk," the Emperor said. "But for this sick groin of mine, I'd go myself and see him, that is, if he'd come half way. But I won't have you lowering yourself to him; I'm all for a direct deal, but he'll have to show that he knows it's a damned condescension on our part for the Emperor's nephew to talk to him. You'll go as the Praefect of the East, to inspect fortresses. It shan't be said that you go to see him."

"Not unless he turns Christian," the Empress said. "These pagans ought to be rooted out, really."

Theodora was amazed at the conversation. Someone had said that the world was governed in a very odd way; she had not reckoned on becoming suddenly an instrument of Imperial policy; yet here she was, chatting at supper and apparently dictating what was to be done on the most important of the Empire's frontiers.

"You see, young lady," the Emperor said, "Tino here said you'd got some sense. I think you have. We'll try what these peacocks and things'll do. If they help him to be a bit whiter, you'll have done a good night's work.

Friend Sosthenes, your two young ladies are credits to your taste. Let's drink to them."

"Sir," Sosthenes said, "I am proud to drink to them."

"I'm going to drink, too," the Empress said. "I like both these girls; they do their hair so nicely. Say what you like, young girls are better than old."

"They can't be," the Emperor said. "Now here's to the ladies Macedonia and Theodora. God bless them."

The party rose to drink the toast; the old Empress stood, waved her little glass and said, "My dears, I love you."

Theodora was aware that the British Count, who had been left out of the conversation, was looking a little lost. He had probably concluded that these were the ways of The City, and had made up his mind, now, to the failure of his mission. She found a chance to say to him, as he sat, after rising for the toast,

"Thank you so much, Count. We were talking about the Eastern frontier."

"It isn't a frontier," he answered, "it is the good-will of the Persian King; that is the only frontier there."

She looked at him with appreciation. The swordsmen of the Body-Guard entered, bearing black cloaks. The men of the party now had to go with the Emperor to Evening Prayers with the Body-Guard. As they passed out, Justinian's Mother gave him her blessing, and added that she would now go to lie down. A maid helped her away.

"Come in to the little room," Euphemia said to the two young women. "We can have our sweetmeats there."

She led the way to a very beautiful room, walled with

black enamel on which someone had modelled a flight of wild geese in low relief.

"What a beautiful room," Theodora said.

"Ah, you like the birds," the Empress said. "They were done a long time since; it is what they call old work, that. Settle yourselves in, now, and be snug. These palace places are all for state, but I always tell my husband, the Emperor, I do like a room where I can be comfortable. What I suffer in these great halls at these functions. This is the only room in the quarters where I can be homey and put my feet up. Though you know, my dears, I've much to be thankful for; being Empress. I don't mind so much for myself; it's for Justo; he likes being in command and taking the salute. I ask for a lot of warmth and sweets after dinner. And I do like a nice brisket once or twice a week. You know, you can have that, when you're Empress. And I do like being called Queen, after being at people's beck and call: 'Lupi, why haven't you cleaned the plates? Lupi, take up your mistress' broth, and see the napkin's clean.' I've had all that, in my time. But what pretty dresses you both have. Ah, it's nice to be young and care what you wear. It's nice of you to come to the Palace to talk with old people. It's nice for the boy, too. I always think he ought to mix more with people of his own age. He's never been young. In a way, I suppose one ought to be thankful, for most young men are only too young. I know they were in my time. But you'll know better than I if they still are. He said to me only the other night, 'I enjoyed meeting those dancers, and their advisers.' I never knew him break out like that about anybody. Now here are the honey-wafers and that. These are the real Sardican honey-cakes. Honey-dix, we call them. They would put this cinnamon in them, which is wrong, but I think I've got them to do it at last. Did the boy say anything about what he wanted you to do for him?"

This question was put to Macedonia, but the Empress looked at Theodora too, as though she, too, were meant. Both young women said, "No. What can we do?"

"He'll be back from prayers in a few minutes," the Empress said. "Evening Prayers only takes a few minutes, but they don't like missing it, because all the officers report afterwards; just a matter of form, but Justo always can tell if anything's been kept back, and then he pounces. They all think Justo's easy going; so he is, but, my, if anyone tries to take a liberty, or to dodge him. There's nothing like being an old soldier, is there, for teaching a general what may be going on? You'd be surprised at what goes on. But Justo was in the business when they were still boys at top-notch. He saw it all; the corn and fodder business, and so much to the colonel, so much to the sergeants. My dear, what pretty hands you've got." This was to Theodora, who had hands of much beauty. "I do like a girl to have pretty hands. I used to long for pretty hands when I was young, and used to rub ivy on them; they say ivy makes a white skin, ivy or lemons : but it never did with me; I had always too much rough work to do, scrubbing and cooking, and all the washing. Let me have a close look at your hands."

She was comfortably prone on a cushioned settle, which was hung with scarlet. Theodora came to her side,

knelt down and held out her hands. The Empress took
them and looked at them inside and out.

"We used to have roamers," she said. "They used to
come about and tell fortunes from the hands. Did any
roamer tell your hand?"

"No, none," Theodora said. "My mother was very
strict against any fortune-telling."

"I go by the face," the Empress said. "I'd say that a
good fortune waited on both you girls. But you haven't
eaten the honey-wafers. I told my cook who makes these;
she is a Sardican, she isn't one of these palace-men, who
are all in the conspiracy to rob the state; it is all that,
really; I told my cook, I've got two very beautiful young
women coming, and if they leave one honey-wafer un-
eaten I shall know my cook's in love with a roamer. She
can't iron linen, isn't that strange, but has the lightest
hand with pastry, ever was. Now have another of this
sort."

Presently, Justinian returned from Prayers with Sosthenes; the Emperor and the Count had stayed to talk
together somewhere. Theodora's heart sank for the
Count. Justinian came over to talk to her.

"You pleased my Uncle," he said. "You spoke up to
him."

"He won't have me beheaded? I said dreadful things.
I was so taken by surprise."

"He was delighted. What was it that the strange man
wanted?"

Theodora explained, and added, "He seemed in desperate need of the things. It is sad to see a good man
plead in vain."

He looked at her, and understood from her look, that she knew very well that the Emperor would never understand what the fellow wanted, and would refuse it, and perhaps later regret what he had done.

"You're right," he said. "He will plead in vain, if he doesn't get a little help. I'll join them for a moment."

As soon as he had gone, the Empress said, "It's sad for the boy to be going East with his mother so ill: she's got her heart-strings gone, poor soul. I suppose he's gone now to see her in bed."

Theodora explained, that he had gone for a moment to speak with the Emperor and the British Count, who had to ask them something.

"I couldn't understand a word that foreigner said," the Empress said. "But then, all foreigners speak gibberish really."

When Justinian returned, it was time for the ladies to put on black cloaks and go to the Chapel for the singing of the Evening Hymn. Coming back from this service, Justinian walked beside Theodora and checked her at a window, to shew her the harbour with its lights, and Sycae on the Asian shore.

"I'm afraid that the poor Count comes at the wrong time," he said. "We could not persuade shipwrights to go all those miles, into barbarism, and how could we order them? It is the same with soldiers, even if we had them to spare."

"Don't you think that a great Empire ought to listen to suppliants?"

"Yes; but as a University listens to scholars, not as a sentimental being listens to beggars. He can always send his people here to learn; we can help him to that; we cannot send to him to teach."

"Cannot we even spare some horses?"

"He might get some stallions from Kallimachus; but what hope is there of that, till Kallimachus has won the Imperial Gold Cup? None, I should say."

At the window they could see the moving lights of another torch procession, and hear the strains of the Green march.

"That brings us back to earth," she said. "The last week has kept us out of the world; but there are politics once more."

"They still interest you?" he asked.

"They interest me profoundly," she said, "because I feel sure that very passionate feelings are stirring in them at present."

"Yes," he said, "you are right; and when certain things have been done, and all these feelings stirred, the settling of them's a problem. What a blessing it would be if old Timotheus could be here to advise."

"O Prince, that would be wonderful."

"Would it not? Still, if I am to be so near to him over this Persian matter, I can perhaps go south to see him. I want to see that eastern world."

"The Count said a thing which interested me," she said. "He said, that we had no frontier there, except the Persian King's will."

"It's very true. You liked that Count, and felt that we ought to help him?"

"I shall be beheaded before morning," she said. "Never mind; yes, I did and do."

"How old Timotheus makes one see things," he said. "You won't be beheaded; your head is a very useful citizen. I believe that the young shipwrights and some younger corporals might be persuaded to go. They might like to have the offer at least."

Soon after that, it was time to kiss the Empress' hands and leave the Palace. Theodora was shocked at what she had said and done amiss. It had been the most interesting evening in her life, to sit there, in the Quarters, the private rooms of Empire, talking with Empire, as an equal, and being listened to, by those simple souls. Then she had seen Justinian's mother and this strange Count; she had been asked to dictate policies, and had done so; and she had had that quiet little talk with the Prince. It was much to her, that he had spoken of Timotheus at that moment. She still felt that Timotheus had led her home, by some insight or spiritual prompting. She thought much of Justinian that night. She had felt that her heart was dead within her; but was it quite dead? Now she brooded on the image of this strange scholar, the disciple of the heretic, who had said to her with such simple feeling, "When certain things have been done, and all these feelings stirred, the settling of them's a problem." What had he meant? She saw presently that he meant that he was in an anguish of mind. The Emperor was a rude, brave soldier, who had killed Theokritos so that he, himself, might rule. Later, he had killed Vitalian, so that his nephew might succeed him. Later still, he had sought to prove Hypatius a traitor, so that his nephew's way to the throne might be clear. Blood had been shed and evil things done, and the rage of all the Green Faction had been stirred; all that blood was crying out for vengeance, and now that the old Emperor was failing, it fell to Justinian to try to allay the Furies. How was any wisdom to act, so as to allay them and make peace? She was sure that that was what he had meant. It was indeed a problem, which would tax the wisdom of the wisest, and perhaps find no settlement then. The greatest of the poets had found no help in such a case, save in the divine spirit. She felt that she would not see Justinian again. He was to start for the East: would he ever return?

Looking out, as she did, daily, upon the increasing insolence of the Green Faction, she wished that he were not going. The leaders of the Greens well knew that he would be out of the way in a day or two. Their marches became more frequent and by much more noisy; their songs became ribald and seditious. It was published abroad, that the Prince Justinian would leave The City on Thursday morning. On each morning in each Church prayers were offered, that the Holy Wisdom might guide his dealings with the rulers of the East so that Justice and Peace might be assured. Coming out of the theatre with Macedonia after a run-through, on the Wednesday, Theodora went to the Great Church and heard the prayer repeated. All The City was now talking with pity of Hypatius who was spending a fortune to get a Consulship which no one could support without a vast expense. Coming out of the Church into the Parvice, she found that the Greens were explaining that matter. There in the Parvice standing on a box was a speaker with a persuasive voice. He stood among henchmen who bore a **Green** banner, with white letters:

HYPATIUS for CONSUL.

———

LIBERTY. LIBERTY.

By the look of the henchmen, they were pugilists of some fame.

"Yes, my friends," the speaker was saying, "the Consul is but a name now, almost a mockery; but he was once the check upon tyranny, and the chief magistrate of the land. His powers have been usurped or checked; they have never been annulled, even by tyranny. Legally he is still the Chief Magistrate. Legally he can act as in the past, he can restore liberty, he can punish fraud, he can avenge blood, he can drive out the usurper."

At this, some twenty or thirty men, who had been leaning against the wall for the cue, started up and shouted, "Yes. Drive out the Blue Usurper. Down with him."

Instantly a drum and trumpet struck up a lively tune. The party burst into a song:

"But the Consul shall return, my boys,
And strike the tyrant down . . ."

They fell into a military formation, and were away at once, marching to the singing, speaker and banners and all, to repeat the process a little farther on.

In the theatre, when she returned, Theodora heard that some Green gangs had been down on the water-

front and had smashed up the wine-shops of some minor
Ward Politicians of the Blue Party. This was a frequent
matter in ward-politics at all times, but it struck her as
ominous, coming when it did. She judged that there
would be a good deal of violence in this election for Consul. The Greens would use the excuse, to work off the
blood-feud-feelings stirring in them. She had not heard
yet if Hypatius were going to be opposed. If he were to
be the sole candidate, there could be no sense in all this
pother.

She was in the theatre for another run-through; then,
in the brief break, she went down to the water-front, to
see what damage had been done; it was but a minute's
run. There was little to see; a few pots and benches had
been broken, a shutter was unhinged and lying askew;
some brickbats lay about in the road. But at the boat-
builders' wharf on the right, where three small ships
were on the stocks, she saw Prince Justinian and the
Count talking to some of the wrights, who had left off
work to listen. Justinian caught sight of her and at once
came over to greet her.

"I am so glad to see you," he said.

"You are going tomorrow?" she said.

"No, tonight," he said. "This evening."

The Count came shyly up; he was not quite sure if it
were good manners to come.

"I tell the Prince, he will have a wet journey," he
said. "It will rain tonight. The one knowledge of my
country teaches me so."

"I hope, Count, that you have now some shipwrights,"
she said.

"I am hoping," he said. "But we want all things; metal-workers, tool-makers."

"This lady was your first friend here, Count," Justinian said. "She backed your appeal from the beginning."

The Count looked at her keenly and said, "I thought that I had found a friend."

She knew that Justinian was looking at her with deep attention, as though he were trying to learn her face by heart.

"You might like to hear," he said, "that the white mules have gone."

"White mules?" she said.

"Yes; and some tusks of ivory, for the Persian King. You remember, you recommended sending them."

"Yes, but Prince, I never thought . . ."

"Twenty white mules; the kettle-drum mules of the Imperial Parades; my Uncle's heart is broken in pieces."

She blushed with pleasure; she had repented in agony her impudence in suggesting these things, but now her advice had been taken. Could it be that now the Prince would make friends with Persia, and settle the Eastern question for forty years?

"As for the pheasants," the Prince continued, "a Persian here says that he is tired of pheasants now that someone has sent him some swans."

A carriage, which was driving along the Front, stopped near them. An old man, with a white beard, yet with a good deal of quiet liveliness, got down from the carriage and greeted Justinian.

"I thought I wasn't mistaken," he said. "I just came

down to see the damage done by the friends of Liberty."

"Ah, Symmachus," Justinian said, "I am glad to see you before I go. Lady Theodora, let me present our Consul-to-be, Symmachus."

"Blue candidate, rather," the old man said. "Not much chance of election as things are. They have smashed up twenty-three little eating-houses in One, Three and Five Wards; a dirty trick to play; just the little places where Blues can meet to talk. They'll do more than smash eating-houses and wine-shops before the week is out. I hear the Hippodrome set are bringing in the A boys. However, they may defeat their own ends. I hope you'll have a successful time, Prince. I shall miss you at the two big meetings. I wish we might exchange missions; I love Antioch. Count, if you'll jump into my carriage, I can shew you all those specifications and you can take your pick."

The Count's face showed, that he felt like a sinner suddenly admitted into Paradise; the look smote Theodora's heart. He had come with nothing, from nothing, to this City with all things. He came to her, took her hand and thanked her with a look which she never forgot. He got into the carriage with Symmachus and drove away.

"Symmachus is standing for Consul for the Blues," Justinian said. "He is a remarkable man. When he was young, he owned all the forests on Mount Ida. He cut down most of them to make standard fittings for houses and ships; all the pieces cut to exact lengths, big size, middle size and small size, according to the size of house or ship wanted. They called him Symmetry Symmachus. He became very rich, and took up the study of law, and held various offices. Now he writes light verse and makes

little model wind-mills. He is going to give the Count
sets of all his specifications. If he can ever get them back
to Britain, they should be exactly what he wants."

"How very kind you have been to the Count," she
said. "You can see how grateful he is."

"He is very interesting," Justinian said. "I had no
idea, till I talked with him, that Britain is quite a big
place. A lot of it is marsh and jungle, of course, but he
says that his bit of it isn't so bad, and is Christian still;
that is so strange to me."

"I must thank you for your kindness to me," she said.
"Now I must go back to the theatre. May I wish you the
very greatest of successes in the East? If you go to
Timotheus, please tell him that I bless him."

"Thank you for your wishes," he said. "I treasure
them. If I see Timotheus, I'll tell him what you say. And
thank you for saying what you did to my Uncle; it had
a good deal of effect."

Several people had recognized Justinian, and stood to
watch at a little distance the progress of the talk.

"There's Tino, talking Law to a nun," a boy called.

"Are you working very hard at the new Ballet?" Justinian asked. "I have seen lights in the theatre till very
late."

"We often stay on till nearly midnight," she said.
"We shall tonight. We open on Tuesday."

"I hope that that will be a great success."

"Thank you, Prince," she said. "Now forgive me, if
I run."

"Let us meet when I return," he said.

They parted, then. She was very glad to be able to

slip into a little street which took her at once out of sight
of him and the watchers. She knew that he turned to
speak to the shipwrights. She knew that she was not indifferent to him, and very clearly knew, that she loathed
and dreaded his going to the East. The City was full of
rumours of trouble; she could not reach the theatre without hearing the Green songs. A band was playing "Up
with the Green Flag," and a party of marching boys
sang "We will rally to the Green flag of our fathers."
She had just seen the wreck left by a Green riot.

When she reached the theatre, she found the door-
keeper with bleeding knuckles. "One of these Greens,"
he said. "He came in just now and said I'd better leave
while I had the chance, since no Blues were going to be
allowed in the Entertainment trade; so I just put him
out." Maron was an elderly man who had once been a
weight-lifter in a circus. If he had damaged his knuckles
in hitting a man, he had certainly hurt his victim. She
had much to do from that instant, and had no time for
thought; but the foundation of her mind was now one
of uneasiness, of trouble near at hand, not yet well de-
fined, yet already affecting all things in the Empire, and
threatening people and things which made her life.

She had one more break just after dark that evening.
Going out for a gulp of air with Macedonia, she found
that rain had begun, with every sign of increasing and
continuing. Together, they ran down to the water-front
to see the lights of the harbour. As they reached the
wharf, a big ferryboat was just shoving off under oars,
with a mass of people aboard. A small crowd of sight-
seers was gathered to see her go, in spite of the rain.

Some of them cheered and some of them called, "The Greens for ever. Vote for Hypatius." One who came in a hurry to the crowd asked, "What is it, boys? What's the fun?"

"It's Tino, the Prince, going to Persia to make peace or war or something," a man answered. "He's there in the boat; you can't see him now."

Theodora could not see him now. She was glad that she had seen the boat going; at least she could watch it diminish, with the grunt of oars and the gleam of water, and send a prayer after it.

"It'll be long before he sees The City again," Macedonia said. "What a night to set out on. Come back or we'll be drenched."

They ran back to the theatre, where plenty of work was waiting. They set to it, with a good will, while the rain come down. Theodora told herself that it was no good thinking of Justinian in that way, and then continued so to think.

They rehearsed with some measure of progress till about half-past ten, when Macedonia said that she was completely exhausted and could do no more. Sosthenes swore under his breath, sent her home in a hired carriage, the last on the rank, and called out her understudy. They went through the entire ballet again, in two runs-through, with the music. Sosthenes was for doing it a third time, although it was midnight. Theodora whispered, that some of the girls were already nearly dead, and that they would never get through it. Iophon also put in a plea for daylight; these artificial lights gave him no help at all. Sosthenes said that perfection was worth dying for, and anyone going in for art ought to expect to die for it, and be jolly proud of dying for it. Still, he was swayed by Iophon's saying that he could not judge the effects in this light. "Very well," he said, "we'll knock off for now and be back to it first thing tomorrow." Even so, he had certain notes against some of his flock and let these be heard before he dismissed. When they had gone, he still had some matters to settle with Theodora; certain things had to be bought, done, or arranged for. When at last he had finished, the bells had stricken one. He had not yet finished his day, and turned to his office to finish it. She was free to go. It was one in the morning and just finishing to pour; the gutters were streaming from the clearing shower, and every eave and penthouse roof dripped. However, as she looked out from the stage-door, she saw that the clouds were hurrying towards Asia, and a star or two gleaming in the gaps. Maron said he thought she'd be home before the next shower if she stepped out.

She was young and strong and had not a very long walk before her. She had some fears of the way, so late at night, but knew enough of the night-world to know that it shrinks from getting wet through. Her mind was full of misgivings about the future, and she was a little tired. She knew that the tiredness was partly the stuffy theatre, the hot air of the stage, with its candlesmoke, oil-fume and reek of hot reflector. In the little square of the Ares fountain, she stopped an instant, looked towards the sea, with its beacons and reflections, and went through a simple breathing exercise, which never failed to give her new life. The pure air filled her lungs, and in a few minutes she felt new life and joy in every vein. A dancer

at the Old Winter Palace had taught her the exercise,
saying that it came from Persia, "but it doesn't work
with everyone." She went on after the exercise, much
refreshed. She came out of the buildings close to the
children's playground. In the open space, she was thrilled
by the beauty of the night, all storm over Asia, all stars
and hurrying, whitish, wispy cloud overhead. She stood
for an instant to marvel at it. Her little house was about
a hundred and twenty yards ahead of her. A light left
burning for her shone through the chinks of her bed-
room shutters. Kallianassa would be asleep in the other
upstairs room. The adjoining house, where the gambling
ladies lived, was dark amid its arbutus. The quarter was
deserted and lifeless, save for a cat moving out towards
John's timber yards. The place had an astonishing moon-
lit clearness and strangeness. Away to her left front was
a pile of new hurdles. She had heard that a part of the
playground was to be fenced off for the winter so that it
might be returfed or resown. She saw suddenly, that a
man was sitting on the hurdles, and that he rose and was
coming towards her. Her heart beat fast, for this was a
lonely place; no civil guard would be near. Perhaps it
might be a civil guard; a keen look shewed that it was
no civil guard.

It was ever her word that a danger faced was half a
danger. If she ran, she would be run down before she had
gone far, and would only be out of breath by the effort.
Every step forward took her nearer to her home, where
a cry would rouse Kallianassa. She moved towards the
man; she felt terrified, yet having moved in a rough
world, she knew certain tricks of self-defence, and knew

well that even desperate men will dread a desperate woman. She thought, too, that it might be some lover waiting for his love in the small hours, or some homeless beggar. The man wore a dark cloak which shone.

"Lady Theodora?" he said.

It was the Prince Justinian.

She had an instant relief at knowing who it was, but at once there came the thought, that those old maids next door might be watching through their curtains. It would never do to be seen or suspected of receiving gallants at night, yet here was the Prince, and she knew that whatever brought him to her it was not gallantry, and that the old maids should, therefore, be dared. She knew, too, that she must not speak his name; he had come back secretly, when all believed him gone upon his mission. He was wearing a cloak of fine canvas, which had been tarred. He swung this from him so that it rested on the crook of his left arm.

"May I speak with you, please?" he said.

"Certainly," she said. "Come into the house. Are you wet through?"

"I've been well protected, thank you. I want very much to talk, if you can endure it," he said. "Are you not too tired? It's been a long day for you."

"Come in; let us talk," she said. She led the way round the clump of garden to the gate, and then to the door. "My maid is in bed, upstairs," she said. "If she wakens, I shall tell her that I have a friend. She is my trusted friend; she would never betray that you are here."

She opened the door and held it, so that he could enter the little living-room barely lighted by a night-light in a dish and some hot coals in a brazier. She lit two candles, so that he could see his way to a chair.

"May I offer you some milk and fruit-bread?" she asked.

He thanked her but would not. She sat on the other side of the brazier from him and looked at him. He was in some agitation; he kept pulling down the left end of his moustache. She knew that he was the heir to the Empire, whom she had hardly seen, yet here he was at her hearth on some mission of desperate need.

"What is it that you wish to talk of, Prince?" she asked.

He looked at her and said, "First, I wish you to forgive me for coming here at this time and lying in wait for you."

Both were talking in low voices; they knew how voices carry in a still night.

"You are very welcome," she said.

"You are a Timothean," he said, "the only one here. Tell me straight out of your mind, without an instant's reflection, ought I to go to Persia?"

"No, Prince," she said instantly, "you ought not to dream of it."

"In the same way, why not?"

"The Greens are going to rebel; your uncle is often suffering; you ought to be here to act for him."

"I'll tell you something," he said. "I think I've been tricked and misled. I do not name anyone, because I can't, but it seems to me that men of the Green Faction, who were trusted to end the Persian trouble, have kept it an open sore on purpose; for two things: one, to get me out of the way, the other, to get the army out of the way. The army has gone, of course. I should have gone, if my uncle had kept well, I was to command the troops. That is my office still, but in these last days, my uncle has considered what you said, and hopes that I may make peace. Thinking me gone, or as good as gone, the Greens have shown their hand. Hypatius for Consul. As before, does that mean anything to you?"

"No, Prince; a few shows and a banquet or two; a speech at the Gold Cup. The Consul never does more than that."

"A little more," he said. "He has some Committees. Legally, he is still the Chief Magistrate. Hypatius is only a puppet, but you may judge if he loves us. No, you cannot judge, nor guess, the hate the Greens have for us." He was silent for a little; then he said, "You've heard the phrase, 'he waded in blood to the throne'. My Uncle killed, in order to be Emperor; then he killed again, so that I may succeed. Those two blood-guilts are on me day and night. That is why I long for a word with Timotheus. How am I to profit by murder? I deserve the hatred of the Greens; their whole party is in blood-feud with us, and will do justice on us when they can. I see their plan. When Hypatius is the Chief Magistrate, he will declare that my Uncle seized the throne by blood and fraud; he will declare the election to the purple fraudulent; we shall be cast out."

She knew that he was confused in the multiplicity of the issues, and that the fable would have to be made simple for him.

She rose and said, "You must eat and drink, Prince, while we consider this."

In the brazier, lightly packed among the embers, was the stone hot-box in use among the Winter Palace people for those coming from late rehearsal. She opened this with the iron hook and brought out the hot milk and fruit-breads.

"Come, Prince," she said. "We can talk much better as we sup."

The break of the mood gave him calm; she had a moment in which to reflect.

"Did you really start for Persia, Prince?" she asked.

"Yes, and went twenty miles. I gave them the slip and came back. They think I've gone on."

She knew that he had come back to talk it over with her; she hugged the thought with joy. She liked this man very much; he was linked to her through Timotheus, and he was her Ruler, come to her for guidance; she would give him all her thought and all her prayer.

"They may have followed me," he said.

"Here? To this house?" she asked.

"I saw no-one, and I took pains; but they beset me everywhere. The Palace is full of spies. But no; they aren't here."

"It might be well to quench the candles," she said, "and screen the night-light. We may show more light than is seemly, through some cranny."

She put out the candles and screened the tiny lamp.

"Tell me, Prince," she said. "I imagine that your uncle does not believe in any danger?"

"He says that Hypatius is such a fool that the more he appears in public the better for the whole Blue Faction. He despises Hypatius. Then, he beat the northerns and killed their chiefs; he thinks that he taught them such a lesson that they will never rise again; he did nothing of the kind. Then, in the west; they are all these racing lords, there, with their serfs. He calls them the amateur cavalry. I probably need not tell you how many of them he has insulted in one way or another; nor of the grudges they bear myself. Then, there is the man Nicanor who is in blood-feud. He has allowed Nicanor to come back to The City. He is an implacable enemy and very able."

"Right," she said. "Now may I ask one other thing? May I say, without offending, how the thing seems to me?"

"Do," he said. "I came for that."

"The Greens mean to fight your House," she said. "Armed forces are on the north and west, among the old rebels and the Nicanor people; they are all getting ready. Everybody seems to know that. The Greens are taking great pains to make people vote for Hypatius for Consul. They must set great store by that. It is plainly a main point in their procedure. They are going to elect him as Consul; they are then going to make the Consul proceed by legal means to get rid of your House. Probably, the Consular powers have never been removed by statute, only by use and wont. Is that so?"

"Sufficiently so."

"I suppose Symmachus has no chance of election?"

"I should say, from what I have heard, that the Committees will all vote Green."

"So I suppose," she said. "But we may take it that they will proceed as I've said, and do nothing very much until the election. When will that be?"

"Just under three weeks; two and a half weeks."

"So you have a fortnight at least before the serious trouble. A fortnight is a long time, Prince; much may be done in a fortnight. Your army is moved to the East; I heard about that at Antioch. How far from The City is it?"

"The advanced base is at Myra at present. The stores at Antioch, Caesaraea and so forth have been filled. The troops are echeloned along the roads from Lycia to Nicaea. Most of them are in the Cities of the Churches; all the five regiments are there."

"That would be a week's march, I suppose? You haven't recalled them?"

"No. My Uncle has refused to move a man. It will take a week for a message to reach them. The rain has been bad; the roads will be flooded and the bridges down."

"The sun will shine this morning," she said. "You can flash orders and use the telegraph arms."

"Ah, no," he said. "They are in the winter-quarters, not expecting to be moved. Most of them'll be in billets, in farms, in parties of half a dozen. It will take the commanders perhaps a week to concentrate, if there come snow or hard frost, and there may be either, or both, at any moment. It is the hardest thing to move troops in a hurry. You see, the difficulty is one of supply. If those four thousand horse are to move back, forage and provision will have to be moved to meet them, and guarded on the way; it is no small task, on winter roads. My Uncle forbids me to move a man, moreover."

"You command those troops," she said, simply. "Your order suffices, your Uncle need know nothing whatever about it till they are here. Order them back to The City by forced marches. You can depend on them, I suppose?"

"All the Five Regiments adore my Uncle; they can be trusted."

"Your Sardicans would die for you, I suppose?" she asked, meaning those men of the Emperor's hills and villages, who were retainers in the Palace.

"They are our clansmen," he said. "They are parts of us."

"Very well, Prince, you have, in them, secret and determined messengers who will carry orders. You can always command post-horses in any number, I suppose?"

"Yes, if I use the proper forms. However, that is only going to the Palace to take them. Still," he said, "I doubt if we could get even the Kingfishers back to The City before the election."

"You will have, perhaps, till a day or two after the election," she said. "They may not strike at you on election day. Has not the Consul to be sworn or blessed before he functions?"

"Yes; he is sworn at once; he takes the Sacrament next day."

"He would not do anything dangerous till the day after that, then."

All the same, she thought of Nicanor lifting the Bays past the Pillars. She judged that spearmen from the North and lancers from the West would be in The City outer wards the night before the election, so that "liberation" might start as soon as the Chief Magistrate had the votes of the Committees. Nicanor would not wait for any Sacrament to be given to the Consul; he would want blood at the first possible instant.

"How about your navy, Prince?" she asked. "The Navy has always been loyally Blue; have you any seamen, to use in The City?"

"Fewer than ever before," he said. "The ships and men are all along Karamania and so forth, wherever there is shelter; the men housed and the ships often hauled up on the slips. They are waiting to move the army in the Spring. I have a few reservists here; and the Coast-Guard Service."

"How many?" she asked.

"Two hundred, somewhat scattered. I am concentrating them," he said.

"Prince," she said, "would you not upset the Green plan if you stood for Consul against Hypatius?"

"That is a new thought," he said, looking up eagerly.

"Had you never thought of that?"

"Never. If I give up the command, of course, I could do that."

"Won't you do it? You would upset all their plans by standing. No one would vote for Hypatius against you. Your policy would be peace abroad; as evidence of that you could show, that you have given up the Eastern Command, and are not going against Persia. You can have no idea of the comfort that would give here and abroad."

"It has much to recommend it," he said. "You are helpful in suggestion."

"It might bring on the conflict here," she said, "but I think not. The Greens have made their plans for the clash to come in just under three weeks from now. They cannot alter their plans at once. Their armed forces are at some distance, just as yours are. They could not alter any plan without consulting their army leaders; and even if they wish to strike earlier, they cannot, without preparation. Is not that so?"

"A good deal of devilry can be improvised," he said.

"O, I grant that," she said, "but not military movements; they are planned. The difficulty is one of supply," she added.

"They control our supplies," he said. "Our army forage comes from them."

He seemed to reflect upon the problems raised by standing for Consul.

She said, "Prince, forgive me if I press this matter. Whether you stand for Consul or not, you must lose no instant in recalling the cavalry. Even if you have only the Kingfishers, they will be more than a match for half-trained men. Send off your Sardican riders at once, in batches of two, with urgent orders to the troops to fall back by forced march on The City. Later in the morning, you can send orders to prepare the magazines on the roads for them. Send the cleverest men you have and tell them it is life and death, and that if they do it in time it will bring them great reward. You can write the orders here."

She pulled out writing materials from the table drawer. "Dictate to me; I will write," she said.

She wrote the orders to the generals commanding and to the Praefects of the regiments; she wrote a good, firm, clear hand, with much character in it. He signed the letters and sealed each one with his seal of the Cock of Dardanos, using her blue sealing-wax.

He said, "These will be on their way in half an hour. I will send duplicates later. If I can find my daredevil seaman, I may tempt him to take some of them south by sea; it will blow hard from the north tomorrow." He rose as though to go. "Wait, yet," he said; "I cannot stand for Consul after all."

"Why not? You are qualified, aren't you?" she asked.

"Yes, I've the means, and am of age, and have held the preliminary appointments; all that; but Hypatius is being nominated at noon today; this is the nomination day. The candidate has to go before a magistrate, and get leave to stand; then he has to appear in public and say that he is going to stand. This is the last possible day for nomination."

"But you have time for that. How long would your examination by a magistrate last?"

"O, only a few minutes, probably; that isn't the point. I cannot stand for Consul while I command the Eastern Army. I shall have to lay down my command, and obtain the Emperor's discharge and quittance from it; that will be no easy thing to obtain."

"You must obtain it. He wants you to succeed him. It is your one chance of succeeding. You know, Prince, your own instinct tells you, that you'll never be Emperor if once you leave this City to the plans and plots of the Greens."

"Then there is the other matter," he said. "I can only come to the throne through the blood of murdered men. God knows, my heart sinks when I think of it."

"You shed no blood," she said. "Your hands are innocent. But if you stand aside now, others whose hands are
not innocent will thrust in. God gives you both a chance.
Are you going to take the chance, which God so plainly
offers to you, or will you let these thirsters for blood
take it? You fail now, and all your friends will be dead
by Christmas, your mother and uncle and aunt and
you."

"The worst of it is, that I'm not a soldier. I'm a
thinker," he said.

"And the Empire is a mess left by successive soldiers,"
she said. "It needs a thinker and a cleaner-up of mess.
Nothing functions here but party-feud and horse-racing.
If your uncle, or any other patriot, killed a few Greens
and horse-racers, so that you may come to the throne
and cleanse the mess, I say he did God's work. God let
him do the work, and it was done for your sake. If you
profit by it, you'll have to remember, with trembling,
every moment of your life, that men died so that you
might rule."

"You haven't quite got my thought," he said, "but
you have been a great help to me. I must go now, to get
these orders sent. By the way, here is a pass to the Hippodrome at noon today, in case you should wish to hear the
Green candidate. The man Theophanes is to speak; he
is a great orator." He laid the metal disc on the table.

"Thank you," she said. "Now, if you are going, I
will listen if the maid be asleep." She stole to the door, to
the stair-foot and listened. In the stillness, she heard the
breathing of the sleeping maid. "Her door is open," she

whispered, "but she is sound asleep. Now I will go out, to make sure that the coast is clear."

Very softly, she opened the outer door and slipped into the tiny garden to a night fragrant from the rain and all washed clear. It was all exquisitely still save for an occasional tinkle of trickling water. There was no sign of man abroad. A little brown owl cried near by. She saw him as he sat perched and knew from him that no man was about.

"I think all is clear, Prince," she said, as she blew out the light. "I shall lead you to the door in the dark," she whispered. "Give me your hand. There are no steps. Make no sound."

There was no question of any romance between them.

"I thank you again," he whispered.

She gave him his tarred cloak, and led him through the door into the little garden and the road. He stood for one moment to make sure that no one was passing; then he slipped silently away. She remembered then that all his movement had been swift and silent. Creeping back to the house, she took a sponge and mopped out all traces of his footprints. It was just as well that not even Kallianassa should know that a man had been there. She lit all her lights, and carefully searched the room for any trace of him or thing left behind. She put away the writing things and then went up to her bed. "Put not your trust in princes," she said to herself. All the same, she gave this Prince a great deal of her thought.

It was very clear to her as she walked to the theatre that morning, that the Green Faction supposed that the

Blue Prince was out of the way. Bodies of lads of about twenty years of age were marching in the streets, in military formations. They all wore Green badges, and sang the familiar songs, and from time to time shot out their hands in an odd way in unison, shouting in a barking manner,

"Vote
For
Hy-pa-tius."

Outside the shops and offices of well-known Blue merchants, they stopped and shouted abuse; they threatened those who entered such houses, and in some cases mildly assaulted them, knocked their hats off or plucked things from their hands. In the theatre, she swiftly arranged a brief freedom so that she could attend the meeting at the Hippodrome. She was busy, like everyone in the theatre, but by giving up her midday interval she had only to plead for a quarter of an hour. The day was clear and bright, but cold, after the passing of the storm. An open-air meeting was not likely to last long. She wondered as she worked, how the Prince had prospered in his laying-down the command and asking leave to stand for Consul. Every detail of the talk in the small hours came back to her; every word was weighed and examined. She was shocked at her boldness, and felt that he would never forgive her, not for her advice, which he had asked for, but for having seen his perplexity. She told herself that she was not in love with him, but she was interested in him. He stirred within her a protective maternal self, which her own children had never touched. She had

shrunk from her own children, as being some of the dis-
carded rags of Hekebolos. Since her return to The City,
she had begun to think of them with some little yearn-
ing, as things not safe in Hekebolos' control.

A girl at the theatre told her that there would be a
big crowd at the Hippodrome, and that she would never
get a seat. "All the whole Green Party will be there, and
Lord Kallimachus is sending all his teams for the procession." This one fact was enough to bring more than
half The City to the streets, for Kallimachus' teams were
famous. His forbears had lived for their horses, for more
than a hundred years; latterly he had thought that the
horses and the popularity they brought him might bring
him more of the power that he coveted. What he wanted
was an Emperor chosen from the nobles of the west, or,
better still, married to his younger sister. With such an
one, he might look for great appointment and influence
which would mean much to him. Theodora knew of
him, as one of great position in the west, whose wealth
gave him much power in The City and in society. He
bred horses and sold forage on a great scale. He owned
several sporting clubs and had lately established and
supported a company of public speakers, whose task it
was to defend chariot-racing whenever a strict Patriarch lifted up his voice against its cruelty and seemed in
the least likely to get a hearing. Theodora guessed that
such an ally might help the Green cause more than
genius.

As she left the theatre, she heard the roar of the crowd
to her right, and knew that the procession was on its way.
She had not far to go to the entrance marked upon her

disc. Long before she reached the entrance, she heard the crash of the massed bands beginning, and thousands of voices lifted up in the song, "Up with the Green Flag and down with the Blue." As she drew nearer to the Hippodrome, she wondered what sort of a seat hers would be. As the Prince had given it, she could not help thinking that it would be a special seat. She looked at the neat, bright disc, marked "Alpha, gamma." As she drew into the approach to the entrance, she noticed a group of well-dressed young men, all wearing Green rosettes. One of them came at once to her, and politely asked what her seat's letters were; she said, "Alpha, gamma."

"A friend of the candidate," he said. "Come this way, will you?"

He led the way through the toll-gates into the Race-Course, close to the Imperial Box. She knew the Race-Course very well from of old. It was now patrol.ed by Green stewards, each one of whom carried a long club. She saw that these men were a pretty evil-looking lot: they were the "A boys" and other gangs, she judged.

"A fairly tough set, the stewards," her guide explained, "but it is well to have them tough; we don't want them too conscientious if there's a row."

He led Theodora past a good many of these to the great central box, hung with green. Here he called from the Course to a young man of great elegance above him.

"This lady is Alpha, gamma," he explained. "Pass her in, will you? I must go back now; he'll see you to a place."

A tough-looking steward opened a gate; she went up the step into Alpha, and then up three steps to gamma:

there she was, in the centre of things, close to the pulpit from which the speeches would be given. She thanked her guide and sat, and then looked about her. The seats near her were fast filling with people; she recognized some of them; the people who always went to gatherings; "Little Byzantium", she called them. "Little Byzantium" had changed somewhat during her absence; the woman who had worn leopard skin now wore zebra skin, and the creature who had dyed his beard purple had now dyed it green. Glancing back over her shoulder, she saw the Green Faction waiting for the show to begin, and among them a girl of outlandish elegance wearing a Persian head-dress of great beauty.

But now the audience rose as the crashing bands came round the curve of the Course. They came on in style and halted, still playing, just opposite Theodora, while after them, amid singing and applause, came the chariots with their teams, the horses glistening and proud, and the famous charioteers, insolent and dare-devil, delighting in the cheering. Car by car, they halted just by Theodora, while the Green Leaders got down: Menippos, the President of the Charioteers, the great sporting club, Pompeius, a soldier, the brother of Hypatius, then Hypatius himself, Nicanor of the Bays with Kallimachus, and about a dozen lesser men, last of all being Theophanes. Theodora was interested to see that the members of the Persian Embassy were there. The chariots dropped their freight and moved on. The Green henchmen got into groups, and cleared gangways. They were going to take no nonsense from any Blue; their eyes roved up and down for someone who might reasonably be clubbed.

For the moment, they saw no one; it was a Green meeting. It was a fair, sunny day, but rather cold; the proceedings were to be brief, for no one wished to sit long there. Theodora had noted that much of the audience was organized, drilled, and even uniformed. There were schools, brotherhoods, burial and benefit associations, each with some leader, each with marks and banners. She saw, too, that the henchmen's bludgeons were all of the make known in The City slang as 'Macedonian ticklers'. They had been supplied from one source, from the same model, a light strong rod, tipped with a swelling of lead. A voice spoke just behind her, saying, "I didn't expect to see *you* here." Turning, she saw that it was Theophanes. She greeted him, but was not well-pleased at his speaking to her. His dress was flashy; he was hung about with the amulets and medals of the political societies of which he was a member, and he had the look of what he was, an insolent, cynical, low politician up to any corruption that was going.

"Ah, girl," he said, "your people were plum good to me in the old days; I just had to greet you. A fair house," he commented. "But I don't hold with morning shows. You can't spread the moonlight before dinner."

"I'm told that you can," she said.

"Don't you believe it," he said, smiling. "Not what I call the moonlight."

"Are you speaking this morning?" she asked.

"Introducing the candidate," he said. "Just saying there's no need to introduce him."

At this instant, a bruiser in charge of some "A boys"

thrust hurriedly into the Alpha seats and up to Theophanes.

"Say, Chief," he said, "the Prinny and his set are just across the way there; d'ye like us to set about 'em?"

"What?" Theophanes said. "Prinny? Here? He's gone east."

"No. He's there," the bruiser said.

Theodora looked in the direction pointed out. Just across the course from her a little party sat in the seats of Alpha, gamma. One was Justinian, two were priests, another was Philip the Pisidian, and a fifth Old Symmetry Symmachus.

"Hell," Theophanes said. "He started east yesterday. He must have come back."

"We'll deal with him," the bruiser said.

"The hell you will," Theophanes said. "Keep all fast with your dealing. Keep your boys quiet; you'll have your fun later."

The smasher seemed grieved at not having his fun at once. He growled, "He ain't got any minders with him," but went back crestfallen and obedient. As he reached the Race-Course, to give his orders, Menippos went into the pulpit, and all the Green drummers below him beat a roll for silence. As they stopped, he shouted,

"Friends, Fellow-Citizens, Fellow-Sufferers from Blue Misrule, this is a great day for The City. Why is it a great day? Because we are here for a great cause. And why are we here? Because we are here for Liberty." (A storm of cheers.) "The Liberty of Free Men. The Liberty our Fathers died for. And which of you here would not die for Liberty?" (A roar of cheers.) And perhaps it may come to that. Who knows? Friends, we are here to restore Liberty. We are here to approve Hypatius for Consul." (Tumultuous cheers.) "You know what the Consulship was. A check to tyranny. A bit in the mouth of avarice. A sword against the usurper."

Here there was loud and long yelling; no one failed to take the hint. The usurper meant was the old Emperor Justinus. "With Hypatius Consul," the speaker continued, "the Consul will be all those things. There will be peace abroad. There will be prosperity at home. The usurper will go down. And there will be Liberty." After uproarious cheers, the speaker cried:

"So welcome the Green Candidate for the Consulship, the hero Hypatius. Welcome our champion, who will lead us to Victory. Hypatius. Hypatius. Hypatius."

This triple cry was the signal for the bands to strike up the well-known air,

"See, see, the Victor flaunting comes."

Amid immense enthusiasm, with song and music, Hypatius came slowly down the steps with his party-leaders. Theodora had a good look at him.

Someone had said in her hearing in the theatre, that Hypatius had a face like a worm, and a dancer hearing this had approved. She saw now that the description was not poetically true. He had a face which did seem to come to a sort of point in a rather wormy way, but it was a set, expressionless face; it lacked the aspiring thrust and enquiring wriggle that gives vitality to the faces of so many worms; it also lacked the colour. A man among the smashers below Theodora said audibly with much disgust, "God, he looks like a milky maggot." His face, whatever it was, had frozen now to an unhappy fixity. He was loathing this business yet determined to go through with it. In his person, he was tall and well-made. He had dressed with foppery in fine white linen, with one jewel of emeralds, very choicely made, upon his right chest. Someone near Theodora said, "He knows a lot about jewels; all his rings and things are very good." His colourless hair had been frizzed in what was then the new fashion for elegant young men; it had also been scented. He bore no mark of rank, though as the late Emperor's nephew he might have worn purple bands upon his robes. He carried a little case of scarlet leather. He had upon him a look of breeding, or at least, of having been bred and tended and groomed. Theodora watching him, wondered if he had consecrated himself to this candidature, or been taken and forced into it. He held his head well up. She thought that he had rehearsed that coming down the steps with a great deal of care. She saw him pause at the foot of the steps before going up into the rostrum. He gathered his robes about him, so that he might not trip. As he did this, he turned towards her, so that she saw his weary and cross face twitching a little from nerves. She thought, "So this is the Hypatius about whom so much was said. It is little wonder that he failed in the employments given to him. His uncle gave him the command of an army; he lost it. He then gave him the command of a second army; he lost that. He then

put him in command of a Province, which he lost to the
Empire. Yet even so, after three major disasters, each
enough to justify a capital charge, he was trusted by the
present Emperor with a most delicate peace negotiation
which he was supposed to have betrayed. What was there
in this milky maggot which caused him to be employed
time after time? Justinus had employed him perhaps in
the hope, that doing so might placate the Greens.
Someone behind her said, "Justo used to think he won
that cavalry skirmish. He did nothing of the kind.
The Q.M.S. won the skirmish as everybody in the army
knew."

Nicanor came with Hypatius, close behind him. Theodora had a good view of him. He had once been the idol
of that Race-Course, and had come surging down it with
a quadriga in a way which shook the heart. Theodora
instantly felt that he was driving Hypatius now, just as
surely, with as cold a calculation and as ferocious a re-
solve as had swept his bays there years ago. He held the
reins now, and had ready the appalling and compelling
scourge. He was the driver of all this, she had no doubt.

Theophanes slipped from his seat and followed them.
Hypatius went into the pulpit. Nicanor stood a step below him, with his cold, stern, contemptuous eye upon
the crowd below. It rested for a moment with scorn upon
the figure of Justinian. As the tumult ceased, Nicanor
took the occasion to speak, though the speech had been
allotted to Theophanes. He slightly indicated Hypatius
with his hand and said, "Our Consul-to-be, Hypatius."
He glanced pointedly at Justinian and added, "Our
Consul-to-be is a native, one born in The City, not

brought in from the wilds of barbarism." This was
cheered loudly.

Theodora saw Theophanes' face. It had been allotted
to him to introduce Hypatius; now the task had been
taken from him and his prepared effects made of no account. However, his face remained steady, he waited for
the applause to die and then began. Theodora had never
heard him speak; she had heard all the best preachers
and some of the good orators of her time, but when once
he began, she knew that none of all these could compare with him. None could resist that voice, so sweet, so
varied, so persuasive, compelling and beguiling. He was
dishonest, unscrupulous, dangerous, but let him once
speak and everyone with ears was at once under his spell;
so it was here. He was very brief, but held the entire
multitude breathless. Hypatius followed.

It had been a jest among the men of the Old Winter
Palace, that if one were called upon to play a patrician of
a certain kind he should do it from the top of his throat,
with a shut mouth, as though his mind were dried grass.
Hypatius now gave what seemed an elaborate parody of
one such performance which had been famous through
The City. Theodora saw Nicanor's face become stern.
She saw Theophanes put both his thumbs into his mouth
and bite them. He had prepared the audience; was it to
be treated thus? Hypatius began, floundered on, tried to
make a joke, said something about freedom, and then explained that by freedom of course he meant liberty. He
said that it was a great pleasure to see so many friends all
wearing the right colour. He did not have to tell them
that that colour throughout the Empire stood for all the

things the Green Party stood for, like Liberty. Here he
stopped in his speech and began to fumble with his case,
which did not open easily.

"I've got a . . . a . . . a sort of duty to do," he said. "I
offer myself as candidate for the Consul, to be your Consul . . . for the Consulship. I have to show that I have
been through the stages of office in the prop ordah. These
are my parchments and commissions and what not. The
first is this one." He read them all in his colourless voice
while the audience began to talk and all attention ceased.
When he had read his certificates, he said, "Of course, I
forgot to say, I was born at the prop time. I mean to say,
I'm old enough to be Consul, that is, if you're good
enough to elect me. I've a record of my birth here." He
read this, then suddenly seemed to reflect that something
had been left out. "There was another mattah," he said.
"I've forgotten what is is, but I'm shaw it's a veh important thing. Yes. Baptism. 'Mshaw we're all agreed that
baptism is a veh important thing. When you see these
fellahs without it you see a thing like that. This is a cer-
tificate of my baptism. Then, of course, another thing.
'Mshaw we're all agreed religion's a veh important thing;
important as anything, you can say what you like;
'mshaw we're all agreed about that. When you buy a
horse, you have a fellah to say if he's sound. When you
elect a Consul you want to know if he's sound, too.
'Mshaw you'll all want to know that I'm orthodox Christian."

There was an outbreak of cheers at this; some of the
henchmen sniggered as they cheered, for orthodoxy was
not important to them; but many there had waited for

the declaration, knowing that the old Emperor, Hypatius' uncle, had not been orthodox, but almost a downright heretic.

When the cheering stopped, Hypatius made his peroration, which he had learned by heart and rehearsed before a mirror. "I have now fulfilled the legal requirements of a candidate for the Consulship. I have only to add, that if elected my every effort will be for the service of the electors. In fact, my motto will be Liberty, and my aim will be . . . I mean to say, that, if elected, it will be my first wish and 'mshaw you'll all agree . . ." Here the poor man was lost, and Theodora had an actress' sympathy for one who had 'lost his lines and dried up'. She heard Nicanor prompt him in a loud whisper, "Restore the functions." "Ah, yes," Hypatius said, "my first aim, if elected, of course, will be to restore the functions, which I'm sure you'll all agree ought to have been restored long ago. When I say the functions, I mean the liberty of this great Empire."

"You don't," Nicanor hissed. "Drop the functions. Get on to the sword. Let our antagonists remember . . ."

"Ah, yes," Hypatius repeated. "Let our antagonists remember that an old sword, and by sword, I mean the Consulate, of course, an old sword, kept by the tyrant from its oppressed owner, is still a sword, and if drawn, however blunt, can be resharpened, and however old-fashioned, can be used, and used with effect, let them remember, by true men, Green men, determined to have Liberty or Die."

He came down from the pulpit. How an old sword kept from its owner was to be used by its owner Theo-

dora did not gather. However, no-one asked, there was
great applause, and directly it lulled, Theophanes cried:
"I have the utmost pleasure in announcing, that Hypatius is chosen as our candidate. May he sweep tyranny
from The City. Hypatius for Consul."

The cheers were taken up and repeated. Nicanor led
Hypatius forward to take the cheers and bow. He took
the cheers and bowed. Then some wandering devil
prompted him to lift his hand, as though he were going
to speak. When the audience hushed for him, he had
nothing to say; the words were gone; all the mass of
human gunpowder in front of him, all ready to explode,
became suddenly quite damp.

In this silence, which might have been made for him,
Justinian rose in his place, leaped on the ledge of the
tier in which he sat and, holding to a stanchion, cried:
"Citizens of Byzantium . . . I am Justinian, the son of
Sabatius. I come as the law directs to offer myself as a
candidate for the Consulship."

If it were not a wise act, it was profound, as a brave
act often is. It came as a shock and a surprise; it took
people's breaths away. A few sniggered at the man's au-
dacity; the rest became suddenly tense. This was a moment of the theatre. What would happen next? Some
turned white. Theodora gasped, expecting to see him
knocked senseless. Half-a-dozen Green henchmen in the
arena just below him shouted, "Yah, you dirty Blue,"
and shook their clubs at him.

Justinian said, "Ah, no; men should keep their clubs
for their wives."

Some of them laughed at this. They came of a class of

society which specially prizes courage. Justinian's nerve, or 'neck' as they called it, in proposing himself at a Green meeting, won their hearts. He laughed at them and added, "I mean it. Here are my qualifications. By age, by office, by order of office, by baptism, orthodoxy and by freedom from other State employ, I am qualified to stand as Consul. I ask you to support me at the polls."

The mob had hardly drawn its breath before he had finished. He remained standing on the ledge, while Symmachus rose not far from him, to say, "I, Symmachus, also qualified in all the demanded ways, also offer myself as a candidate for the Consulship."

Theodora looked at the Green chiefs. They had been taken completely by surprise. Hypatius had looked at Nicanor, who looked as if he had been shot suddenly in a vital place. In an instant, however, he wrote something on his tablet, called one of his runners and told him to fly with that to some person or place which she could not catch. The man saluted and fled. Menippos, who had been taken by surprise as utterly as the other two chiefs, made an injudicious remark.

"Friends," he called, "you need not pay any attention to the Emperor's nephew."

Justinian, who was quick in debate, replied, "Your own candidate is an Emperor's nephew."

The crowd laughed. They were of the Green Faction; but a mob follows the winner, even if the victory be but for twenty seconds; they laughed, and turned with quick anticipation to hear what Menippos might reply.

"Run home and learn some more catechism," Menippos said. "You're not old enough to be Consul."

"I beg your pardon?" Justinian said.

"I said you're too young," Menippos replied.

"You did not," Justinian answered. "You said I was not old enough."

The crowd laughed again.

"Nor you are," Menippos said.

"I was born in the same year and the same month as your candidate, Hypatius," he answered.

"In hell you were," some of the henchmen cried. "Take that."

They had picked up stones and now let them fly at Justinian in a volley. It is never easy to fling upwards with accuracy in a crowd. The stones were not sent with accuracy; they were sent with the thought that anyone near Justinian would be a dirty Blue and, therefore, a fair mark. The people near Justinian dodged below the backs of the seats in front of them. The one man hit was a minor Green politician, an elderly tavern-keeper known as Old Father Abraham because of the length and whiteness of his beard. He was hit on the head. Theodora saw Justinian and the two priests lift him up and support him into the near-by exit tunnel. Other people closed in behind them. The henchmen made some attempt to follow, but Theophanes, who was not going to have the meeting ruined, called to the bandsmen to play. They struck up "We will rally to the Banner of our Fathers," and at once formed up; then they struck up the old march of "Up with the Green Flag". At the signal, the waiting chariots advanced to pick up the leaders, everybody sang, and so the meeting came to an end.

Theodora was sure that Justinian had escaped unhurt

from the stadium, but had some anxiety, lest Nicanor's sudden note had been to henchmen to waylay him at the outer gate and beat him out.

Theophanes was at her side speaking to her. "Well," he said, "they made a pretty mess of that between them. Did ye see the way they chucked away the house as soon as I'd made it for 'em? The whole house was just wax for them and the crazy creatures made it tallow on me."

Theodora knew what he meant. She had seen the audience ready for any wild enthusiasm, and the prepared mood had been caught, surprised and used by Justinian. Then Menippos with his coarse and clumsy interference had completed Justinian's triumph. She found her heart leaping strangely at the thought of Justinian's courage and success. It had stood still when the men flung the stones. It had leaped again when she saw him escape. It was thrilling now with anxiety, lest he should have been met at the stadium gate. If this were not the love which she had abandoned forever, what was it? She found no clear answer to the question as she went back to the theatre. All the crowds in the street were talking of the meeting. "That shews how important the Blues think it. Justinian's given up his command and come to contest the election for Consul." It was her doing and it was wonderful to her. She caught snatches of talk about it: "It took Nicanor clean by surprise. Hypatius didn't know what to do or say. Now there'll be trouble. Now the fat will sizzle." She thought that this was so. Whatever trouble had threatened would now be precipitated. Would the Greens wait for the election? She thought not; she judged that they would use violence at once. Nicanor

had looked violence itself. What he had written on th
note was doubtless an order to murder. Cooler thought
came into her mind after an hour or so. Nicanor's fur
might well have been with some spy who had not tol
him of Justinian's return. "The Palace is full of spies,"
she repeated. "Yet this secret was kept and took then
utterly by surprise." She judged that the spy who ha
failed Nicanor would have an uneasy five minutes when
next he faced his master. Who was the spy responsible
Could it be Philip the Pisidian?

The Green bands marched with the chariots throug
The City. The leaders got down at Kallimachus' City
house or palace, where there was going to be a banquet
Doubtless, the banquet became an anxious council of war
Going out with Macedonia for a little air later in the
afternoon, when it was coming towards sunset, she heard
that the Green orators were already speaking about Jus
tinian. They were asking: "Is it lawful for a man ap
pointed to high command in the east to stand for Con
sul? It has not been done before. By what presumptio
does the heir-apparent claim the right to do it now?"
Another was less questioning. He was saying: "And ye
the usurpers are not content. They stole the throne, they
snatched the purple, they annexed the commands, they
pillaged the treasury. Yet even that, brothers, is not
enough for their greed, which is like the fire or the sea.
No, they demand the Chief Magistracy, also. And why?
Because, they know that Hypatius and the Greens are
determined to end this menace to our peace and liberty.'

Going back to the theatre, she heard from Iophon that

little groups had been passing the theatre door shouting,
"Impeach the Usurpers. Liberty. Hypatius."

She wondered much what effect the candidature of
Justinian had had upon the plans of the Greens. In the
rush of rehearsal, she had little time for steady thought;
but gradually she came to see that the Greens knew the
helplessness of the Blues and meant to profit by it. She
judged that Nicanor's note had been sent to hurry on the
armed forces waiting to the north and west of The
City. Meanwhile armed gangs in The City began to
make their presence felt. The next morning, as she went
to the theatre, she saw some Green henchmen set upon
a young man and pluck from his tunic a Blue favour that
he was wearing. This they tore and flung into the gutter.
The same party, having done this, and told the lad to
get out of it if he did not want his head clubbed open,
suddenly charged at a shop by the roadside, which bore
a Blue sign. They hit the shop-keeper into the midst of
his goods, three of them swarmed up and tore down the
sign, while the others flung the goods within reach into
the street. It was all very swiftly done; there was no re-
sistance. She was deeply indignant, and cried, "How
dare you treat the poor man so?"

The men laughed and said, "You better not inter-
fere, lady. This doesn't concern you at all."

Some loiterers, who were Green partisans attending
the bullies, gathered at once and said, "That's the truth,
lady. This is no concern of yours. You get away and
keep out of this."

A man, who was older and quieter than most of them,

came up to her and said, "Just walk with me, Madam.
I'll see you where you wish to go."

She was glad of his protection and walked with him.
As they drew away from the gangs, he said, "It is going to be a dangerous thing to try to check these gangs of
the Greens. They'll be the rulers of The City."

"Why?" she said. "Surely the Guards will be called
out and sent to patrol the streets?"

"Don't you believe it, lady," the man answered. "The
Emperor will never use troops in an election riot, when
his nephew's one of the candidates. It would be said at
once that he meant to crush liberty. That would be the
way to bring down the whole house."

She thought that possibly there was sense in this, and
that the riot and threatening would continue on the plea
that thus free men exercised the right of free speech. She
had seen some stormy elections in the past, but nothing
promising to be quite so lawless as this. Indeed, what
passed that morning was but the prelude or foretaste of a
reign of disorder which was soon sweeping through The
City. In every public place there were Green orators,
always supported by bullies, who frequently used violence. As the days passed, they became more violent.
They went to the lengths of seizing people whom they
knew or suspected to be Blues, and making them make
public profession of belief in Hypatius. They made men
display Green banners or knocked them senseless for refusing. They broke down all Blue symbols and stand-
ards; they went boldly in gangs into the shops of Blue
merchants and demanded subscriptions for Hypatius'
Fighting Fund for Liberty. In some cases, they insisted

on payment to the Green cause for permission to keep
the shop open. In some cases, they flung the Blue partisan
into the Bosphorus. They were well organized; their policy had been ably planned and was brutally enforced.
Much license and disorder had always been permitted in
The City at election times; this was worse than anything
hitherto known. The Blues seemed powerless. The Guards
were not called out, not for any dread of what the Greens
might say, but because they were out of The City.

It was soon plain that the Greens had established control of The City. Every committee man had been told to
vote for Hypatius for Consul, and warned that a Blue
vote would be a death vote. Theodora heard of a shop-
keeper who was told to house and feed two Green henchmen for a fortnight. He refused, and appealed to one of
the magistrates for protection. The magistrate advised
him not to press for relief from the law, but to give what
was asked and be glad to get off so well. On leaving the
magistrate's office, he was set upon by Green agents,
taken to a central hall or headquarters of the Greens and
there questioned, as to what he had said to the magistrate. He had then found that his questioners knew the
very words he had used. This story was but one of many
such during those days of the Candidature. Murder,
which had been secret and of the night, now came into
the streets by day.

She heard nothing from Justinian in those first days;
then she heard that the Blues were holding a big meeting
at the great Palace of Varieties, at which both Justinian
and the Patriarch were to speak. She learned later that
the Greens were indignant at the thought, that their

enemies had forestalled them. They took the Palace of
Varieties for the day following, and at once began to ad-
vertise a monster meeting of the Greens. However, they
could not have the Patriarch; their chief speakers were
to be an old politician named Theophrastus, who controlled the weapon-works in the Western Province, and
Kallimachus, with the support of a new body known suddenly as the Macedonian Trade Mission, of western land-
owners and ranchers, who were about to come to The
City to arrange a trade agreement. Theodora judged
that these men were the leaders of the trouble in the
West.

The rehearsals kept her busy daily, but Sosthenes had
postponed the date of opening till The City were quieter.
When that might be was not very clear.

Theodora suddenly received an invitation to the meeting of the Blues. Two discs of admission to the seats
Alpha, gamma were sent to her by some Palace messenger; she could only suppose that they came to her at Justinian's order. As she was freer at the theatre than she
had been for days, she arranged to go. However, on the
morning before the day of the meeting, Philip the Pisidian
appeared at the theatre asking to see her. She found him
elegant as ever, though somewhat white and anxious. He
explained, that the Prince Justinian would be most deeply
obliged, if she could come to the Palace of Varieties to
give some advice about the arrangement of the stage. She
asked Sosthenes, if she might go. He said, "Surely;"
Philip helped her into his waiting carriage and drove off
with her.

"The Prince is very anxious to have your advice about

the stage decoration," he explained. "The Palace of Varieties is not exactly the stage on which the Patriarch and the heir-apparent should appear, perhaps, but as they are to appear there, we must do what we can."

"It is the biggest theatre in The City," Theodora said. "I suppose that that is why it has been taken. Who runs it now?"

"A man named Pappus."

She knew Pappus as a famous low comedian who had been a success as a manager.

"I suppose it will be full?" she said.

"Well, it is the great effort of the Blue Faction," he said. "This sudden standing for Consul has to be explained to the Party, who, between ourselves, are not too well pleased. It is the maxim, not to meddle with the Greens in little matters. Who regards the Consulship? It is a fiction, an anachronism. Besides, we need the Prince in Persia. However, it is his wish or whim or impulse, it must go through. If I might dare to suggest it," he added, "might you not do a real public service in suggesting to the Prince, if you ever have an opportunity, that much of the present unrest is due solely to resentment? People are saying it up and down; I have my reports, of course: 'The Prince is doing it from spite'; or, 'doing it from jealousy'. Why should he grudge the Greens this chance of winning an empty honour with much expense attached to it? That is what is being asked; that is what is so lowering. He gives up a great and necessary State appointment to shew his spite against a rival Faction; it is on everybody's tongue. And it is so inopportune, and so ill-judged. He has made countless enemies by it and lost dozens of votes in the Committees. I have heard of over twenty Blue Committee men who will vote against him. He may have committed political suicide, believe me. You can see from the Green parties in the streets how they are taking it. I don't think that he has any chance of being elected Consul. The Committees will bring in Hypatius just to spite him. It will be a blow from which he may never recover."

He babbled on, hoping, as she thought, that some of what he said might be passed on to Justinian as advice or comment. She was not likely to be asked for advice or comment, nor was she likely to give either so far against her own feelings. The talk increased her suspicion of Philip, and had one other result, that it made her for a moment wonder if she had not given very dangerous advice to the Prince and perhaps brought him to ruin. As the carriage stopped at the front entrance to the Palace of Varieties, she put this last thought out of her mind. If danger threatened the ruling House, it was here, in The City, not on the remote frontier a thousand miles away. Justinian's place was here, and she had done well to keep him here. As she passed into the theatre, she thought for a moment, that this elegant courtier, so skilled in the game of life at Court, may have heard some little praise of her from Justinian or his uncle, and may have decided that she was worth watching, flattering and perhaps using.

But now she was in the great empty house, in front of the stage, where men were arranging palms in pots and ranking blue chairs. Half-a-dozen women were on their knees scrubbing the stage, one half of it at a time. On the right, in the Imperial Box, men were folding the Imperial Banners in swags. Justinian stood on the stage, giving instructions to Pappus, the manager, who had a clerk beside him taking note of what was needed. A party of Greens, wearing their badges and headed by Menippos, stood in the auditorium, to the left of the stage. The Green Faction was holding its meeting a day later in this house; these men were now rapidly noting what would be needed for decoration. All theatres then had little doors between scene and house, in the boxes at each side of the stage. As the Imperial Box was full of the men arranging banners, she passed the group of Greens, entered the box on the audience's left, crossed it and opened the little door onto the stage. She heard one of the group say, "There's a way through there; the girl's gone straight through. That ought to be good enough." She heard the men follow her into the box and open the door behind her to peer through. In another instant she was being greeted by Justinian, who thanked her for coming so promptly; he introduced Pappus. She was always glad to meet people of the theatre. She had often seen Pappus in the past, when he had done his gigantic sleep-walking act and the equally famous skit of Phalaiktos of the Phalanx; but he had been among the stars when she had been among the walkers-on. He had the shrewd eyes of success, and the smiling good nature of the variety stage. He said that he was pleased to meet her; she said that she was glad to see the real Phalaiktos. He was pleased at having his old act remembered; ah, those had been the days.

She asked swiftly what had already been ordered and

arranged for the stage decoration; then, what curtains Pappus had ready to hand. These were technical points which she thoroughly understood. Justinian followed her about as she examined the back-cloths. She chose some painted hangings which Pappus said had gone with "a little sentimental act we done, called 'The Golden Heart'. " She asked for the stage hands to get these into place. All the time, the women were scrubbing the stage, men were folding and nailing flags, others were arranging the palms and chairs. Justinian was watching her as though nothing else mattered in the world; the party of Greens in the box on the spectators' left watched him and commented. She took in all these points. She was one who always thought it well to know her possible enemies. She led the Prince to the actors' left, close to the Imperial Box, so that she might take a good look at these people. After watching the effect of the hangings, and giving a couple of directions about them, she stole a glance at them. There was Menippos, a cool, big, stupid bully, a soldier very good in a tight place, and quite certain to get his troops into one, as many poor bones in foreign earth could have testified. He had been responsible for the disaster at Little Hill; it had been forgiven him, because of his personal courage and the lies of his friends in high place. She saw instantly that the men with Menippos were not patricians; one or two might be charioteers and another a boxer, for Menippos was a sporting peer, but three who hung back from the rest seemed an ugly lot. Well, the Green Faction was employing plenty such at that election, what were three more?

When the hangings had been set and approved, and

the other matters explained clearly to Pappus, she took them both to the front of the house where she made a suggestion, for flute-players just below the front of the scene, to play some solemn movements before the Patriarch spoke. She stood close beside the box in which Menippos was.

She said: "The Patriarch will be in the centre, and you, Prince, on his right. Who will be on the Patriarch's left?"

"Nicaea," he answered, meaning the famous Bishop, "and Symmachus just on my right. There will only be the four of us on the stage."

"In that case," she said, "could we not have the boy choir from the Cathedral, in the wings at each side, to sing as you take your places, and to go off singing as you reach the seats?"

"Say," Pappus exclaimed, "that would take. That would be a sure draw. Those boy voices are a dream."

She knew that Justinian was deeply pleased by the suggestion.

"I told you that this lady would give good advice," he said to Pappus. "I will go to the Dean at once about it. That would be a very beautiful effect."

"They could wait off-stage and come back to sing you off and the people out at the end," Theodora said.

"That will be beautiful," Justinian said; "the one thing we need."

They moved towards the door together, Pappus assuring them that he would have the palms and everything else set and the stage ready in case the choir-boys wished to rehearse that afternoon. Justinian said that the choir

would be well used to walking in procession. Theodora
said that they had better rehearse all that afternoon and
the next morning in their surplices, for so much depended on their taking position accurately and with grace;
still more, on their leaving position well. This had not
occurred to Justinian; he said that he saw how it must
be so. "I'll be on the stage," Theodora said. "I'll help to
marshal one wing of them at least." With this they
reached the door; the Prince saw Theodora into her carriage. Philip had long since disappeared.

"I thank you most sincerely," Justinian said.

"All shall be fixed, just as you said," Pappus cried.

As the carriage drove off, she was aware that not less
than a hundred people had watched the heir to the Empire see her into a carriage, and had wondered who she
was. Word had gone about that the Prince was in the
theatre; the entry was beset; some of the Sardican guards
were there. She thought that if the choir and the flautists
could be had, the meeting might be lifted out of the common.

Later, she thought of Menippos and his company, and
again wondered who the men were who were with him.
The charioteers and the boxer would be his chosen associates and friends; he was also their patron and master,
no doubt. The other men would probably be his heelers
or minders. Perhaps no Green leader would go about at
election time without a body-guard. Later in the day,
she wondered again; she felt somehow uneasy about them.
When she left The Swan Maidens that evening, she
walked to the Palace of Varieties, and asked at the Box
Office if they could show her a plan of the house for the

norrow's meeting. They handed the plan to her. She
noted that the Imperial Box had been lent to the Persian
Embassy; the front stalls had been given to Blue families
of Praefectual rank and to important City people of either
Faction. She saw that Nicanor was sitting in the third
row, and that a strong party of Green partisans held the
left front of the house, including the three boxes on that
side.

"Have the Greens bought these seats?" she asked of
the attendant.

"No," the man said. "They were invited and accepted;
it is thought that they will not turn up, in which case
their seats will be used for others. The Patriarch urged
that they should be invited. In fact, the Patriarch made
it a condition of his speaking, that they should be asked."

"If they know that the Patriarch asked for them, they
will certainly come," she said. "I suppose the house will
be crammed?"

"We couldn't seat another soul," the man said. "And
the same with the Green meeting next day. A waiting
list a mile long for both meetings."

She went home strangely relieved. She felt that the
situation had changed for the better. The Patriarch was
making his presence felt. If he could persuade the Greens
to the meeting, then, doubtless he would persuade them
to reason. "Ah," she thought, "if Timotheus were here,
he would have reconciled the two parties long ago; but
certainly it does look now as though the Patriarch might
do it."

At her home she found waiting for her a note from
Justinian thanking her for her help, and adding that the

boy choir would be at the meeting, and that if she could help in marshalling the boys, it would be a great satisfaction to himself and the greatest possible help to the Precentor. He also named the hour at which the boys would be there.

She had feared that Sosthenes would not spare her the next morning; however, he let her go. She rehearsed the entrances and exits of the choir-boys until it was almost time for them to appear. She then paraded them in their surplices, to make sure that they were ready to go on. By this time, the curtain was down; the stage was set for the meeting, and The City was flooding to its seats. The Patriarch and Justinian were both waiting in the Green Room for the house to be declared ready. The choir-boys were ranked in the wings, pulling faces at each other and mimicking the Patriarch and higher clergy. Theodora noticed that one little boy did the benevolent Nicaea to perfection.

There were little spy-holes in the curtains, through which those on the stage could see if the house were ready for the performance to begin. Pappus had his eye at the spy-hole on the actors' left. Theodora walked to the other, and looked through at "little Byzantium", taking its place for the show. From the plan she remembered clearly where Nicanor was to sit. He was not there yet. Hypatius was in the front row, with his brother, Pompeius. The box just beside her nearest to the stage was empty. The one next to it was empty. The one beyond that contained two ladies, in green costumes. She thought that the Greens shewed very poor spirit, in accepting invitations and then not using the seats. The Pre-

centor called her to the back of the stage for a moment.
He said that someone in the passage wanted a word with
her. She hoped that this might be Justinian, but it proved
to be Theophanes. He was in the dark and narrow passage which led to the dressing-rooms.

"I heard you were here," he said, speaking thickly.

He seemed scared of being seen; he kept huddled from
the light.

"Are you ill?" she asked.

"I hoped I might have a word," he said.

"Certainly," she answered. "Was there some message?"

She was more and more puzzled by him. He was scared,
agitated and shaking.

He bent very close to her and whispered, "That door
onto the stage, actors' right. Get it wedged."

"Wedged?" she whispered.

"Here," he whispered. "Quick." He had a heavy package in his hand, under his cloak; he thrust it into her
grasp. "Never say you saw me," he said.

He slid away from her at once, keeping his face
screened, with his hands over his eyes, as though he had
received dreadful news. She heard him pause at the stage
door before slipping out; she looked at her package. It
was a piece of cheap green cloth, such as made countless
hangings on the election waggons; it contained a heavy
wooden wedge and a mallet.

That door onto the stage, actors' right, led into the box
where Menippos and his friends had been. She was suddenly aware that shocks of terror were running through
her. She told herself that she must keep her head; usu-

ally she was cool, but now she was shaken. Theophanes had been terrified. He knew of some plot against the Prince, or the Patriarch, or both. She wrapped the things in their cloth and ran to the stage. The house, beyond the curtain, was falling still; it was almost time to begin. Pappus was tense at his peep-hole. She glid to the other and peeped through it. Nicanor was not in his seat, which was conspicuously occupied by the notorious and outrageous Mother Glycera. He must have sent her to occupy his seat, as an insult to Justinian. She glanced swiftly to the box beside her, though now Pappus was hissing to her, to get off the stage as the curtain was to go up. She saw that some men were at the back of the box; certainly three men keeping well out of sight; they looked like the three doubtful men who had been with Menippos the day before.

"Sst. Sst," hissed Pappus. She turned a ghastly and imploring look at him. He violently signalled to her to get off the stage. "Off the stage," he hissed at her. "Get off. It's curtain up."

At that instant, the Precentor at the back of the stage struck up his processional; the choir-boys' exquisite voices struck in, the lines of the lads turned. She had only just time to slide into the wings at the actors' right as the curtain slowly rose upon the choir advancing in two double lines, with the four speakers coming down stage in the midst. She saw then that the positions of the speakers had been changed. The speaker nearest to her on the actors' right was Justinian; next to him was Nicaea, next to him the Patriarch, and Symmachus at the left. "Who changed the order?" she muttered. An instant's thought told her

hat Symmetry Symmachus would have changed the or-
ler, so that the Church might hold the positions of hon-
ur, and the two candidates for the Consulships be visibly
umbled. "Yes," she thought instantly, "and so that the
Prince is nearest to the box with those three men in it."

She said to herself, "Of course, Symmachus couldn't
ave planned that;" then added, "Who can tell? Treach-
ry is everywhere, what with blood-feud and faction."
However, a look at Symmachus as he came down stage
old her that he had no thought of evil; he was a gen-
rous, good and clever old man. The House had risen at
the first sound of the hymn; it stood now, waiting for the
Patriarch to signal them to sit. All shaking as she was,
she slid back into the wing, close to the little door which
ed to the box.

She had noted that a key had been in the lock, on the
stage side, the day before. There was no key there now.
Usually a bolt had been upon the door, on the side of the
stage. It had been torn off. It had been but a small bolt,
running into a small catch; but bolt and catch were gone.
The removal must have been very recent, for the little
splinters broken by the jemmy were still fresh prickles
there. There was nothing to keep the door from opening
onto the stage at a push. The plan was clear. Three or
more men were inside the box. At a signal they would
come onto the stage. When they were on the stage, they
would be within a few feet of Justinian's chair, and on
his right side, so that they could beat down his effective
arm before he was aware of their coming. All this crossed
her mind in a flash. Something of the kind was planned.
Theophanes had been sick with terror of it. He had

known all the details. He had known that there would be neither lock nor bolt upon the door, and had somehow come with the only possible means of keeping the door shut. She stood in the wing there, touching the door, and wondering what she should do. She wondered for a moment, if murderers were in the Imperial Box on the other side of the stage. No, she could with some craning just see into that box, and be sure, from the head-dresses and the gleam of jewels, that the Persian Ambassador was there with his glittering staff. The murderers, and she had no doubt now that they were murderers, were on her side, where their victim would be, with no-one near him except herself and the frail and gentle old Bishop.

Then she began to think of the time when. They would not attempt it now, when the choir-boys were between them and their victim. They would not attempt it when the Patriarch was speaking, or probably would not, because they would expect the choir-boys to be still in the wings, then, listening, and because even the most abandoned partisan would shrink from interrupting the Patriarch; a kind of divinity hedged the Patriarch. After the Patriarch, Symmachus would say a few words, a very few; then Justinian would speak for at least half an hour. That was the danger-time, when Symmachus sat and Justinian rose. They might wait, perhaps, till Justinian sat, and the gentle old Bishop of Nicaea rose to hope that the meeting might prove fruitful of blessing. But no, they would know that the choir-boys would be tiptoeing back into the wings then. It would be before them. She had no doubt whatever that the men would stab Justinian and then escape by the wings and back-

stage passages to the stage-door and some waiting horses
or chariots. They would no doubt have agents in the
wings, perhaps on the stage and certainly in the passages, to help them to escape and stop pursuers.

She looked along the wings on her side, to see what
accomplices were there. She saw one of the dressers, a
woman, at some little distance, staring from cover at the
Patriarch. Beyond her, a stage hand stood; he was not
paying much attention to the stage, just looking at it.
His bearing was a little like that of a negligent sentry. It
struck her that he might well be an accomplice. It struck
her as suspicious, that he was stripped to working kit,
while all the other men in Pappus' employ there were
dressed up in honour of the Patriarch. This one man
lolled there, watching the stage, and sometimes casting a
glance at herself; he was wondering what she was doing
there. From her place Theodora could see across the
stage to the wings on the actors' left. The windlass for
the curtains, with the windlass crew, were on that side.
By this time the choir had sung the speakers to their
places and were moving off. They were doing it well,
she thought; the lines of slowly moving singers went up-
stage in time, drew into groups off-stage, and hung in
groups there. They would wait for the Patriarch to speak
before going to the Green Room for the refection of
cakes which the Prince had provided for them. As the
singers cleared away, Theodora saw that the wings on
the actors' left were full of sight-seers. Pappus was there,
with his wife, holding a bouquet; the Pappus family was
there; all the theatre staff was on that side, all in their
Sunday best. The Patriarch did not usually frequent the

Palace of Varieties, but now that he was here, the house meant to show that they felt it. Of course, they were all on that side because the Patriarch was there.

Now the speakers were alone, standing, facing the house, in front of their chairs, while the Patriarch told them that he wished them all to take their seats; he had not meant to say much, but felt that certain things needed to be said. He waited, while all in the house took their seats. The Patriarch turned to his fellow-speakers; they, too, sat. Theodora gasped, for the sands were running swiftly. The singers had gone; soon the Patriarch would end his talk; then Symmachus would speak; then, if not before then, the terrible thing would be. She was used to war; she had seen it close-to during these last months; but she was feeling lost, helpless and unable to act or to plan. The Patriarch was talking of the need for Peace upon the eastern frontier, and the dire need of Peace at home. He was one of the best speakers then living; his words came pelting out like sand-grains in a dust-storm, and with every arid grain the danger came nearer, and she could do nothing but hug the green bundle and stare and quake.

She was standing, staring in a lost way at Justinian and the Patriarch, when she knew that the door beside her was opening. She turned, with a gasp, to see that it had opened wide. Nicanor stepped out from the box into the wing. He was very silent. He cast a cold, insolent eye upon her, with perhaps, though this was doubtful, some shade of contemptuous memory of the creature who had tried to sell imitation jewellery at Antioch. She saw him look searchingly along all that side of the stage. All was clear enough; the choir-boys were gone to their cakes;

there was no other person on that side, except the stage hand, if indeed he were a stage hand. To her horror, Nicanor spoke.

"Who is the fellow there?" he asked.

Could it be that he did not know? Could it be that he was not an accomplice, but one of Pappus' men?

Instantly, she answered, "A stage hand."

"Well, tell him to get over the other side."

Her heart beat. Nicanor spoke again: "You are with the choir-boys? Well, would you mind moving from this place? You can see quite well from the next division. You see, the Bishop of Nicaea and his friend will come through into this box when they finish. I want the way clear. Shift that stage-hand."

She nodded. Something prompted her to move as though to do his bidding. She saw now what might be done. She was sure now that the man in the wings there was not an accomplice but one of Pappus' handy men waiting to be of use. The Patriarch was in his peroration, and would be done in a minute; there would be a minute of applause, then a minute of Symmachus; then danger. But Nicanor was now on the stage, holding the fatal door ajar. The time had gone by for driving a wedge under the door. She had lost her moment. Now the enemy had been beforehand with her, and had snatched the Time, which is all-important in affairs. He held the vital point. The enemy was within eight yards of Justinian's chair, and Justinian's face was turned away, watching the Patriarch. She knew that the house was listening with bated breath to the Patriarch, who was speaking with intensity in an hour of crisis. She saw Nicanor's lip wrinkling with contempt for the old fool.

As she moved, Nicanor also moved a little to make way
for her. Having moved, he continued moving; he held
the door open, so that she could see the men inside it.
For one instant, she thought, "This is the instant. Now
they are coming in a rush. I must stop them and scream
alarm." But she was wrong; Nicanor slipped within the
door, back into his box, and drew-to the door behind him;
she heard it close, though it could not catch.

She was ever swift of foot. She sped like the young
gazelle to the stage hand in the wing. The Patriarch sat;
a tumult of applause broke forth. She was at the stage-
hand's elbow. He turned to look at her; he was a man of
about thirty-five, prematurely bald, with a grave, kindly
face, and a most beautiful pair of arms. No doubt he was
one of Pappus' handy men, who could do stage-work and
bear a hand, when needed, at acrobatcy and clownage.

"Please," she said, "do stop up the stage-door. People
will be coming through on to the stage. You saw that man
then."

"I bolted the door just now," he said. "Someone must
have unbolted it. It only needs the bolt pulling."

"The bolt's been taken off," she said. "I've got a wedge
here and a mallet. O, do please stop it."

Already, he was moving towards the door, with a look
of incredulity. She went at his side. Her speed made him
quicken his step. He stared at the splintered wood from
which the bolt had been wrenched.

"Who could have done that?" he said in wonder.

All the house had risen to cheer again. The speakers
on the stage had risen; all were clapping the Patriarch.

"Please wedge the door before they come through,"
she pleaded.

He looked at her, marvelling at her earnestness, and smiling at this elegant little dark woman, who carried a wedge and a mallet onto a stage. He pulled from his belt one of several tools stuck there for instant use. She thought that it was a butcher's steel, but it was a big screw-driver. He thrust the flat blade end under the closed door at the end of the threshold. The blade went an inch or more into the crevice between the little raised sill and the door itself. He then took her wedge and placed it under the screw-driver, so that the handle was slightly tilted upward.

"Drive it in with the mallet," she whispered.

He shook his head. "It's closed," he said. "No one could get that open."

"They'll try," she said. "Do beat it home with the mallet." He took the mallet and turned it over curiously; it had been a good deal used; it had been painted red and black on its head and had two white lines, as an owner's mark, on the handle. "A very little tap will be enough, if they shove," he said. The noise in the house had stopped, now. Symmachus was speaking.

"That'll stop any door," the stage-hand added, "a screw-driver properly put in and turned a bit up."

She felt that Justinian was safe for the moment. She could not doubt this quiet, good man who spoke with such certainty.

"Do tell me your name," she said.

"I'm Rhesus," he said. "I used to do the knockabout in *Megabyzus the Mede*."

She pondered this, while her mind began to wonder what the murderers would do when they found the door jammed. If they could not get through the door, they would try to clamber up from the front of the scene.

Could they do that? Three or four active men, helping each other, might do it. But there would be a counter to that.

"Tell me," she whispered, "if there's a row . . . there'll be a row . . . how can you get the curtain down?"

"See old Megabyzus yonder?" he said, pointing right across the stage to a placid, stout man, in Sunday best, staring with wonder at Symmachus. "He's the curtain man. He'll let the curtain down, if there's a row."

"He's not on the rope," she objected. "It might take him a minute to cast it all loose."

"That's the old way, lady," Rhesus said. "We got the new way, with a lever and a tumbler. It only needs one jerk of the arm to bring it all down bang."

"It's the next speaker there'll be the row about," she said. "Could you possibly warn the curtain man?"

"That's the Prince, the next speaker? I'll try to catch Mega's eye."

He made a sudden swift jerk of his hand. Megabyzus, used to such signals, looked across with an amused contempt. Instantly Rhesus began to telegraph with the swift silent alphabet in use among the stage hands. Megabyzus followed the message with an amused neglect.

"I told him to stand by to drop the curtain if there's a row," Rhesus said. "He don't seem to pay much heed. But there won't be much row, lady; these are all lords and ladies here; besides, the Patriarch's guards are here."

The Patriarch seldom went abroad without his Guard of Religious Knights, or Company of St. George, who wore white, with a great red cross. Theodora had not seen any of them at the theatre.

She said, "Here? I have not seen any of them."

"They've got them there," Rhesus said, jerking his head to the back of the stage.

At this point, Symmachus cried aloud, that his duty was, after all, not to speak but to introduce to them the speaker of the meeting, His Royal Highness, the Prince Justinian.

He remained standing, as Justinian rose. All the hundreds of devoted Blues in the house rose to greet Justinian with cheers and the refrains of songs. Theodora half expected to see arrows dart from the box close to her and Justinian falling. He stood for ten seconds, fifteen seconds, twenty seconds, bowing to the cheering. It lapsed a little, and Symmachus sat. Justinian held up a hand for silence; as the house stilled, he began: "Most Holy Father, Right Reverend Bishop . . ."

Instantly, all the hundreds of Greens in the house lifted a concerted cry of,

"U — surping Dog.
U — surping Dog.
Yow. Yow. Yow."

Some of them had clappers, bugles, bird-scarers, rattles, bells, metal boxes with pebbles in them. Every such instrument was at once in full roar and clack and every hostile throat was screeching, and as the tumult rose up, the men inside the box hove at the door and found it jammed.

Theodora heard Nicanor's voice say, "Push it. It's not bolted. Open it. Open it."

A voice said, "It's jammed."

"It's not. It's only caught. Open it. I was through it a second ago."

Rhesus stooped and lightly tapped the driver's blade home. The men inside heaved, pushed and swore.

"It's caught at the foot," one of the men said.

"Are you all children?" Nicanor cried. "Open it." Theodora heard him leap at the door and smite it. "Open on that side," he cried. He seized the handle and shook and wrenched, while the house broke into battle. The Blues struck at every yelling Green mouth, and every yelling Green mouth bit at the avenging hand. What stewards there were were fighting in the gangways. Stale eggs, pieces of orange, fig, dead fish, began to fall upon the stage. Theodora heard a crash, as seats in the house fell or were torn over. She heard Nicanor screaming like a maniac, "Come, over the box, onto the stage, that way." She heard the men in the box leap from the box into the hollow below the scene, and leap, to heave themselves up onto the stage.

She had never dreamed that a theatre could make such noise. A sort of salvo of small missiles came out of the house about the speakers. Theodora saw the heads and shoulders of three men struggling to get onto the scene. Across the stage the pale and placid Megabyzus watched their struggle with amused contempt. She saw his right arm reach over and thrust something. This was the lever which released the tumbler. Instantly, with a muffling of rattle and bang the curtain fell, to shut away the uproar, as though it did not exist. The Red Cross Knights were on the stage. In a moment, as it seemed, the speakers were off the stage, and probably out of the theatre.

There could be no shadow of doubt that the meeting was done for. Nothing could have restored it. A roaring battle was raging in the house. A dozen Red Cross Guards came at the double across the stage towards Theodora, who stood with Rhesus there, still guarding the door. It had been assailed half a dozen times since the battle began. The leader of the Guards asked Rhesus if they could get through into the house through that door.

"Why, yes," Rhesus said. "What d'you want there?"

"Open up," the man said. "These fellows may attack the Persian Ambassador."

Rhesus withdrew his screw-driver.

"Pass, friends," he said, opening the door. "But don't let anyone in onto the stage."

The Guards ran through. The box was empty. Theodora slipped into it, with Rhesus, to see the mêlée going on in the house.

All the lower half of the house was in confusion; terrified women had drawn to the sides; in the house itself seats were lying about, men were grappling and fighting in the ruins. It was liker a battle than a public gathering. In the box opposite, the Persian Ambassador sat in unmoved dignity, with his staff about him. She saw one man guarding the door behind him with a drawn sword. She knew at once that the Blue cause had had a frightful set-back and defeat. Their chief had not been allowed to speak, even in the presence of the Patriarch and Nicaea. The Persian Ambassador had been shown, that the heir to the throne was loathed and despised; and unable to get a hearing, even from his own party, in his own City, within a mile of his Palace. She saw all this. She knew how to reckon an immediate situation.

Then she glanced about the box, for evidence of who had been there. At least four men had been with Nicanor there; she had heard their voices. They had left no traces, she thought. Groping under the seats, she found and pulled out a small grass tool-bag, such as carpenters used. On opening this, she saw, that the handles of the chisels were painted in dull red and black like the mallet, and had the same owner's marks of parallel white stripes. Among the tools were the bolt, catch and screws removed within that hour from the door.

She gave these to Rhesus. She could see nothing of Nicanor nor his four assassins. Her heart leaped up with the thought, that all this work of prepared riot had failed. It had been prepared to divert the attention while the five men rushed the stage, killed Justinian and escaped by the stage-door. Then her mind leaped further. They had certainly hoped to kill Justinian. They had expected to kill him; they must have reckoned that he was a dead man. In that case, they would be ready to follow up the murder by seizing The City. Their men from the north and the west would be even now in The City, taking charge. The City would now be a Green stronghold. Then again, her heart leaped. That was not so. The armed forces were probably not there. The plan for the murder must have come from rage at Justinian's sudden change of plan, which had so taken the Green party by surprise.

By this time, the Red Cross Knights had started to clear the house; some civil guards had fought their way

in to help to quell the riot. Theodora left the box and
thanked Rhesus again for what he had done.

"It was nothing, lady," he said.

She went up-stage. Some of the Pappus ladies were
there in tears and agitation.

Theodora said, "They are clearing the house now. It
will soon be quite quiet."

After all, what theatre can hope to escape a row? This
was only a political meeting, broken up by the other
party.

The choir-boys had gone. In the Green Room she
found the sweepers eating what had been left of the
cakes. She asked if the Patriarch and other speakers had
left the theatre safely.

"Yes, lady," they said. "They went away with the
Holy Guards."

She went out at the stage-door and round to the front,
where the last of the fighters had now been flung out. A
sullen and unruly crowd hung about near the entrance;
they were mocking some members of the Blue Party who
were waiting outside the theatre for their carriages. Some
civil guards and Red Cross Knights stood by them. The
Greens were confident that they had won a victory. Had
they not broken up the Blue meeting and silenced the
Emperor's nephew? As she went back to her theatre, she
heard enough in the streets to know that they believed
that Justinian would never speak in public again. As she
went home that evening, she heard singers at various
street-corners singing of the triumph. The Green poets
had already put words to familiar tunes. One snatch of

song, to a well-known march, stayed with her for years:

"But we made him hold his jaw, my boys,
When he asked us for our votes."

Word of an uproarious Green victory was everywhere.
Kallianassa, who had not left the house save to buy three-
pennyworth of milk at the dairy fifty yards along the
road, had heard all about it, with the addition, that Justinian had run like a hare out of the theatre, directly a
piece of dead cat hit him.

"Well," she thought, "I believe that the gang meant
to kill him. That was the real intention this afternoon;
and but for Theophanes and Rhesus, they very likely
would have."

It chanced that she needed some sewing silk. Going
out to her mercer's shop, she heard something more like
the truth, that Justinian had escaped from the theatre,
at the Patriarch's order. The man who told her this, the
mercer, knew it for a fact. His daughter was married to
young Pappus. She had been on the stage, in the wings,
and knew the Patriarch's very words: "No, Prince; nothing can save this meeting. Come out with me. You can
do nothing here. We must begin again on different lines.
As your Pastor, let me urge you not to stay one instant
more." The mercer said that this wise advice had probably prevented bloodshed.

"It shews you to what depths our City has fallen," he
said, "when men will riot even in the Patriarch's presence."

She wondered sometimes during the night if she had
really helped to save Justinian's life. Had those men

planned to kill him? If they had, they could have done
it, beyond doubt, when the door lay open. Nicanor could
have done it. Her own share in saving him had been con-
temptible. Rhesus had done it all, by a little practical
sense, done it as a matter of course, to keep the audience on
their own side of the stage. If those men had meant to
kill, why did they not do it when Nicanor came onto the
stage? They had tried to rush the stage later. Could it be,
that Nicanor had come to gloat over his victim? Certainly, Theophanes had been a sick and shaking man well
aware that bloody deeds were planned and that a bloody
end would be his, if his friends suspected that he had betrayed them. She knew that she loved Justinian. She
thought that she had loved Hekebolos, but that was the
folly of youth and a degradation. This was a flaming up
within herself of every talent that she had to help one
who seemed to lack all that she had, and to have at the
same time all the faculties she herself wanted. Yet she
told herself, that she was not likely to see the Emperor's
nephew again, save afar off, on some stage or in some
procession. She was not in the political world as Macedonia had thought, but out of it. As she thought of the
meeting and the riot, she thought it likely that the Emperor's family would be swept away in the next few days.
She could only wish that she might be mixed up with
them in that destruction. She slept ill, thinking thus.

The morning was full of the exultation of the Greens.
At an early hour, their young men were marching in the
streets to music. Hundreds of them had learned the new
poem during the night. Going to the theatre, Theodora
heard half-a-dozen companies singing aloud,

"But we made him hold his jaw, my boys,
When he asked us for our votes."

The City believed that, firmly. The Emperor's nephew had been silenced, his meeting broken up, and even the Patriarch threatened. The general feeling was, that The City had shewn a righteous indignation against a Blue, who had tried, out of pure spite, to stop a prominent Green from obtaining the Consulship. This point of view was spread by a hundred speakers in every public place that day.

That day was a day of rejoicing for the Greens. The Patriarch's Guards had arrested some of the rioters at the theatre. These men were charged that morning at the courts. The magistrates in the court which tried them were not altogether of the Green Faction, but they were impressed by the fact that their Court was surrounded by some thousands of Green partisans, who would without doubt kill them and wreck the building if they tried to be severe. They bound the prisoners over to keep the peace, and so dismissed them to a roaring and cheering mob, who at once bore them in triumph, shoulder-high, down to the Palace, round the Hippodrome, along the main streets, and then, in bravado, to the wharves, where good old One, Three and Five Wards came out to give battle, and drove them back. It came on to rain early in the battle, and the armies melted away.

The Green triumph had been very real, but only for the moment. Theodora soon saw that it had been nothing but a successful riot, followed by an unduly loud exultation. It had not been instantly followed by an irruption

of armed men from the west and north. She began to
doubt whether a murder had been planned for the meeting. Yet, if the murder had been done, and Justinian
killed, the exultation would have served very well to
usher in a new order.

She found a chance to visit Pappus' theatre, to speak
to Rhesus and thank him. She found that not very much
serious damage had been done in the theatre. Some chairs
had been smashed; some stuffings cut; a variety of missiles flung at the stage, and some paintwork and gilding
defaced.

Rhesus said, "Some plug-uglies came to ask who had
fastened the door, lady. I said the door was unfastened,
as I'd seen a man come through it; and it was unfastened
later. They tried to find out where I'd been. I said a lady
ordered me off the stage and I'd gone, so that I was not
around when the row began." Theodora was pleased to
think that this reply exactly squared with Nicanor's orders to her.

Rhesus continued: "They went to old Megabyzus, to
ask who was near the door when he let the curtain down.
But Megabyzus said, 'All that side of the stage was empty.'
So they learned nothing from us, and thought that the
lock must have somehow caught. They were only a set of
plug-uglies, from the Sixth Ward."

"Did anybody come for the carpenter's tools?"

"Nobody asked for them, lady; but they disappeared
from the office where they'd been put."

"And the mallet and the wedge?"

"No. I kept those. I just altered them a little."

All the Green Faction turned at once from rejoicing

over Justinian's discomfiture to the great Green mass meeting at the Palace that afternoon. Kallimachus was to preside. With him on the platform were to be Menippos, Pompeius, Hypatius, Theophanes, and other leaders of the Party. The City was thronged with men who announced these dainties. Banners proclaiming them were hung from many windows. Theodora learned that the great attraction would be the procession and a speech by Theophanes.

During that morning, Theodora went out, as usual, with Macedonia, for a breath of air between the runs-through. They slipped from the stage door and then round the corner, meaning to run to the wharves. Just at the corner, they came upon Philip the Pisidian, who greeted them. He was smiling and dapper as ever. He asked, if he might walk with them to the water-front. As they could not well refuse, they agreed. The talk went at once to the destroyed Blue meeting. He shook his head over that.

"Of course, it was only to be expected," he said. "The feeling is running very high against the Prince, I'm afraid. You were on the stage, I understand," he added suddenly, looking at Theodora, "with the choir-boys? You had a remarkable view of the battle, I suppose, like the gods above the Trojan plain."

"No," Theodora said, "I could see very little. I was at the side."

"It might have been a very serious matter," Philip said. "The story goes, that a party of rioters planned to rush the stage and assault the Prince, by coming through the door there; but that at the critical moment they found the door held or secured."

"But the door wasn't held," Theodora said. "I was standing near it, listening to the speakers, when someone came through the door and listened beside me, and asked me to keep people away from the door. I went to tell the people on that side to keep well away, and the man went back through the door. I suppose he was one of the stewards and locked the door behind him when he went back. An instant later, the riot began, and I'm afraid I ran for it."

She was thankful as she spoke that she had heard in time what Rhesus and old Megabyzus had said. Philip kept his eyes upon her. The tale agreed with what he had heard, and yet, he had a suspicion: it was plain that he had a suspicion.

Macedonia said: "When we were in Athens, one of the men from a rival company came round the dressing-rooms just before we were to go on for the second ballet. He had a master-key, and locked us all in; the ballet was half-an-hour late in starting; people were stamping and raging, and Sosthenes had to explain."

"You need fear no rival company here," Philip said. "You are without possible rival."

"To go back to yesterday's meeting," Macedonia said. "Probably the stewards locked both the doors between the house and the stage the instant the riot began. That was a standing order at the Old Winter Palace, if you remember."

"I remember well," Theodora said.

Philip seemed satisfied that this might have been the case. At any rate, he now had another line of enquiry to follow. Theodora felt certain, that he had come to the theatre to ask her about the door. She had never trusted the man. She was sure, now, that there had been a plot to murder, and that Philip not only knew about it, but was much concerned by its failure.

"Will you be at the great meeting this afternoon?" she asked.

"O yes, in diplomacy one attends the functions of the enemy."

"It will be a grand procession, I hear," Macedonia said, "with bands and horses."

"O yes, the enemy knows the effect of display."

They lingered at the water-front for a while; it was always lovely, changing, and unlike what it had been the day before.

"Now we must run back," Macedonia said. As the two friends ran, she said to Theodora, "I had to devise some way of shaking him off; he is such a bore."

"He seems to me much more of a gimlet," Theodora said.

As they neared the Palace of Varieties, they were surprised to find a gang of navvies roping off a portion of the road. They had the iron rails and notice-boards of the Street Repair Board. Within the roped-off portion, they had already begun to pick open a trench. At the other end of the street, another gang was doing similar work. Theodora and her friend stopped for an instant, to watch the driving-in of the wedges between the paving blocks; it is ever beautiful to watch the rhythm of the rising and falling mallets and the splendour of the arm and shoulder muscles. A civil guard came up to the workers and said:

"The procession'll be along here in an hour. You'll be done and cleared away by then?"

"O, long before," the man said. "It's one of these new water-pipes; we shan't be more than a few minutes."

The civil guard watched them for a minute and then moved on. The navvies lifted the paving blocks, and then set-to with picks on the earth below. One of their number asked the spectators to clear away.

"This work's got to be done in a hurry," he said. "The procession'll be here at a quarter to two. Please leave the men to do their work. They haven't much time, and people talking distracts them from their work."

The watchers moved off. In a few minutes, Macedonia was on the stage again and Theodora intently watching a new effect. She was now coming to understand some of the ways in which she could help her friend; she was masseuse, dresser, adviser and encourager. Her little suggestions to Sosthenes were never seen to be suggestions, but she knew now that they were acted upon; she was a prop to the company.

That afternoon was memorable in The City. When the bands, banners and stamping horses reached the end of the street, on their way to the Palace, they found a deep trench dug right across the road in front of them. It was not attended. The space had been roped off, and bore the notice-boards of the Street Repair Board. The paving had been lifted and neatly piled; the trench driven deep, the workmen gone. A fine rain had begun to fall;

the head of the procession was suddenly halted; the entire moving mass closed up, marked time and then halted,
while men hurried to find if they could make a detour
and reach the theatre by the other end of the street. But
at the other end a similar trench had been run across the
road by navvies who had disappeared. Meanwhile, the
rain fell and time passed, while the procession stood singing their songs indeed, but with less and less enthusiasm.
At last, parties of the Free Fellowships and Sodalities,
who were mostly in unions controlled by Green ward-
politicians like Theophanes, broke ranks, trussed up their
Sunday best as well as they could, and set to work to fill
in the trenches. This was a slow job, for they had first to
find some tools. The rain increased as they worked; the
job took longer than they had thought; and all the time,
the leaders of the Greens sat in their carriages, cursing.
The crowds melted away; the great meeting fizzled off
like a wetted firework. Those who did wait till it began
were cold, wet and angry; no one wanted to listen to the
speeches of the noble lords, and, indeed, many left in the
first half-hour: the house was almost empty for Hypatius. When she left the theatre that evening, Theodora
called on Comito, and learned that it had been a wretched
meeting. Comito, who had been there, said, "If they had
had a real orator there, it might have been different, but
none of those lords can speak; except Menippos, they've
all got pebbles in their mouths, and he's got nothing to
say. They were to have had Theophanes. They had him
billed for it. But at the last minute they decided that he
wasn't enough of a gentleman to be speaking in the same
bill with them, so they threw him out on his ear: dirty,

what? nor he is; but when it comes to talking, he could make a dead rabbit get up and fight a tiger. Give the devil his due, he could talk St. Paul clean off the pulpit. But, say, Thea, you ought to have heard what was said about those diggings."

"But who dug the diggings?" Theodora asked. "I saw them being dug, and the civil guards saw them and let them be dug. They said the water-pipes had broken underground, and that they would have them repaired in half-an-hour."

"I'd like to think the Blues did the digging," Comito said, "in return for the Greens breaking up the show yesterday. But it wasn't the Blues. It was the lads from the Medical Schools of the University. They had it all worked out. They stole the notice-boards, and practised with the drills and picks to get the hang of it, and to harden their hands. Kallimachus is the Lord Warden of the University. If he ever gets to know which of them was in it, he'll break them to a man."

"What I cannot understand," Theodora said, "is the apathy of the Blues."

"Plenty of people cannot understand it," Comito said. "But it's very simple: the present Imperial family isn't respected. The Emperor got there by fraud, the Empress by following the regiment; neither can read; and Tino's said to be a eunuch; you know how people talk. Besides, the Greens have pretty well scared the Blues in these last days. And who's going to stand up for the Blues, when all they think of is to go plunging in an Eastern war? And what strength have the Blues, with the army gone? The Greens have it all in their own hands. You ask anybody, one of John's men, or anyone you meet. He'll say, 'If the Blues can't keep order, let them give way to the Greens who can.' I wouldn't mind betting, that if Theophanes had been speaking this afternoon, he'd have roused such a cry that the Palace would have been sacked and Justo scuppered."

"I daresay that a good orator can always make lawless men do desperate things," Theodora said, "but this question really is which of two parties shall hold the Consulships. You do not mean to tell me, that the Committees would choose Hypatius rather than Justinian?"

"You ask John," Comito said. "Every Committee has been got at in some way, with money or flattery or promises. Tino will be outvoted seven to one, or more than that, ten to one. He hasn't got a friend in The City."

"I know one or two," Theodora said loyally.

"Well, the Fifth Ward might vote for him," Comito said. "The Fifth Ward'll vote for any Blue who offers, but even the Fifth are shy about Tino. As one of John's men said to me, 'We don't mind a rogue, and we don't much mind a fool; we're used to both; but these odd fish we do mind, for we don't know where to have him.'"

The maid came into the room and asked if Comito would see Theophanes.

"What, here?" Comito said.

"He's in the door, Madam," the maid answered.

Indeed, Theophanes entered as she spoke, but humbly and as though expecting an outburst. The maid withdrew and closed the door behind her. Comito and Theodora stared at Theophanes. He was looking very white, sick and ill at ease. He was wet and much splashed with mud. He stood cringing, and dripping, while Comito stared and said nothing. Theodora knew that she was raging at his coming there.

"Why do you come here?" Comito said. "How dare you come here?"

Theophanes turned to Theodora; one of his many orator's instincts told him that apart from that little link of the mallet, she was now profoundly interested in his coming. She was. She said at once, "Comito, darling, let us take his cloak and have it hung to dry."

Years before, the address "Comito, darling" had been code between the sisters only to be used in certain most urgent cases. Comito remembered this, and knew that for some reason Thea wanted to speak with this man. She stifled down her rage and said coldly, "You would be more comfortable without that wet wrap. Will you leave it on a chair outside, and then come in?"

He did this; she offered wine and cake, which he refused; and a chair, which he took. She stood at some distance from him, coldly and angrily staring. Seeing that she would not sit in his presence he rose.

He said, "Lady Comito, we've had many sets-to in these last months. You won't want to see me here: I understand that. But there's truce henceforth between us on my side, believe me."

"I've got reason to believe you, haven't I?" Comito asked.

"No," he said, "none. I came here in despair to see

your sister and you. Your sainted mother helped me
when I was lost before. Now I come to see her daughters."

"Leave Mother out of it," Comito said.

"Comito, darling," Theodora said again, "I believe
that but for Theophanes the Prince would have been
murdered yesterday. He will deny it, and will not want
more said about it, but I believe it."

Comito seemed impressed by this sudden shot.

Theophanes said, "I heard from your friend, the
dancer, that you had come to your sister's, so I came on.
I walked for a long time, to shake 'em off, if I was followed. You'd better both know what I've got to say. Your
sister is right, Lady Comito, the Prince was to have been
murdered. Why he wasn't, no one rightly knows; it was
just the act of God. Four of the 'A boys' were going to
hold him and the fifth was there with a knife. Mind,
I'm no saint, but murder is damnable to me. I've come
here because I've been made a fool of from the first, and
only now see how I've been fooled. Look here, Lady
Comito, I've caused you trouble, God knows, you and
your husband. Now you can get me hanged, or my throat
cut, whichever you like, by what I tell you. Either way,
I put my life in your hands. Tell Tino, and he can have
me hung; tell Nicanor, and I'll be feeding fish in the
stream before dawn. But I tell you, because you and
your sister and the dancer may get into the Palace and
warn Tino and Justo what they're up against. It isn't an
election, it's a revolution. I've been led into it, little by
little, not seeing what the game was, and now that I'm in
it, I know, and it's the thing I've fought all my life."

Theodora knew that Theophanes was a born actor, able to play any part and persuade on any occasion. She was not by any means sure that murder was damnable to him; she reckoned that as unlikely; still, it was certain that he was angry with his present political allies. What he said about warning Tino made her heart beat.

She said, "You know perhaps, that we are both out of politics, and I have been little here for some years. Will you tell us what is happening?"

He seemed pleased at her tone. "I'm a ward-politician," he said. "You know what that means. I've got a hand in a lot of dirty games, and I can swing a vote in three wards, and have the boys just where I want them; but in the main, I'm for the workers. I keep down the rates, but I starve The City services, so that I've always a pay-chest handy. What's the sin in that? I've been poor. A lot of chance the poor have in a city like this. What chances have the poor? They take what jobs they can find, and can be pretty sure they won't be good ones. They won't care if the garbage isn't swept or the alley isn't lit or the sea-front isn't a carriage-drive. I go to them and say, 'You vote the way I tell you and I'll be by you like a friend.' So I am. There's something for them out of the chest when the baby comes; and a wreath and a head-stone, and sometimes a band when Father dies, as well as a purse slipped into the widow's hand; yes, and the orphans are looked after, too. We stand by our people. All the human things they get from us, and well they know it.

"Before this thing began, they came to me and asked me if I would bring in my boys to help them work

Hypatius for Consul. They told me, it was the usual Green ticket, but they wanted to make sure of it, so would I bring in what I could. I believed what they told me. I brought in all my boys. I've got a lot of fraternities and so forth. I've swung elections, and have the tools, singers, speakers, smashers, anything you want. A lot of what you've seen about the streets is my doing. I've worked this, like a stage-piece; they gave me endless money; so I did things on a scale not yet seen. It's been well done. I've got this City Green-conscious and hardly broke a head doing it. Now, when I've done it, I find what sort of a game they've brought me into. Lord, I've been easily fooled. This isn't any Consular election; it's a revolution. I didn't so much as suspect, till I was in Pappus' theatre just before the meeting and heard them talk as the carpenter took the bolt off the stage-door. They were going to walk boldly onto the stage and kill Tino as he spoke. It made my blood run cold. I may be bad, but murder in the presence of the Patriarch and a sort of Lord's anointed, for you could say Tino was that, is something beyond me. That was why they'd had me in and buttered me up and used my boys—for cold-blooded murder. I just sat and shook.

"The carpenter had brought some wedges. He hadn't known which way the door opened; he came prepared to wedge it. As a matter of fact, you couldn't have wedged it, with that sill; but I sneaked away a wedge and mallet and later, I got to the back of the stage and gave you a word. I don't know what you did; I don't ask; but Tino owes his life to you."

Comito looked at Theodora, leaned across, and patted her hand.

Theodora said, "Of course, the whole Consular election is a blind. The real plot is to make Nicanor Emperor."

"You've guessed it," Theophanes said. "But there's more to it than that. Hypatius is to be made Consul first, that is, the Chief Magistrate, so that he may order what they choose. Nicanor has been in Persia planning this for a year. He's worked it all, so that the army has been moved from here. He expected that Tino would be out of the way a month ago. Tino's staying-on upset him rather. He thought he would get rid of Tino at the meeting. But he doesn't regard Tino as anything more than a law-student. Justo is the man he wants to kill. He means to kill Justo with his own hands and take an hour doing it."

"If he'd killed the Prince at the meeting, would he have attacked the Palace?"

"No; they aren't ready yet. They would have looked on Tino gone as just a stepping-stone on their way. The northern chiefs, who are bringing down an army, have not begun to march yet; and the western lords, who are up for the Trade Mission, as they call it, and they're all in the plot to a man, are still bargaining for rather more place and power than Nicanor wants to give. Nicanor is a bit jealous of Kallimachus, or doesn't like him or doesn't trust him. Kallimachus is the big dog among the westerners and swings their vote."

Theodora saw now why Theophanes so loathed the plot.

"In fact," she said, "it isn't an election at all, but a plot by big business and possession to take all power again."

"You've said it. It's what I've been fighting all my life; these great lords, who want slaves in The City and serfs on their estates, with all the great appointments in their hands or in their gifts, and not enough humanity to endow a school or use a genius."

"I take it that Hypatius isn't much in their councils?" Theodora said.

"That thing? No. He's only in the pay department, and only in that as the ladle. But all the same, that thing with the frozen face and the rock in his gullet thinks he's cousin to God, because he was the last Emperor's nephew. He will believe that till he's a public nuisance, and then he'll get his wind-pipe slit.

"Now I've come to you, because you can help me. You helped me save Tino at the meeting. You can help me save Tino now. He wants help. The Palace set have got no real friends anywhere; but there's time to make some. I want you to go to the Palace, first thing tomorrow. You can always get in to their early chapel; it's a public service, but so early very few ever go to it. He'll be at it. You get to him afterwards, as a suppliant, and tell him all I've told you and say from me, that I'm through with Nicanor and his lords. I'm not to be despised, say. I can swing Two and Four and most of Six Wards; and I can pull strings up and down, say. You, Lady Comito, you know whether I can."

"Yes, you can," Comito said. "Pretty dirty strings, too, if you ask me."

"Maybe, opponents don't show each other their best
sides. Maybe, you won't be so troubled another time.
But, Lady Comito, don't let us have feud now; I want
you to urge your sister here to do as I say : get Tino alone
and tell him the game that's set. He doesn't know it.
Half the Palace staff are in the Green pay. Philip, his
sort of Chamberlain, has told the Greens everything the
Palace plans or does; and he's only one of twenty. I
know no other single soul in all Byzantium that I'd dare
trust with the message. If she can let him know the
danger, maybe he'll be able to meet it. Meantime, I'll
steady down the Wards."

Comito knew more of Theophanes' power than her sister; she looked at him with a growing interest.

"Suppose my sister does go to the early service," she
said, "how is she to make sure of a private word with the
Prince?"

"The Prince knows her," Theophanes said. "It's
known that he likes her. If he sees her, he'll speak. Besides," he added, with some hesitation, "he has some reason to speak to her."

"What do you mean by that?" Comito asked.

Theophanes spread his hands abroad. "If you see him,
little sister," he said, "you tell him I came in against
him not knowing. He may think it's too late to do much.
You tell him from me, it isn't. Say this, 'One word from
him, that he's out for the poor—really out for the poor;
that they're to have good schools and universities and a
chance for all appointments, as well as water and decent
homes and proper food—one word of all that and he'll
have all my boys behind him to a man.' And I can tell

him a good deal of what may surprise him, further-
more."

He rose to go. "Can you slip me out the back way?"
he asked. "I may have been followed."

"I can get you out into the passage," Comito said.
"Since you try crossing Nicanor, you may try crossing
the Prince; you may come to a sticky end."

"Comito, darling," Theodora said, "you must see that
he has risked much already."

Comito shewed Theophanes through the timber-yard.
She let him out into the night and returned to her sister.

"What was all this about your saving Tino?" she said.

She listened to the story, then said, "I do so hate that
man. He's got a nerve, thinking he can use you as his
go-between. He always was just about as poisonous as a
pole-cat. I wonder what his dirty game is now. 'It's
known that the Prince likes you.' How is it known? By
whom is it known? You be very, very careful, Thea; they
may be trying to get you in as a spy."

"I don't agree," Theodora said. "He was sincere in a
lot of what he said. He is a very vain man, like most people who depend on popular favour. He has a great gift,
men say, for oratory; a very great gift. I've heard him a
little; it's true. His present associates have never let him
speak. They've passed him over. They are just using his
organizations and not trusting him. He has seen that; he
has felt that he has been tricked; his vanity is outraged,
and he is now furious. I shall go to the early service."

"No great harm will be done by that," Comito said.
"Do tell me, if Tino makes any dishonourable proposals."

Theodora parted from her sister, and ran home. As

she reached the door, Kallianassa opened to her, closed
the door behind her, and whispered, "The Prince Justinian is here, Madam, waiting for you."

"What? Here? Since when?"

"Twenty minutes, Madam."

"Never mention it, Kallianassa."

She went into the little sitting-room. The Prince rose
from his seat by the spinning-wheel and greeted her.

"Forgive my coming in this way," he said, "but I
have to speak with you."

They sat facing each other. The Prince produced a
page of parchment, and said, "This was brought to me
this evening. It was so interesting to me, and so important, that I had to come to speak with you about it."

She held the page to the little lamp. It was written in
a disguised but clear hand not recognized by her. It ran:
"Prince, at the Green meeting, you would have been
murdered, but for the lady who marshalled the choir-
boys. You speak with her and learn the truth of this, and
a lot more. A well-wisher."

She knew that his eyes were fixedly on her as she read.

"Can I hear the truth of it?" he asked.

She told him of the meeting, and of Theophanes' story.
"From what he said, Theophanes must have sent you
this letter," she said.

She was thinking hard, wondering what that tricky
politician's game might be. Comito's phrase, "he always
was as poisonous as a pole-cat," recurred to her. Might it
not be, that all was a subtle plot, to bring Justinian hot-
foot, after dark, to this lonely house on the hill, so that
the Green gangs might kill him at ease, and afterwards

proclaim that a rival had killed him in the house of his paramour? It might very well be. If it were so, then they might look for the murderers within a few minutes. She mentioned her fear to the Prince.

He said, "Yes, the thought occurred to me a moment ago."

"We'd better get out into the open," she said. "Theophanes may be sincere. But if the Greens suspect that he betrayed them the other day, he may be betraying you now to save his own life."

They slipped out into the hallway.

Theodora said to Kallianassa, "I have to go out for a few minutes with the Prince. Do not let anyone in, and do not tell anyone that the Prince is or has been near here."

"I am my Queen's servant and my Prince's servant," Kallianassa said simply.

The two passed out into the night, crossed the road, and the open space beyond it, to the edge of the hill. It had not yet been built upon; there were benches there; the view from the point was famous. No murderers could approach them unseen.

"First," Justinian said, "I owe my life to you, Theophanes and this man Rhesus."

"Not to me at all," she said, "to Theophanes and Rhesus. I was useless. I was stunned, so that I did not know what to do."

"You shall not find me ungrateful," he said.

"Prince," she said, "never think of thanking me. I was like one paralysed. I was like the bird held by a snake's eye. You might have been killed, if Nicanor had not come on, and gloated over you, and then given me orders as though I were his servant. That roused me. It was almost too late."

She wanted no more talk about the saving of the life. She determined to change the subject.

"Prince," she said, "will you tell me if I can help you with Theophanes?"

"What do you think?"

"Some of what he has said has been true, and very helpful. He is not a man to trust very far, but it would never do to slam that door now that it has opened a little to you. If I may say so, it is the first little gleam of light in your affairs."

"You think that?" he said. "I think so, too. I came out from the Palace feeling that our cause is dark enough. I want to tell you. Things are black. For instance, I found this morning that the secret arsenal in the Palace has been emptied within the last two days, perhaps only last night. Weapons for two thousand men have been taken right out of the Palace, by men disguised as masons and workmen. You may have noticed that we are buttressing up Constantine's Tower. Bromion, the trusted Keeper of the Keys, must have been the traitor. He has been bought by these fellows; he has disappeared. Then, I had despatches from the army command. You don't know what soldiers can be in the way of making difficulties. The men are scattered in billets, the horses aren't fit, the forage magazines are not full; then the state of the roads; excuse after excuse. I will tell you what I have done. I have relieved the cavalry commander from his post and given the command to a captain, with orders that he cannot ignore. He is a young man, Aristides. He will move. But there again, time has been lost. Time. Time. That is the enemy. They say Anger and Lust are deadly sins, so they are, but they are at least swift. Apathy is a deadly sin, and what old fool will ever believe it to be deadly?"

"It is a deadly sin," she said, as she reflected; then she added, "I suppose twenty men were engaged in the shifting of the weapons?"

"Probably."

"Do you think that the weapons have left The City?"

"I'm trying to find out, but it is hard to learn anything, when so many are in the Green pay or in the Green camp."

"They would have gone west, to the western levies," she said, "or been scattered among the Green fraternities here; the northern levies are said to be already armed. You may be sure, that they are for the westerners, or are for the gangs here. Theophanes said that the western lords are all up for the Winter Races. Might not the weapons have been brought to their palaces and hidden there?"

"Possibly," he said. "I've no evidence yet. At present, they seem just to have melted away. But you are wrong about those lords being up for Races; they are really up for what they call the Western Trade Mission; that is, they are spending a good deal of money in the Green interest, and squeezing any Blue dealers in their particular goods, corn, hay, hides, meat, tallow and so forth, oil, wine, and honey, right out of business. At the same time, I am interested in what you heard tonight that they are bargaining for appointments and place before they commit themselves with Nicanor."

"Prince, will you go to see Theophanes and give him some assurance of the sort he asked for?"

"I want to do that tomorrow upon another point. The Patriarch and I mean to make a great appeal for civil peace. We are planning a great Peace Meeting at the City Hall for two days before the election. We are asking all the important Greens and Blues to it, and if they come we shall appeal to both sides to put an end to Faction. The Patriarch will ask Kallimachus, Nicanor and perhaps Pompeius to speak. I intend to ask Theophanes also. That will be four Green speakers, though they will not all agree to speak. The Patriarch and Nicaea and perhaps Smyrna will speak for The Church; and Symmachus and myself for the Blues. You see, we must offer the Greens every advantage. They may refuse to come to the meeting; somehow, I think they will come to it."

"I am sure they will," she said. "It is a wonderful thought of yours."

"Symmachus thinks they will refuse; the Patriarch thinks they may come. He is charging the priests to preach the end of Faction; that will have great weight."

"There is a thing I would recommend," she said, "that you send Philip on some mission to Smyrna or Athens."

"I was thinking Trebizond," he said. "It is colder; he does not like cold."

"Could you send him overland?"

"It would be better."

"It is often said," she said, "that women betray conspiracies. I have the chance of hearing certain things from Theophanes. I warn you that what he says may be false, and wilfully misleading. That we shall be able to judge better as time shows his faith. He may be employed to deceive us. Still, we ought to act as if he were running great risk in coming to see us. We ought to devise some way in which he can communicate."

"Would Sosthenes help at all?"

"No," she said. "He loathes politics of every kind. He says that they are sham oppositions invented by the devil to check progress and fetter genius. He says that nothing enlightened has been done in the State since the Factions began."

"He is not far wrong, perhaps; but I was wondering if he would do this: Theophanes is a great speaker. Could you not suggest, that he come to the Swan Maidens Theatre, to give your announcers some hints? No man living speaks better in public. He has taken great pains with his gift. He went to Athens to teachers there; it is profoundly taught there. You have no announcers yet, but you will find them necessary. I throw this out as a suggestion. Could you suggest it? If he agrees, then Theophanes could be in the theatre possibly two or three times a week. If that could be arranged, there would be his chance to communicate."

"I will suggest it," she said.

"That leads me to another point," he said. "My uncle, the Emperor, asks me to ask you to sup at the Palace tomorrow, as before, with Sosthenes and Macedonia."

"O Prince, that will be a great honour."

"I have told him something of what that anonymous

letter said. But apart from that, we have been considering the great beauty of what you gave to us and to The City, and we all wish to speak to you about that. Certainly the Emperor does. The two others will have had their invitations by this time.

"Do not feel that our Peace Meeting will certainly bring Peace. The Greens may say that we are only trying to gain time. It may make them strike before the election; perhaps on the very day of the Peace Meeting. I have not told this to the Patriarch, but I mention it to you. If they do, of course, our chance will not be big."

"You say, if they do; ought you not to say, if they can?"

"They will be more able for it, than we can be to resist them."

"Prince, you must not lose hope. This morning, perhaps, things looked black for you. The black was an unbroken line. Now, if Theophanes be really going to fall out of their Faction, the black is broken."

"He will not dare to fall out openly."

"Go to see him and try," she said. "I say that the last few hours have been incredibly for you. I see hope now."

"We left it rather late," he said. "It is never easy to get back an advantage. But I must not stay longer here, keeping you in the cold, however much of new hope I get from it. I had to come here to tell you of the letter. As to thanks for what you did, what thanks are possible? Things are remembered and wondered at, though they cannot be thanked."

They walked back towards Arbutus Terrace.

"Theophanes must be remembered and wondered at," she said, "though as yet he cannot be thanked. Thank him when he is surer, and thanks are safer."

He pondered this as he walked home, and presently came to her meaning.

Theodora was met at the Palace Door the next evening by Philip the Pisidian, who was cloaked in warm things as for a journey. He seemed perplexed and anxious.

He said: "I am glad to welcome you once more. Unfortunately, I shall not have the pleasure of talking with you, as I am about to start upon a mission. But come in for a moment, to the Little Library."

The room was hung with painted plaster busts of the human types found in the Empire. "You see there the Libyans of the Pentapolis," he said. (So he knew all about Hekebolos, of course.) "I grieve to be leaving at such a time," he added. "I sadly fear that the Prince has made a big mistake by not starting for Persia. This standing for Consul, you have seen what storms it has provoked. This is but the beginning, I fear."

"I hope that you are going to some sunny place for the winter," she said. "Is it Athens?"

"No such good fortune," he said. "But before I start, and I am even now setting forth, I wonder, if you could suggest to the Prince, in some very tactful way, the deplorable lowering of the Imperial prestige which his candidature has brought about. One hears of nothing else."

"Alas," she said, "I could not presume to."

"Ladies do not presume," he said. "They are privi-

leged. You little understand what a great opportunity
you have for serving the Prince's welfare by a suggestion
of the sort. But I have to start at once. Good night."

She wished him a speedy return. She wondered what
crooked policy he was scheming as he went. The Palace
maids now took charge of her. Soon she was led by
Father Serapion to a room where the Patriarch stood.
She found herself talking alone with the Patriarch about
the great beauty of Macedonia's dancing. On that topic,
she could always talk; so, it seemed, could the Patriarch,
who said he had danced much as a lad, before he had
studied for the priesthood. He said, "I can never think of
dancing save as a holy thing. It happens to be linked
with the deepest experience in my life." She felt that
he was going to tell her this experience; he was at point
to begin upon it, when Serapion came in with Sosthenes
and Macedonia. Justinian followed them and welcomed
them. Then the Imperial Pair entered, limping, both
looking very old and weary; they took the obeisances
from their seats. The Patriarch also sat. The rest of the
party remained standing, while two Sardican servants
swiftly brought in a table, on which were three dishes
bearing what looked like rolls of linen. Theodora thought
that they were now to be offered olives, or some dry wine
before the supper began. At a sign from the Emperor,
Justinian spoke:

"Most trusty Sosthenes, most honourable ladies, Macedonia and Theodora, His Imperial Majesty, having seen,
with deepest pleasure, the noble and pure art which you
have brought back to the Theatre, and having, in his
wisdom, determined that such service pre-eminently

calls for the approval of the Throne, now, therefore, bids me to declare it. It is his wish that you be henceforth spared the annoyance and ignorant prejudice which the brutality of past times has bequeathed to these against members of your profession. He has, therefore, decided, that there shall no longer be question of your right of entry into any Society in this City and within the Empire. It is his Imperial Will, that you be from this time en-nobled. It is my pleasure to present to you your Acts of en-noblement.

"First, to you, most trusty Sosthenes, with these words, that in your synthesis of the arts, you have revived that art of the Theatre, which was for so long the glory of our race. Then, to you, Lady Macedonia, with these words, that beauty, grace and elegance should ever be privileged, and doubly so, when they are linked with gratitude to friends. Then to you, Lady Theodora, with these words, that wisdom and courage are the en-nobling things; this title does but show that we know this.

"To you all, His Imperial Majesty bids me say, that this en-nobling is but a small thing; it gives the recipient little; but being one of the few things which Fate has not already dowered you with, he knows that in each case it is your due."

He handed the titles to each of the three in turn. It was but a small thing, being a roll of vellum slipped into a ring of flexible gold chain. He had given to each with a singular, charming grace. Theodora loved him for it. She had thought him awkward and lopsided; indeed, there was always something outlandish and odd in his movement and approach. She saw now that his real nature showed in giving; he loved giving; and gave with his whole nature with a charm which touched the heart. What he had given was something which overwhelmed them all.

They had first to kneel, to receive the Patriarch's blessing; then, to kiss hands and return thanks to the Emperor and Empress. Then, still kneeling, they heard the Patriarch pray, that these three newly en-nobled might grace the order. A moment later, Justinian was saying that he wished to be allowed to congratulate them, and to say how glad he was that this little act of justice had been done; then servants led them away, to the tiring-rooms, to affix the marks of rank. The two women could then unroll their scrolls and read that, "Despite the fact that the said Lady —— is of the profession of the Theatre, We, Justinus, by the Grace of God, Emperor, now decree, that she is hereby en-nobled to the degree of the Most Illustrious, and shall enjoy all rights of entry and of precedence accorded to such rank." Each scroll was marked with that stencil of red paint, which Empire used in lieu of writing; the Imperial Seal had been affixed, and the Praefect of Ceremony and Respect, the Warder of Privileges, had numbered and signed it. There was no doubt of it; they were en-nobled. Both had exceptional talents; both had been born into the despised profession of the Theatre, and both had suffered bitterly in it. How many times they had both been cut to the quick by the assumption of all the other classes, that the actress was not even Christian, might even be without a soul, and certainly need not be regarded as other than an outcast and pariah. She might be admitted to a house to perform, but not to a meal, not to social intercourse, not always even to a church, and frequently not to Christian burial. Now here without any effort made, without any application, it came to both of them. They could never have dared to supplicate for any such privilege. Even had they supplicated, petitioned, prayed, all would have been vain. Now here they were en-nobled; they could enter with the proudest; they could marry with the noblest. Theodora could, if she wished, write to Hekebolos and demand that he should marry her, so that her children might be made lawful. She did not see herself doing this. She looked at Macedonia who was weeping with joy of such a gift.

"This is what comes from being the peerless dancer of your time," she said, "and of being the friend of such."

"It all comes from your standing up for me against that old brute, Anthrax," Macedonia said.

"It does nothing of the kind," Theodora answered. "Come, mop up your tears now."

They returned to the Presence, wearing the badges of their rank.

"See," the old Emperor cried, "here they come. And well they set off the badges. And well they deserve them. Dammy, I wish one tenth of the women of the noblesse had one tenth as good title and could set off clothes so. But, come on now; though it's the fast, we must sup. I've got my wound, but what of that? The soldier who can't sup is like the jackass who can't kick; he's past braying for, as the she-ass said."

After supper, the Empress asked Theodora to read to

her from a book of simple love-poems. She soon fell asleep under the treatment, but woke presently to say, "My dear, you read those poems just as though you were making them up. Go on, dear, you're so soothing, and sleep is what I want. I lie awake so, thinking of when Mother and I both had iron collars on."

Later, Theodora had the happiness of a chat with the Patriarch. He told her that the Peace Meeting at the City Hall would certainly be well attended, that he could not yet feel very hopeful of Peace from the meeting, and that he deeply dreaded a Green rule.

"I cannot feel that it will be permitted," he said. "It would be a going back to the very worst days of the Empire. It would mean a rule by terror and delation and brutal debasement, with these frequent chariot-racings, with men and horses killed in them, as sops to the enslaved mobs. Consider the nature of their leaders. Kallimachus was saying only last week, and saying it to a crowd with great applause, that he could not see the use of schools for anyone not going to be a school-master. Yet that man aims at helping to control the Empire, the man who says that it is false and unfair to call chariot-racing brutal and degenerate. However, let us not talk of these things. Our choir-boys said, 'They did like the lady who drilled them at the Palace Theatre; she kept us in order and no mistake.'"

Just before she was to leave the Palace, Justinian spoke to her in the Little Library.

"I have sent Philip overland to Trebizond," he said. "He will never go, you will find. I am wondering, if you will consent to this arrangement. . . Sosthenes is having

Theophanes three times a week to the Swan Maidens, to teach the announcers. In the evenings of those days, say at five or six, will you come to read to my Aunt? Then you can tell me if there be news."

This was agreed upon.

Though she had hoped much from the meeting of Theophanes with the Prince, she was disappointed. When she went, on the next evening, to read to the Empress, she learned, that the Prince had not seen him.

"I went to his place, the Roost," Justinian said. "He was not there. The man who saw me is one of these ward-attorneys. He says that Theophanes has gone out of town on business for a few days; he does not know where; he thinks to the vineyards at Sycae. I told the man that I wished to invite him to speak at the Patriarch's meeting. He said he did not know when he would be back; not for a few days, anyhow."

"I wonder if they have killed him," Theodora said.

"Possibly. If they suspected him, they would have killed him. The attorney was not telling all the truth, of course. He is one of these shady political lawyers who keep men like Theophanes just clear of the galleys or the gallows. It is quite likely that they have sent him to speak to their supporters west or north. They are sharp enough to see that they have offended him by not letting him speak here. It is disappointing, but it may be all for the best. I asked the attorney to the meeting, and said, that I would be very glad if he would tell me when Theophanes returns. He promised to do that, but of course won't. There is another sad thing to tell you. The shiploads of corn and hay which I was sending by sea to meet the Kingfishers have been run ashore and lost, either by treachery or negligence."

"That is unfortunate. Have they no magazines to depend on?"

"I can only hope. I don't know. There should be plenty on all the post-routes; but at this time, beset as we are, who can tell? These Greens seem to have thought of everything and to be beforehand with us everywhere. And when I try to do a thing, there seems always to be a broken axle or a wheel come off."

"You could send some wagon-loads of forage to meet them by road," she said. "If you saw the contractors to-night, the wagons could be on the roads by dawn."

"Not so," he said. "The Greens know perfectly that we have sent for the troops. It is no use going to any contractor here in The City. These western lords own all the forage businesses. They make it impossible to buy forage. They hold up the supplies. Hardly any is coming into The City. They know perfectly well that I want to make sure of the magazines. Apart from that, they are making sure of their own supplies."

"I was a little in the postal-relay service," Theodora said. "I did help to examine some of the Gulf roads and their supplies. Three years ago, there was a woman running a great dairy-farm at Pirene-under-West-Wood. She was named Elpis. She had marvellous hay, and used to supply that thirty miles of road. If you sent a galloper or two out to her, starting now, ordering her to send some tons to the post-house at King's Pirene, she would do it. The messengers would be there the day after tomorrow. If I might add a word by your messenger, it might help.

I felt that that woman was a friend. She may be dead, but the place will still be a dairy-farm, and there must always be hay there. Nicodemus, of Sycae, had good forage in those days."

"He has none now; I've tried him."

"Elpis will know the farmers near Pirene. She would help to collect forage from them. They are right outside the infection of this rebellion at least."

They wrote the orders; Theodora wrote to Elpis; letter and orders were sent off. It seemed natural to them both, that they should be working together.

"This anxiety makes one see what ought to have been done years ago," Justinian said.

"It is no use thinking of the past," she answered. "Its faults are plain; they need not be repeated. I am not without hope."

"You give me hope whenever I see you," he said. "It is odd, that the whole situation hinges on the election, and yet we never think of the election at any time."

Indeed, the election was nothing now to either party. Theodora thought only of whether the Kingfishers would be in The City before the Green armies came down upon them. She was sure that the Greens would strike before the Election Day, probably just after the Peace Meeting.

"Even the election may go in your favour," she said. "The priests have helped your cause more than you think. It is known through The City that you have tried to bring peace. But surprise is a great thing in war. You have been surprised successfully in your Palace arsenal. Mind that you are not surprised at the gates. Be sure that your gate garrisons are not tempted by women, or drugged with drinks. And remember this, that the enemy on the north is ready now. It may move down upon you now. A surprise attack may come down by ship from the Euxine. They've always got ships and barges enough to move some hundreds of men. They might drop down with any northerly wind, and be tied up at the wharves, landed, and attacking the gate-guards, from within The City, by dawn on any morning. So have the booms drawn across the channel. You have your naval reservists still. Have them on guard tonight at the wharves, and be sure that the booms are kept closed, and the entrance guarded by patrol-ships."

She knew by this time, that rumour had spoken truly. The Imperial family was not respected in The City. It had very few friends, and most of them were doubtful. As she lay awake that night, she felt that she was the one friend to the dynasty in the Empire; well, she was a friend, and would show that she was.

She thought much of Theophanes. The hope which had sprung up in her, when he had come to Comito's house, was now sunk. Yet some part of his promise seemed to be fulfilled. There were fewer Green speakers and musicians in the streets; there were now no riotous gangs. Had Theophanes really called-off his boys, or were the Greens cutting down expenses? Or was this only the lulling of suspicions before the storm broke? And where was Theophanes? She suspected, that he had been suspected and murdered. But the next evening at the Palace Justinian told her that he had heard that Theophanes had been sent north to speak to Green supporters there. She wondered later whether any suspicion of the man had crossed Nicanor's mind. She decided, "No. If he had been suspected, he would have been killed." However, she had a mind which could not rest when a problem had been presented to it. She could not feel at ease about Theophanes. He had come to her, to betray the Green cause, and the next morning he had gone from The City. She could not believe that he had been chosen to speak to the northern rebels; he was a City politician, skilled with a City crowd, but wasted in the country, where a sportsman like Menippos, with a boxer on one arm and a kennelman on the other, would have more success. She judged that Nicanor had perhaps been a little jealous, or a little suspicious of him; not enough to have him killed, for he had been? and still was, very useful; he could swing a big City vote, and had all these drilled fraternities; but still enough to wish him out of the way. If he had felt that Theophanes was hurt at not being used as a speaker, and a less shrewd man than Nicanor could hardly have failed to feel this, he might have taken this way of dealing with him. She could almost hear Nicanor explaining his scheme to Kallimachus: "That fellow Theophanes has had his use, but like all these fellows, is inclined to think himself too important. It would do him good to be taken down a little and made to feel his place. He is sore at not being called upon to speak here. I mean to send him north to speak to the fellows there. He will be good enough for them, and won't be much of a success, but, all the same, he will think that the northern rising will depend solely on him. Meantime we shall control his people here."

For a day, this satisfied her; then she found herself wondering again. She took her walk with Macedonia past Theophanes' Roost, in Philemon Street. It was open for business. Men were going in and out for their morning drinks and gossip; it had a flash look as such a house usually has. The men going in and out had the look of low political agents, "rather too like the lilies of the field," she said.

A little later in the morning, a thought occurred to her. She was lunching in Macedonia's dressing-room; she poised the little anchovy sandwich she had just made, while the thought flashed into her mind, that possibly Theophanes had been put out of the way while his gangs and premises were used. What if some suspicion of Theophanes had crossed Nicanor's mind? Might he not have sent him out of The City, while he used the gangs to rob the Palace arsenal? Might he not have stored the stolen weapons in the cellars of the Roost? Might it not suit the Green party to have evidence on which to hang Theophanes if need arose? The thought came with such suddenness and brightness into her mind that it seemed like truth. Macedonia asked her why she was suddenly so thoughtful. She said that she had been suddenly wondering about the cellars in The City.

"Well you might wonder," Macedonia said. "You get my father to take you to the Warehouse Cellars someday; he could always pass you in. You wouldn't believe what is underground there; Solomon's pride and the Queen of Sheba's glory and almost one tenth of Theodora's dowry."

That evening at the Palace, after she had read to the Empress, she was joined in the Little Library by Justinian.

"I've been thinking about Theophanes," she said. "I cannot justify what I say. I just feel that some of his boys, as he calls them, have robbed the arsenal. He may not have known it when he spoke to me at my sister's house, and he may not have known that the weapons were put in his cellars; and they may not be there. But a cellar is a good store, and it may be, that the Greens would like to have Theophanes in their power. They may have put the weapons in his cellars without his knowledge, so that they could force him to be faithful to them. It would be a hanging matter to be found with them there. They know what a wily knave he is."

Justinian listened with close attention to what she said. He said: "That is a very interesting explanation of yours. It may be the right one. There are many cellars in The City, though. Each City-palace of the lords has room in it to hide a small army, let alone the weapons. But the point is interesting. There were vintners' men in the Palace precincts on the day the arsenal was cleared. But we can get no further than that. You will be interested to hear that Philip never went towards Trebizond. He got away from his escort and fled to the south somewhere."

The City went about its daily work, as the communities of men will ever attempt to do, even in revolution and in war. All felt, in a dull way, that something might have come of the Peace Meeting, if it had been pushed years before, but that now it was too late.

Theodora as she went to and fro to the Theatre, or to chat a moment in the Markets, felt that in its dull way The City would have preferred that the Blue rule should have continued, but that since it could not keep peace either at home or abroad, the sooner the change was made the better. Certainly, very few in The City wished to fight for the Blue rule, though a good many liked the thought of breaking a Green head or two.

The meeting was to be on the Monday. The City priesthood, led by the Patriarch, did much at every service to turn the thoughts of men to Peace. Theodora saw that they had much effect; as the days passed the tone of talk became more hopeful; so much more hopeful that the Green musicians and speakers reappeared to say that the rightful claims of the Greens were not to be set aside by any ideology, but were going to base themselves, once for all, on freedom and justice.

They were not in such numbers as formerly, Theodora felt that thrift was at work, but they came about the streets and made her wonder if Theophanes had returned. The next morning he came to the Theatre, and gave his lesson to the announcers. His attorney, a shrewd, secret pale man, with much mottling of freckle on his face, which gave him the look of being pock-marked, came with him. Theodora had no word with Theophanes, but saw him and listened to a few minutes of the lesson. Indeed all the Theatre came to the wings during the lesson for the joy of hearing that great effortless exquisite voice. She could not be sure whether Theophanes looked upon the mottled man as a friend or as a spy. "A little of both" she decided. Certainly the creature watched him closely, though Theophanes with the easy friendliness of the bagman and the publican treated him as a comrade, and asked his opinion. Later in the lesson she decided that the man was there as a spy. Theophanes made no least attempt to look for her or to speak with her. "They suspect him a little," she thought. "He is not to be allowed out alone again."

The next day, Theophanes came to the Theatre with his attorney and gave his lesson as before. She decided now that Theophanes was almost a prisoner, almost a slave, doing what he was told. She avoided him altogether, and heard later from one of the dancers that the mottled man had asked, "Which is this woman they call Theodora?" She wondered what message had come from Philip the Pisidian or another to bid a Green spy have an eye upon her.

She read to the Empress that evening and saw Justinian for a moment. He was depressed by the want of information and by the badness of the news that had come through from the returning cavalry. Aristides had written that the roads were under water and the bridges down, and that they had made bad time and lost many horses. This letter was already a week old. It had been dated from some village, name illegible, on the wrong side of the gulf; and bore rude notes to say that it had been shot by arrow across the floods at some place not known to them. Theodora was resolved not to leave Justinian in that mood of gloom. She said that the letter was a week old, and that the floods then must have been at their height, and that no flood in those parts lasted more than three days. Probably an active man might have

swum troops across the day after the height of the floods,
that is, the day after the letter was written. After one
day, or one day and a half, further march, the way
would be clear enough. She was sure that the horse
might be very near The City before the meeting. "Yes,"
he said gloomily, "in the meantime our enemies are in
The City. My Praefect of the Wharves was here an hour
ago. A big barge came down from the north this afternoon and was followed by two others which made fast
at Number Five Wharf. All three were supposedly and
ostensibly laden with larch-poles. But I had given him a
warning not to trust his searchers, so when these barges
tied up, he took the naval reservists and searched the
larch-poles. The ships were full of armed men from the
rebel villages, 35 in one, 25 in another, 20 in the third.
Eighty picked men with food and drink. They were to
have lain in the barges till the signal came, then they
were going to secure the wharves. You can imagine from
that how near we are to the signal."

"What did you do with them?" she asked.

"They were battened down securely below the deck,"
he said. "Then the barges were towed across the water
and moored in the harbour under guard. The naval reservists are either doing that or watching for other
barges. 'More come,' the men said."

"I begin to understand the Horse of Troy," she said.

"The boom is across now," he said. "No more can come
in. From now on the boom will be across all the time;
any ships coming down will have to pull across to Peter's
Point and moor there till we see a little. That is your
boom, of course."

"One thing I would like to say if I may," Theodora said. "You may be sure of one thing. The Greens have been really scared at the influence the Patriarch and the clergy have shown. It is that which has made them send out their speakers again."

"Yes," he said, "the Patriarch has impressed a great many. Tomorrow he will have a very great day with processions and intercessions. I put more hope now in him than in the meeting, and rather more in the meeting than in the cavalry's return in time."

"I put a great deal of hope still in all these things," she said.

"Theodora," he said, "you put the only hope I have into me; I know that; God bless you for it."

When she reached home that night at about ten o'clock she found Kallianassa at the door. "Madam," she said, "let me tell you very secret and strange things. The man, the speaker, Theophanes has been here to see you. He could not wait, nor hope to return. He would not write, but said that he knew well that I would not betray any secret of yours. In that he is wise. Listen, Lady, let me whisper. The Palace weapons are in the cellars of his tavern, The Roost; the young men put them there. They have been hidden there ever since. They are to be served out to the drilled bodies after the great meeting. But the important thing is this: The western lords have now made their pact with Nicanor; the agreement is made but is not yet sealed. It is to be sealed tomorrow morning when the copies are ready. The western lords will all take the Sacrament together tomorrow morning, then go to the Palace to take their leave of the Emperor. They

will then set forth out of The City to meet their men
who are already on the march. Some of the weapons will
go in their baggage wagons headed up in casks."

"Wait," Theodora said. "The wagons will have gone
already."

"He did not say that, Lady."

"No," Theodora said, "but the wagons move more
slowly; they will have started. I wonder if they got them
away before the gates closed."

"He did not say, Lady. He said that the all-important
thing is this. The rising will begin just before dawn on
the morning after the meeting; not tomorrow, not the
day after, but the morning after that. The gates will be
seized; the rebels will march in from the north, ride in
from the west; the boom will be lifted and all the important points taken before day has fully dawned. The Palace will be stormed. The workmen who are renewing
the buttresses on Constantine's tower will leave ladders
for that."

They were in the little sitting-room, lit by one candle.
"You are my brave girl," Theodora said. "Thank God
he saw that he could trust you. You know that you hold
the safety of the Empire in your brave head."

"Lady," Kallianassa said, "what I tell you will not
harm the speaker? He told me these things upon my
gold cross."

Theodora stroked Kallianassa's hair which was lus-
trous, very thick and of the darkest brown. "Friend," she
said, "he risked his life to tell it. If he saves us all, be
sure we shall be glad and grateful."

"Lady," Kallianassa said, "he is a great speaker. Great

power has been given him by God. What he told me with his very life is a sacred thing."

Theodora saw that Kallianassa had been swept off her feet by the speaker; she was not surprised. Theophanes could sweep most people anywhere, for a time.

"Friend," she said, "will you come back with me to the Palace? This news must be told at once. And know that all that I can do for his and your safety shall be done. Will you put on your shoes? If we take sticks the dogs won't attack us, and probably all the bad men are in bed by this time."

"I'll see that no one lays a hand on you, my Queen," Kallianassa said. "No dog nor man shall touch you; though both are the same if you ask me."

They went out into the swift dark night.

She could at all times enter the Palace now. She was shown to the Empress' rooms where presently Justinian came to hear the news. He had not yet gone to bed.

"I need little sleep," he said, "and latterly the situation has not led to much sleep. I am sure that you are right, that the wagons with the arms have already started. And your instinct was right from the first about the weapons being at The Roost. You have always been right. It seems an absurd thing, but it is true, our dynasty depends on about two hundred naval reservists and Coast Guards; they are the only men in The City whom I can absolutely trust. There are seventeen men of my clan in the Palace here. I trust those, of course. The full half of the reservists are on guard at the booms and wharves. I sent another thirty this evening after you had gone, to take over the northern gate and close it to all traffic. That

does not leave many for all that is to be done. I will now
send some of them to search the cellars at The Roost and
arrest the people there. If that can be done quietly so
that no word of it passes it will be something."

"You can spare Theophanes? He has helped your
cause greatly, Prince."

"For his own safety to clear him from suspicion by
his party he had better go into close confinement. He
will be a political prisoner here until we see."

"Prince," she said, "you say you are closing the northern gate from tonight. It seems to me that there is just a
chance that the signed and sealed agreements may go
out of The City by the western gate tomorrow morning
early. The agreements will not be left in The City, be
sure. Do not search any wagons at the gates, but send
some of your sailors to the Customs Search Posts half a
mile outside the gates, at Fair Waters and The Old
Bridge. Everything going west must pass those points.
It will be a Holy Day, few will be passing. Search everyone and everything, just in case."

"Yes," he said, "that seems a wise precaution. And if
I replace the western gate guards with sailors all my little force will be employed. It's not many, two hundred,
to defend an entire Empire."

"Twelve were not many to upset an entire Empire,"
she said, "but they did it."

He came near to her and gazed into her eyes. "You
are rightly named The Gift of God," he said. "In all this
perplexity you give me hope and cheer and light. My
mother's dying; my uncle is in pain, breathing fire and
slaughter which cannot be dealt; my aunt thinks me a

boy; my servants are traitors except my seventeen; my army is God knows where, and my Navy not much better, and all my Empire falling to bits and my City thinking I'd better be killed. Then you come night after night, saying, 'Things are brighter.' When my seventeen are killed, and my two hundred reservists worn out, and myself drummed forth from The City, I do believe you will find me in the ditch and say, 'Things are going splendidly; one more little effort and all will be yours.' "

"Yes, Prince," she said, "if I live you may count on me there."

"I believe I may count on you," he said, "and it's the one light and joy of this time."

"Oh, Prince," she said. She flamed out against his enemies. "Could you not arrest all those western lords, all this Trade Mission as they call themselves?"

"Come, come," he said. "That does more credit to your heart than to your head. I am a legalist, and care for the thing called evidence, and the thing, procedure. I have only the word of Theophanes against ex-Praefects, and the sons and grandsons of such. If we could find one of these agreements, signed and sealed by them, then we might proceed."

"Could you not hold these lords in The City, not under arrest, but by invitation? Could not the Emperor order them to stay? They are leaders about to leave The City to command a rebellion. When they come to take leave could not the Emperor refuse the leave?"

"The Patriarch asked them to the Peace Meeting; they said they would not be here. My uncle has made such frightful mistakes lately by acting on suspicion, which is an old man's usual failing, that I don't think he would do any such thing. No. It seems to me that the agreements, when signed and sealed, will be put into the secret strong-rooms in the palaces of these men. It might take us weeks to find them, even if we broke in to search. Theophanes cannot know where nor when the signing will take place, even if he knows that the signing is to be, which is by no means sure."

"But if you do find the agreements," she said, "then you would arrest them all?"

"If?" he said. "Shall we have enough reservists for that? That is what I ask. Living in this hand-to-mouth Empire, that is what I ask. How many faithful remain?"

"My maid one," she said. "Myself a second. You, Prince, many in yourself, if you would only believe so. That is plenty to begin with."

"Theodora," he said, "when I'm with you I think the game can be won."

"It can be played," she said, "yes, and won. It is a royal game with a royal prize, which isn't going down to a jockey and some race-course bullies."

It flashed into her mind that at that moment one of the conspirators might well be saying, "It is a royal game, with a royal prize, which isn't going down to a private's book-worm nephew."

She had been told that the western lords would take the Sacrament on the morrow, but had hardly expected that they would proceed to their Saviour like the Three Kings of the East. They went to the Cathedral in chariots, behind their racing teams, with the drivers in their racing colours under Green favours. All the myriad lov-

ers of the races came into the streets to see their favour-
ites pass. Drivers and teams were greeted with roars of
cheering; but Theodora was driven to wonder who would
notice if all the owners were removed and only horses
and drivers remained.

She went to several services on that Sunday to calm
her anxiety and to pray for help to her cause. Wherever
she went, outside all the Churches, she heard men of
middle age talking about the need for calm. These men
were all quietly and decently clad, well used to speaking
in the open, and all using the same arguments, almost
the same words. They were saying that a great deal of
nonsense had been talked about the ambitions of the
Green Faction. The wishes of all citizens were for Peace,
both at home and abroad. The Consular Candidate, Hypatius, had striven for peace abroad and was pledged to
peace at home. All the Green leaders were going to the
Peace Meeting on the morrow fully resolved to accept
any reasonable offers for peace that might be had. It
therefore behoved all citizens to be of good cheer, because peace was certain; the citizen who went about saying that there would be civil war was doing his City a
grave dis-service, and trying to bring war about. There
would be no war but peace. Let all men support the good
and wise Patriarch, who was so nobly striving to main-
tain peace. On the whole this talk of peace from men
who were plainly not peaceful frightened Theodora more
than any threat. She knew that it was false that all the
Green leaders were going to the Peace Meeting. They
were not. Most of them were riding that afternoon to
join their armies already on the march. No doubt the

speakers were in the pay of the Greens, spreading rumours of peace to put citizens off their guard. The surprise was being made all the greater. In the afternoon
she heard announcements that on the second morning,
the Tuesday, which she knew to be the day planned for
the rising, there would be a grand display of all the winning teams at the Hippodrome in aid of the Patriarch's
Christmas Charities Fund. All were invited to be present
to help this deserving cause. She knew from this that the
Greens expected to have complete possession of The City
by noon on the Tuesday; the festival would be the rally-
ing of the entire Green party, and the declaration of
Nicanor as Emperor. There was no need for Theophanes
to tell her this.

She went to the Palace that night to read to the Empress, who could listen to nothing but the first two verses
of the 37th Psalm.

"Fret not thyself because of evil-doers, neither be
thou envious against the workers of iniquity.
For they shall soon be cut down like the grass, and
wither as the green herb."

The use of the word "green" gave the old woman
deep satisfaction. In fact those two verses were the con-
solation of most of the Blues among the women in the
Palace.

Theodora continued to read long after the old woman
had fallen asleep. Presently the Empress woke and seemed
confused. "Ah, it's the girl," she said. Now that reminds
me I've got such a pretty thing to show you. It's a hair-

jewel of silver and birds' feathers which look like jewels.
It was sent to me from Persia. It came days ago, but I
never unpacked it till this morning. It's always well to
keep these Oriental fellows in suspense and make them
feel that what they send isn't valued. But I unpacked it
today and when I heard you were here I thought: 'It must
go on her dark hair.' She led Theodora to her room where
half a dozen lovely things were displayed on a table. She
picked up the loveliest which shone with the iridescent
breast feathers of exquisite tropical birds, and placed it
on Theodora's dark hair. "Ah," she said, "it needs youth.
You can see for yourself how it looks. Ah, child, I'd like
to be young again and have my hair dark again, and
have the men coming round me again. It's all folly of
course, but I'd like to be a fool again and free this time.
Ah, dear, with your eyes and hair, and then your hands.
You do keep your hands so good. I do like to see girls
with nice hands. You must take that hair jewel. You become it; my yellow-white wool never could. That's for
you, dear. I forget your name, Massie something."

"Theodora, lady."

"Yes, it's the other was Massie, wasn't it? Now I wonder if you really like it."

"Oh, Madam, it is one of the loveliest things I ever
saw and how can I thank you for your goodness to me?"

"Tino says you saved his life, dear. Now I wonder if
you like sweetmeats. I told my cook she must have some
honey-dix for you, fast or no fast. I didn't say that really,
I said I must have some honey-dix."

"Oh, Madam, no," Theodora said. "I promised my Father Timotheus I would keep the fasts."

"Well, you're right to keep the promise," the old woman said, "but I always get dispensations now. Tino says things don't look too promising, but I always say things blow over, generally, in politics. He worries too much, I always tell him; that's what these scholars do. He keeps looking for news. Well, the pigeons'll come, I say, if the hawks don't get them or they don't miss the way. If the sun were to come out they could work the signals, but when it's wet like this you can't expect that. What do you use for your skin, dear? I expect I asked you that before, but I expect it's only youth you use." She babbled on for a long time in her kind way; she loved youth; she had never had much of a youth herself, and knew now how she had longed for it.

Presently when the Empress wearied of her she was sent to the Little Library where Justinian joined her. She had expected to find him moved, shaken and anxious, like the Palace attendants. Instead she found him quietly confident and more alive and alert than before. She remembered how Timotheus had said that if a man showed readiness for great things the spiritual powers blew strength into him so that he might attempt them.

"Well," he said, "you may have noticed some anxiety among the Palace people. They are anxious because Philip has been taken and will be examined. All those white faces that you see here are expecting to be the next. Now I do not know what you will feel about it, but I hope that you will come to the Meeting tomorrow, you and your friend, will you?"

"Indeed I will," she said, "if you could contrive a pass. Macedonia will come if I go."

"Here are passes," he said. "I would like you to be there if you could endure it. When one puts a thing to the touch, one needs the few people of one's camp."

"I hope that you will always reckon me as one of those," she said.

"One of the chief," he said. "You would like to hear the situation. We have some thirty more men of our clan from Sardica; they are parts of ourselves who will live or die with us. My Uncle is very ill and suffers much from his wound, but if things go ill with us he will insist on being hoisted on to a horse; he'll go out with the clan. Then my riders have brought in the news that the men are marching on The City from the north and west. Some seven thousand foot from the north, and about eight hundred horse from the west. They have had camps and watering places with fodder and so forth prepared for them. There has been plenty of rain, as you know, but both armies will be in sight from the walls tomorrow afternoon when the Peace Meeting begins."

"And, Prince, what strength have you?"

"I have Theodora," he said.

"You know that, Prince," she said, "but what other?"

"What weakness?" he said. "We've a lot of young men of the Blues who have been drilling in back-yards and places lately; there are some Green agents among them too. They will not be any great use. As to the horse under Aristides I've sent all possible fodder along the roads and all the young sappers from the Engineering Schools to see to any bridges which may be down, but the floods have been bad and out there at the gulf floods can be very destructive. I've sent out all the remounts that can be scraped together. I just forestalled the Green agents in that, by the way; just beat them by half an hour."

"But, Prince, will your men be in time?"

"We shall soon know," he said, "shall we not? It will be touch and go. It will be the one race in which I shall be able to take some interest."

"Prince," she said, "may I ask you one thing? You said that if things go ill your Uncle will be hoisted on a horse and go out with the clan. I know that is the Sardican way, to gather round the chief, men and women, and go out in a body and get killed round the chief. I want you to let me go out with the clan."

"Why," he said, "it wouldn't be much of a clan without you."

He came over to her, kissed her hands and said, "If you won't be of my clan, and of my blood and my house, I will go out and die by the road. You are the loveliest thing God ever brought into my sight. I'm lopsided and queer. I'm only the half of a puzzle; but you're the other half, and when I'm with you I see a sort of Kingdom of Heaven which I believe we could make."

"O Prince, O Prince."

"What d'you say, beloved, don't you think we could make it?"

"We'd die trying," she said. "But let us not talk or think of dying. You will know that the Greens are preaching Peace now. I suppose that is a blind?"

"Yes; a blind; they mean to attack at dawn, the day after tomorrow."

"They'll try to rush the gates of course, from both sides?"

"Yes. I have seen to it that they cannot rush them. The gates will delay them for some hours. I have arranged some of my young men to support the gate garrisons."

"The speakers were saying that the lords are staying for the Peace Meeting. Is that true?"

"Yes, curiously, it is true. They have arranged this chariot race or something in the Hippodrome, for the day after tomorrow. The horse-race at Hector's funeral games and a coronation circus all in one."

"Could you not arrest them all on suspicion? Oh, why did you not seize them when they came to take leave this afternoon?"

"They are staying on, so that they did not come to take leave. They know that they are suspected. But as to arresting them I have no evidence, and until I have I cannot act. I will not give them that handle against us of tyranny and so forth. Besides, each of those great City Palaces of theirs is a fortress with from seventy to a hundred retainers in it. I have not the men for it. They would resist, arrest and defy us. When one has no strength one must be more than usually careful. If I sent forty men to arrest upon suspicion and the forty were well beaten as they would be, there would be a fine exultation. No, there are two things which may help us, evidence that can be used and men of The Kingfishers here in time."

"And in the meantime," she said, "there may be a sudden blow by the Greens even before the meeting?"

"Yes, why not? It might be successful. The more surprises a man can spring the better his chance of success. I'm shutting all the City gates at noon tomorrow, and only known people will be allowed in before noon. But now I have to go to hear reports. My aunt bids me say that a room has been prepared for you if you wish to stay here tonight."

"No, Prince, thank you. I must go home. Theophanes may have left some word and my maid Kallianassa expects me. May I say one word, Prince, that I hope and pray for your success tomorrow. I think your star shines bright, Prince."

"You make it shine, my gift from God," he said. "Sometimes I think we may just do them; at other times I wonder. Sometimes I seem in a great stream drifting to a cataract and certain to go over. Well I've learned that apathy's a deadly sin. But you will come to the Meeting if the Meeting is held, and after the Meeting your maid and you had better be in the Palace here until we see."

"We will be of your clan then," she said.

"You are now," he said. He went to a drawer and pulled from it a piece of stuff. "We come from a mountain lake," he said. "Our ancestress was a swan maiden. Our colour is this blue of the lake with the white swans flying over it. This makes you one of our clan if you will wear this; and no lovelier spirit ever wore it." He took the blue jewel from his shoulder and pinned the cloth upon her shoulder. "There," he said, "now you are pinned to us. Our word is 'Truth shines.' " With that belief they parted on the brink of the cataract. He kissed her hands again and glared into her eyes. He was unlike any man who had made love to her in the past, but she was never near him without feeling shattered by the vehemence of his feeling. He went swiftly out of the room; she flung herself down and kissed where his feet had stood. "I never thought that I could do that for a man," she muttered.

The night was somewhat showery till after midnight, then clearing winds blew till dawn; after that they died and the sky cleared for fair weather.

Theodora asked Macedonia to come to the Meeting with her, but Macedonia refused. Her father had had word from someone that the Meeting might not be very safe for a woman; besides Sosthenes wanted her to rehearse. Sosthenes was not polite about Theodora's going to the Meeting. "Isn't the illusion of an art enough for you?" he asked, "but you must try the illusion of politics? Well, go to your Meeting if you must. The sooner the two gangs of fools and scoundrels cut each other's throats the sooner we can start here. Comito's sister and Macedonia's friend ought not to go whoring after politics. However, go; only do come back before dark. Politics, when you might go to a dress-maker's or to see the new conjurer."

The City Hall was an old and not very convenient building used for civic functions and discussions. It was long, well lighted and could seat five hundred people. A long broad table ran down three quarters of its length in its centre. This had seats for about forty people. Behind these seats were open spaces with two inconvenient tiers of raised seats against the side-walls. At the head of the table was a President's throne. At the foot of the table there was a space and then six tiers of raised seats. Theodora sat in row Alpha, seat seven, of these. She was a little to the right of the centre facing the Presidential chair. There was a gallery above her head. A young man, a good-looking secretary of some kind who had been sent there by Justinian to look after her, explained that the Patriarch would be in the Chair, and that the Blues would be on her side of the table, Prince Justinian about three chairs down from the Patriarch and Symmachus beside him. The Greens would be on the left side of the table. Up above in the gallery were the wives, widows and daughters of Praefects and Governors. Theodora saw that only three other women were sitting below in the main hall.

The City had been very tense as she came to the Hall; many people had been in the streets and almost all had obeyed the request of the Patriarch not to prejudice the success of the Meeting by wearing favours or shouting party cries. She knew that everyone now knew the certainty of civil war if agreement were not reached at that discussion.

The Hall quickly filled up. She heard above her the drawl of the speech of the world of wealth and influence, whose members knew the gossip of the moment and called all prominent men by nicknames, often with terms of endearment, "darling Gugu," "that charming Ron-ron," etc. Some of the important women came in at the wrong door into the main hall, and caused a good deal of disturbance at being asked to go into the gallery. Theodora noted the dresses of these, with wonder that so few of them had any sense of dress. She saw that they considered a woman well-dressed only if she plainly bought her things from certain people. They had no feeling for beauty of line or of colour. She reflected that the squaws of the Libyans and every woman in the bazaars of the East seemed better dressed than these. In the midst of the chatter, and the occasional bursts of cheering outside and inside the Hall as prominent men came in to take their places, she prayed for Justinian and his cause in a wordless passionate hoping that he might triumph.

Punctually at the appointed time the Precentor entered with the cry "Be reverent all" and as people rose and bowed their heads, the Patriarch entered with Nicaea and another Bishop not known to her. "Probably Smyrna," she thought. They went to their thrones, while Justinian, Symmachus and the other leaders of both sides entered by the side doors and stood at their seats. Most of the speakers carried tablets, despatch-cases or sheets of notes. Nicanor was with the western lords; he bowed very low to the Patriarch and gave a charming smile to Nicaea. Theodora thought that he had extraordinarily bright eyes and teeth; he looked lean, keen, handsome and master of the situation. Justinian looked somewhat worn. Someone rang a silvery little bell; the Patriarch lifted his hands and began his prayer.

It had been said by some that the very sound of the Patriarch's voice was like an eleventh commandment:— "Thou shalt not go on doing what thou art doing now." Certainly no one could hear that noble voice uplifted in prayer unmoved. He prayed that the meeting might be abundantly blessed, so that from the offers and forbear-

ances of all Christian citizens their City might become
liker the City of God and a more fitting resting-place for
His angels. When he ceased the Bishop uttered a response
that God might hear them.

When the Patriarch and the Bishops were seated, the
audience sat; the Precentor, who was acting as Master
of the Ceremony, called upon Justinian to make his appeal. Justinian moved behind his chair, bowed to the
Patriarch, glanced to his left and bowed to Theodora,
took the attitude of one pleading in a Court of Law and
began his address with clear force and some humour.
He showed how Faction had begun, and what evils had
come from it; he told of the neglect of public services
all over the Empire, of the dangers on every frontier, of
the stupidities, meannesses and crimes which sprang daily
directly from it. He assured his fellow-citizens across the
table that his Faction truly wished to end the struggle
and that each member of it hoped that that Meeting
might end it. He assured them that any offers likely to
lead to lasting peace would be welcomed, at once carefully considered or debated (if they had to be debated)
in the friendliest possible way. He had no wish to try to
whitewash his party; it had been guilty of crimes; there
was no sense in denying that. Well, let that acknowledg-
ment show that the wrong and the folly of crime were
now recognized. Let both sides have done with crimes
and see if frank friendship might not achieve what cen-
turies of bitterness and bloodshed had not achieved. He
asked that the proposals of the Green Faction might now
be laid before the Citizens.

Theodora thought that he had spoken perhaps two

minutes too long. Her theatrical past had given her a
shrewd sense of how and when to leave off. She wished
that she had had the rehearsal of him; she would have
condensed and pointed his remarks, and ended on a
stronger note. There was much applause for Justinian
from the supporters sitting beside him; the House was
silent though it had approved him. The Greens were
silent; the women in the gallery chattered. In the silence
Theodora could hear disparaging remarks about Justinian, why was he not wearing purple, why was he always reading law or talking to priests. "A very feeble
speech, if you ask me," one woman said. Another said
that he had this Sardican accent which made every
one sick. "This man to come dictating to a man like Nicanor to make peace. I hope Nicanor puts him in his
place."

The talk buzzed for some moments, then all saw that
Nicanor after whispering to some of his friends and
casting a glance or two over his shoulder, was about to
rise. He had a waxen tablet in his hand; on it, he had
jotted some heads of paragraphs. He rose suddenly to his
feet, twitched his green scarf down over his chest, twisted
his left-hand fingers into its silk, glanced at his tablet
and stood still, while his Party rose and cheered him.
When they had done, he bowed very low to the Patriarch,
then gave a nicely graded bow to the Bishops, then with
an inclination of the head to Justinian, he began. Peace
and War were in the balance of his mind. However light
and foolish some of the audience had been till then, all
now were serious and hanging upon his words. Theodora looked at him with the intensest interest. He was a

beautiful looking man, with this clear-cut noble profile, the fine, proud mouth and the eyes shining like silver. His speaking voice was not good; it did not win nor did it command. It was somewhat thin and hard; there was too much of the throat in it. It struck Theodora that his teachers must have been legal men, used to arguing cases in small courts. However, it was plain that he had an intensity of feeling which made what he said effective. All there wanted to hear him; that, too, gave him power.

"Most Holy Father," he began, "and you, Most Reverend Fathers, and you my fellow-citizens, we are met by arrangement to listen to suggestions and to make proposals for the prevention of further civic dispute. You have heard from the speaker there that Faction is disturbing to The City, that it prejudices commerce, intimidates the administration of the Law, violates Christian injunction and makes impossible the creation of that City of God, which you, Most Holy Father, long to see builded here. The Party for which I speak has long had reason to grieve at the results of Faction. It has felt the effects of Party legislation, of Party administration, of Party favour in the choice of Officials, of Party prejudice even in such matters as public and private amusement. We, therefore, of the Green Party, may well be believed to be glad to hear that our opponents seek a reconciliation and offer, if I may say so, the cheek of the aggressor to the kiss of the victim. But while accepting the principle of the need of a reconciliation, we, of the Green Faction, ask ourselves why it is that our opponents choose this time of all times for the friendly offer. The Empire is at peace. True, there are lands within it which the ruling

Faction has provoked into rebellion or reduced to a chaos; but still, in the main, the Empire is at peace. It is true that the ruling Faction threatens Persia with invasion; but that crime has not yet been perpetrated. For the moment, the Outer Empire is at peace. At home here in The City we have other images of peace. We have an Emperor beloved by at least all those of his subjects who share his limited outlook and illiteracy. We have also those other signs of peace, a large and growing body of unemployment; a systematic thwarting and starvation of all those arts of agriculture which alone can enrich a state; a vicious fostering of that fictitious commerce in unwanted and unnecessary articles by which a few are enriched and the rest impoverished. Still outwardly there is peace, is there not? The tree however rotten in its heart presents an outer shell to the world, which seems sound. Yet at this moment the dominant Faction asks us to conclude a lasting agreement, to kiss and make friends, put aside all criticism, all judgment, all condemnation, and rally to the task of propping what neglect, folly and incompetence have made crazy."

He paused a while; his supporters applauded; he smiled a little, with a sneering smile; he was relishing his talk; he knew that he was galling his enemies, and had as yet only begun. "Yes," he went on, "they want our friendship. Is it not strange that they should ask for it? At this moment of the Empire's History they ask the Green Faction to cease to agitate for a state of things other than the existing state. Is it strange that we should ask why they should choose this moment? Did they offer peace some years ago when the Green Faction despairing of redress took up arms to fight for it? No peace was offered nor invited then; now it is offered; it may be had. Why? We ask why?

"In asking we must consider the present situation. In Persia on our Eastern frontier we have a powerful and proud sovereign, the Persian King, who disbelieves the words of our Ruler which have been belied by his acts." There were cries from Blue supporters of "No, no, it is not so." He smiled and said, "But my friends and fellow-citizens, it is so. I have had the honour of talking with that sovereign. I have seen with my own eyes our fortresses built upon his frontiers in defiance of our pledged word and solemn treaty. I have but newly come from Persia. What can you expect from such treachery but hostility? How can you blame him for suspecting us, and for arming to forbid any further act of treachery? It was common knowledge in Persia when I was there, so zealously are our state secrets kept, that our Emperor meant to invade Persia in the Spring, and was already gathering his army along the coasts of Asia Minor ready to attack as soon as sailing recommenced. The positions and compositions of our forces were known, as also the interesting fact that the Emperor's nephew, a man perhaps more learned in Church History and the complexities of obsolete laws than in the conduct of war, was appointed to command, and had even started upon his journey."

Here the Blues interjected cries of "Stop all this insolence." "Come to the point." "Make your peace proposals." "This is a Peace Meeting." "Tell us what you suggest as a basis for lasting peace." "Have done with all this. We want your help not your sneers."

Nicanor smiled, bowed to the Patriarch and said, "Most Holy Father, before I come to consider the future as I hope to do, if not interrupted, I wish to make a clear statement of the present. All proposals made by my Party must be based on our view of the present. I must, therefore, be permitted to say exactly how we view the present."

This silenced the interrupters. He continued: "I was saying that our Emperor's nephew, filled with hopes of military glory, had started for the East to take up his command. However, it reached this soldier's ears that the Green Faction, stirred by repeated request, by overwhelming social need, and by its own hope of social improvement, had determined to contest the election for Consul. He learned that it was the intention of the Green Faction, the strictly legal intention, to restore to that Office, if it so chanced that the will of the people returned their candidate to the Office, to restore to that high Office, the Consulship, all those old powers still lawfully attached to it, to make it again what it always was before successive despots stifled it, the citizens' defence against the tyranny and iniquity of brutal, treacherous and illiterate wearers of the purple."

Here all the Greens present broke out into enthusiastic cheering. Nicanor allowed them to applaud while he watched the effect of his words upon Justinian. Theodora saw the smile of relish on his face; he was enjoying this attack. Justinian watched him with cool good humour; the touch about his illiterate Uncle had not been missed. As the applause diminished, Nicanor again twitched his green silk, dug his fingers more deeply into it and continued.

"Such, Fellow-Citizens," he said, "were the positions of the two parties a few days ago. On the one hand, a bloodthirsty, treacherous, unscrupulous, illiterate tyrant, resolved to shed the blood of innocent and harmless foreigners and to waste the treasure of the Empire under the banners of his nephew, and in this, Sir," he added to Justinian, "I speak with the moderation forced on me by the presence of our most to be revered Fathers in God. On the other hand, a few dishonoured, tricked, crushed and humiliated men, faithful to old friends, and to old traditions, who feel that Liberty is worth the struggling for, by legal means, by laws, Sir, not obsolete like the many you know, but set aside and daily outraged by usurping despotism and ambitious nepotism."

Here the cheering broke out into a roar for several minutes.

"Such, Sir, was the situation only a few days ago. And now, may I beg you all to consider the situation now? No sooner did word reach the usurper who now wears the purple—" Here there was almost a riot. The Blues shouted, hissed and booed; the Greens cheered. Nicanor with the utmost coolness continued.

"No sooner did illiterate authority gather from the lips of an ambitious relative that his position and assumptions might soon be legally challenged by those with not only law but right upon their side than he at once made that smear of red paint which with him passes for a signature, and cancelled his nephew's appointment. Why did he do this? Was it to save the lives of Imperial troops certain to be sacrificed by the bookworm's ignorance of war as of those sports which we hold to be the image of war? The question might be asked—was it because he felt that his Persian policy was too strong a mixture of iniquity and imbecility even for modern statesmanship? That question, too, might be asked. No; it was neither of these things. It was the fear that at last a law-abiding population was roused to protest, and sought legal means of self-defence. It was because he saw that he could thwart, trick, terrify and destroy this people no longer. The balance which he had overset was now being restored. Spiritual powers, long outraged, had at last prompted the Avengers. Was it not curious to see how this usurping tyrant, in the purple through an act of treachery, and confirmed there by acts of murder, should have trembled at the thought of Law? 'Ah, if Law be the need,' he seems to have said, 'Law shall be here. We will make our nephew Consul.' No sooner was this thought of than it was put in practice. Almost at the last moment at which a candidate could lawfully be nominated, the nephew was nominated. He appeared at a meeting organized by the opposing Faction to plead his cause and to display his qualifications. 'You seek to restore the Consulship in all its old splendour,' he seemed to say. 'You seek to bring the people the defence of this great Office. I, too, the Emperor's nephew, who hope soon to be the Emperor, I, too, seek for the Office. Without it my chances are in peril. With a Consul opposed to iniquity, what chance will iniquity have? I hope therefore that you will make me the Consul, with my friend, of course,

the well-known jerry builder, who has ever voted as iniquity has asked or usurpation bidden."

Again there was a tumult; he smiled. When it had
subsided he continued, "But it was not enough to ask for
the Chief Magistracy. Others, more worthy, had already
asked. Others, more worthy, had the support of the voters.
Consider for a moment what steps the Blue Faction took
when the certainty of defeat at the polls dawned on what
passes for their brains. What step did they take? They
called a meeting at which they told us that Faction was
wicked. Little choir-boys sang of the beauty of brotherly
love. Holy voices urged unity. Not a word, mind, not
one single word was said about restoring what had been
seized or offering to election what was snatched by force.
No, we were told that Faction was wicked and opposed
to Christian principles, and that therefore our Faction
should not seek legal redress, should not try to restore
that old folly of the Consulship which only made trouble
between the Wolf and the Lamb. There was some indignation at the meeting, but I gathered, in spite of the
noise, that we were asked to take a little time to consider
this great question, for upon our decision the peace of
The City and Empire depended. It was to us, so we were
told, before popular fury stopped the teller, that The
City and the Empire looked for peace. Was it? Ah,
friends, when the offer was made to us what measure
of peace was in our opponents' hearts? Even as we were
begged for peace, even as we were besought to establish
peace, these hypocrites' messengers were galloping to re-
call the troops so rashly sent from The City. All this talk
of peace was but to gain time while the troops returned

to help them to crush liberty. I say boldly to this nephew of a tyrannical usurper that his offer of peace is due to dread and craft because he fears the justice of an outraged people. He seeks time to bring here his hired assassins. Meanwhile he offers us the kiss of Judas the traitor. I say to you, Justinian, that your Uncle, the Emperor, is a thief and a murderer. I say that you hope to profit by the murder as you have profited by the theft. I say that your offer of peace is craft and policy while you and your Uncle plot our destruction. By what right do you talk to us of peace while the State's troops gallop at your orders to destroy us who seek only to defend our liberty. How can you talk of peace and ending Faction when at this moment your minions shut the City Gates and search all comers to The City lest they should seem to favour the Green Party. Your troops hurry hither, your ships scour the narrow waters, your guards molest and rob us, yet you talk of ending Faction. I say that we of the Green Party know your iniquity and see through your guile. You are one of those other miscreants of the purple, who slaughter as soon as they have deceived. We are not so simple. We will have our Consul, we will have our ancient safeguards, we will have Liberty, and no craft, no treachery, no theft, no murder shall rob us of these things."

After the tumult of applause had died, he continued, "I have little more to say, Fellow-Citizens. To you, Most Holy Father in God, and to you, Right Reverend Pastors, I offer my apologies if I have spoken with more bitterness than is seemly in a Christian. But to those of the Blue Faction who desire an end of Faction, I say only this:

if you seek an end of Faction, give up some of those things which have been the prize of successful Faction. Surrender the purple to popular election, pay into the Treasury the golden spoil of bribery and theft. Make a lasting peace by generous dealing on your Eastern frontier. Seek not to check or influence a free election by calling soldiers post-haste from their stations. Show the peaceful Party that you mean peace. Dismiss your cruisers; end your hateful use of the State's resources for the benefit of one party, and that the youngest and the least beneficial. Show us that you mean peace, and the Green Faction which has always stood for peace, which seeks only peace, will by all its strength and all its fervour work with you to make a lasting peace."

He had been speaking with much greater power and clearness as he proceeded; he ended with a clear ringing power very moving. He was applauded even by the Blues. Theodora thought that he had done well, much better than she had expected of him.

When he had ended, the benign Nicaea rose and spoke for some minutes with elegance and charm. He said that he wished both parties to clear their minds of hatred in the first speeches of the Meeting. When the rancour had all been emptied out, if any rancour had been brought to that Meeting which he, for one, would never like to think, then friendship would prevail, and the brotherhood within us assert itself with fruitful suggestions on which policies might be framed.

While he was speaking one of the Green ex-Praefects sitting on the Left began to make himself a souvenir of the Meeting by asking his neighbour to sign his name upon a tablet of parchment and pass it along the table for the signatures of all the other leaders there present. When his parchment had gone to three places, others on that side began to do the same thing. When Nicaea ceased and sat, half a dozen parchments had accumulated at his chair. "What is all this?" he asked.

"People know that they have your prayers and blessing, Right Reverend," Justinian called. "They want also your signature."

"That is a little thing to grant," the old man said, "but let me see now. I am somewhat short-sighted; perhaps someone will kindly point just where my name must be put."

Pompeius who was sitting next to him did this. There was some little pause in the proceedings while parchments passed. The audience tittered a little at the sight. Symmachus felt that perhaps the Meeting was being wilfully made absurd by this trick of the asking for the signatures. He rose with the customary bows to the Patriarch and the Bishops and said, "This Meeting has been called to promote peace. It has begun with an assumption which should not be allowed to pass unchallenged. The last speaker has assumed that all the evils of Faction have proceeded from the Party which wears the more beautiful colour. It seems to us that the purpose of the Meeting might be better served if both parties would frankly admit that certain things have been done by them and encouraged by them and paid for by them. . . . I am speaking deliberately . . . which do not look well upon reflection and would sound very ugly in confession. To one, who, like myself, has lived for the last

few weeks within this City, it has certainly seemed that
the Party led by the last speaker has promoted civil strife
by every means in its power, by organized insult, terror-
ism and brigandage."

The Green adherents cried, "No, no. Order. Shut up.
No insults here."

"One moment, please," Symmachus said. Somewhere
outside the Hall in one of the passages a little mechanical
peal of silver bells began to chime. Many such were in
The City then. As the bells chimed Symmachus waited,
as though not liking to speak through the noise. When
the peal ended he said, "I have no wish to insult. I would
only ask the leaders of the Green Faction if they have
not known of gangs of bullies who have within the last
weeks smashed and pillaged the shops of Blue supporters
and cruelly beaten their owners?"

Menippos answered, "A certain amount of horse-play
takes place at every election. Who complains of that?"

"People who care about Law do complain of violations
of the Law," Symmachus said. "I would also ask the leaders of the Green Faction if they have known of any
organized, drilled and armed bodies of supporters in the
Northern Province whose avowed aim has been to support their Faction with spears?"

Kallimachus said, "That fairy-story has been told all
over The City. The truth of the matter seems to be this.
The Blues some years ago suppressed an armed rising in
those parts with such barbarity that they have been afraid
of the Avengers ever since. But my Son was riding
through the Northern Province last week. It may interest
you to hear that he found no sign of rebellion. The prov-

ince is quiet and, indeed, too cruelly impoverished by Blue rule to think of rebellion."

The Greens applauded this. The House was listening very intently. There was a feeling that an explosion might not be far off.

Symmachus continued, "I am interested in hearing of your son's report, Lord Kallimachus," he said, "I do not of course ask what your son was doing in that province."

"No," Kallimachus answered, "I will tell you. He was learning the truth of the report circulated by Blue emissaries, that the province is about to rebel. He wished to nail yet another lie of the Blues to the post of infamy."

"I am only sad," Symmachus replied, "that he did not stay nearer his ancestral home, the reward, I believe, of the successful concubinage of an ancestress. Had he but stayed nearer home he might have learned the truth of yet another report, that the Green leaders there are about to ride upon The City with the 'amateur cavalry' as it is called of your friends and henchmen. But perhaps that also is a fairy-story, known by you all to be such?"

"You impudent hound," Kallimachus cried.

"At least I am not of your kennel," Symmachus said. "Answer me. Are your men riding on The City?"

"Really," Nicanor said, "what measure of peace can come from a Meeting like this?"

"That is what we are here to find," Symmachus said.

"Perhaps," the Patriarch said, "perhaps the Lord Kallimachus would offer a formal denial?"

"No," Kallimachus said, "this Meeting breaks up."

"One moment please," Justinian said, "may I beg peo-

ple to remain for one moment? A matter of very great
importance remains. Please keep your seats."

The tumult ceased. The angry leaders sat again.

Justinian opened his despatch case and took from it
various papers. Seeing at his side some of the parchments covered with signatures, he lifted one of these
and looked at it while the House fell still. The House
became deathly still. One of the Greens, a little man with
a vivid face said, "Don't look so solemn, Tino; we regard
you with pity more than anger."

The House sniggered at this and then fell again to a
dead silence.

He seemed to expect some more comment from the
Greens; as none came he made the customary addresses
to the Patriarch and Bishop and at once began to speak.

"Fellow-Citizens," he said, "I had hoped that an offer
of settlement, fairly and sincerely made, might seem so,
and might be met in a similar spirit of fairness and
eagerness to settle. Disputes within a city can but ruin
both sides. This City, which should be the fair Queen of
all the world, remains uncrowned, not because her citizens do not love her, but because they hate each other. I
am twitted with reading the Laws and the Lives and
Writings of the Saints. It is true. I study both these
things; the one, to find what basic stones of liberty and
equity need still to be laid beneath our Commonwealth;
the other, to find the guidance which has inspired simple
men in the past to the search and the discovery of truth.
We have all listened with interest to the eloquent speech
of the champion of the Green Faction. Among the many

charges brought by him, some stand out pre-eminently. His speech is hardly the welcoming of friendly discussion for which we had hoped. It is little more than an arraignment of persons and policies. Among the arraignments are these, that I hope to profit by a murder, and that my offer of peace is craft and policy."

There came loud cries of "So you do. So they are" from the Green side. He waited till the Greens had finished and continued, "We were told at the end of the speech, that if we seek the end of Faction, we should give up certain things which have been the prize of successful Faction. I gather that he meant that our Emperor, who has been crowned and consecrated, who has taken the Oath demanded of our Emperors, should abdicate, so that his position might be voted for. It is true that I have read many laws, but I cannot name any law by which any such procedure could be countenanced. Next, we were told to make a lasting peace by generous dealing on our Eastern frontier. That is and has been for two years the endeavour of the Emperor. That it has been subtly thwarted, time and time again, by unscrupulous agents, who have remained undetected, is well known. We have as yet no proofs against those agents, no proofs, that is, which would satisfy any Court of Law as to their iniquity, but their doings and their names are known. They are the names of men of the Green Faction. Next, we were advised not to try to influence a free election by calling soldiers from their stations; we were to dismiss our cruisers, and end our use of the State's resources for the benefit of one Party, meaning, I take it, the Blue Party, which he calls for some reason, the youngest in

the State. He means, I think, that the Party of Commerce
and Marine Adventure, the Blue Party, is younger than
the Party of Agriculture and the Sports which seem to be
its solace. Lastly, he made use of words which I noted
down and now repeat, 'Show us that you mean peace, and
the Green Faction which has always stood for peace,
which seeks only peace, will by all its strength and all its
fervour work with you to make a lasting peace.' Only
show us that you mean peace, and the Green Faction
which has always stood for peace, which seeks only peace,
will by all its strength and with all its fervour work with
you to make a lasting peace. There you have the Green
Faction's declared policy; is that so?"

"Yes," the Greens cried, "but show that you mean
peace first."

"Do you repeat," Justinian said, "that you have always stood for peace?"

"Certainly," many voices cried.

"You declare before this Assembly that you seek only
peace?"

"Of course we do. Peace is only kept from us by the
Blues."

There was some roar of disturbance which lasted for
a couple of minutes.

"I have often wondered," Justinian said, "at the claims
so often advanced for what is called the honourable school
of war. That a man should risk his life for his City, his
Faith, or those dear to him, nothing is more noble. To
lay down your life for a friend, or for an ideal, what is
more beautiful? Yet when you consider the conduct of
any war, what of nobility do you find, and how much

barefaced, outrageous lying, treachery, double-dealing, deceit, fraud, meanness, cruelty, baseness? I rejoice that the Green Faction stands for peace, seeks for peace and will work for peace, yet though I rejoice to hear these declarations, I wonder that they should be made by such persons at such a time. It is in the knowledge of every Citizen within the City boundaries, that the Green Faction for the last few weeks has filled our streets with violence, woundings and oppressions, the prevention of free discussion and with murder and attempted murder."

Here the Green Faction rose and shouted at him. He remained calm; he looked Nicanor in the eye, and presently when the noise lapsed a little, held up his hand for silence and won it.

"I wonder," he went on, "at the assurance of politicians who say that they stand for peace, seek for peace and mean peace, when their aim, desire, pledged word and plighted hands are for war and bloodshed. I have here within my hand a remarkable document, drawn up only a few hours ago by you very men who now sit opposite to me and as one declare, in the presence of our spiritual leaders, that you seek only peace. In this document, you men, you there, sitting opposite to me, you Nicanor, you Kallimachus and your son, Kallisthenes, and you Menippos, covenant and agree with Archidamas and his friends, that they shall come down upon our Northern gates with seven thousand foot this afternoon. At the same time, you Nicanor agree with Kallimachus and his friends that they shall come down upon our Western gates with seven hundred horse, all equipped, armed, officered, and already upon the march hither. You covenant with them that you, by means of your gangs here, shall have the City Gates opened to them, and that together you will seize the person of the Emperor and the executive power and at once set up a provisional Government on the lines detailed in this Schedule. Here are the documents, three copies of them duly signed by you all and sealed with your private seals. These documents are your acts and deeds, they are evidence of the extent to which you stand for peace and seek it. Let me in justice gladly add that the names Hypatius and Pompeius are not among the signatories."

"Shew me that document," Nicanor said; "forgery is a very easy matter."

Justinian tossed a parchment across the table. "Forgery is by no means easy to honourable men," he said. "I hand this duplicate parchment deed to our Spiritual Father here. He will see that it is throughout in the hand of that man opposite, Philemon, letters from whom, for the easier comparison, are now in our Spiritual Father's hands. This agreement, signed and sealed by each one of you, is Archidamas' copy. I defy you to deny your signatures. Your usual signatures are here on the parchments lying on the table. Any one here can see that these documents are your acts and deeds. I defy you to hand me your signet rings. That ring upon your finger, Nicanor, is that of the Quadriga and Nike, here impressed. Your ring, Kallimachus, is the Persian Seal of the Running Gazelle, here imprinted. Yours, Theophrastus, is the double Corn-Ear, peculiar in this, that your seal has a chip in its left upper quadrant. Dare you show your ring to prove that it is not so?"

There was utter silence in the House. The Patriarch looked at the writing, compared it with some parchments already at his side, and then looked at Nicanor for some word of protest or explanation. Nicanor was calm. Kallimachus was clutching the table; Menippos was whispering curses; Philemon was as white as a ghost. Nicanor was the first of them to speak.

"I should like to look at that document, O Holy Father," he said.

"There is no need for you to take the Holy Father's copy," Justinian said. "I have here the copy belonging to Kallimachus, a duplicate in every way except in the colour of the seals. Kallimachus, as is well-known, uses always green wax instead of red." He held out a second parchment, but Nicanor did not offer to take it. He sat with a stern face staring at Justinian.

"Of course I must add," Justinian said, "that the Gate-Guards bribed by you to open the Gates to Archidamas and the others, were removed yesterday and the Gates closed. The arms stolen from the Palace for your gangs in The City were replaced within the Palace the day before."

The Green leaders sat confounded.

"Come then," Justinian said. "Is it not time that we threw aside our pretences? Is it not time to end these differences and the wars, confusion and ruin which must spring from them? I do not speak to you, Nicanor, but to you, Kallimachus, and you others. We are all men who love our City and her Faith; will you not take my hand and let us make a friendship? Here is our Holy Father, who is to all of us the representative of the God

in Whom we have our being; he, I know, will be our
help in the making of a peace. For this parchment, Kallimachus, I crumple it and fling it from me. See; that is
done; that is over. Now then, what about peace?"

Philemon was weeping; many people there were weeping. Pompeius was the first to speak. He came up to
Justinian and said, "Sir, here's my hand. I was ignorant
of this pact; since you cancel that parchment you cancel
all that might have made me support it."

"I am going out from here," Theophrastus said. He
rose unsteadily, and went out. It was strange to see people moving aside from him as they might from a leper.
Nicanor still looked at Justinian. In a dead silence, he
rose up and said,

"Your uncle or you, or the two between you, killed
my Brother, Theokritos. Do you think that I will accept
from you either the atrocity of that murder or the infamy of your forgiveness? I am Nicanor of the Bays.
You get no truce from me." He glanced to his side with
a sneering lip at the weeping Philemon. "What a puddle
some souls are, my God," he said. With this he thrust
aside his chair and bowed to the two Prelates.

Something made him look fixedly at the Patriarch.
Every eye in the house was fixed intently upon him. His
lip lifted in a sneer. "So, Holy Father," he said, "there
you are between your two thieves again. I am the im-
penitent one." He gave a little inclination of the head to
the Patriarch. He looked then at Kallimachus; again his
lip lifted. He saw that Kallimachus was both false and
mean. "For he had great possessions," he said. Theodora
then saw, what she had not before seen, that in the door-

way behind him certain men were standing. They wore the uniform of the Kingfishers, with blue birds broidered on the chests of their tunics; they were much splashed and caked with mud, and had neither washed nor shaved for days. These men closed in upon Nicanor and removed him. The House sat in utter stillness.

Suddenly the most marvellous voice in the Empire shouted from the gallery: "Well done, the Prince Justinian," and at once all burst into a storm of cheering. No such cheering had ever shaken the City Hall. Theodora saw Justinian very white, but smiling a little. She clapped her hands and wept and prayed while the cheering rose and roared. Presently it lulled, the Patriarch rose and said that all should give thanks, that plots against the Peace had been brought to nothing. "An offer of Peace is an offer of Christian Brotherhood," he said; "such an offer always triumphs in the end. Let us pray for Light and Peace."

Theodora had longed for a little word with Justinian, but there was no chance of that. When the Patriarch dismissed them, the Blue supporters came round him, lifted him aloft and bore him out, cheering. The house emptied. She saw white, terrified faces and radiant and ecstatic faces going out of the doors. At last she rose, weeping, and went somehow back to the Theatre. She was one of the last to leave the House. In the Theatre she went to Macedonia's dressing-room and sat there for a long time. Going out at last she ran into Sosthenes.

"Well, for once," he said, "your politics weren't so bad. I was there. Tino did well, didn't he? It was great luck the Kingfishers coming in as they did just before the curtain rose. I wonder how he got those documents."

"Wasn't that effective?" she said, "to bring them out like that and sweep them all off their feet. It was like a surprise in a play."

"I suppose some woman betrayed them," Sosthenes said; "generally there's a woman in it. There's a Persian proverb, 'Look for the woman.'"

"I won't let you say that a woman betrayed them. Women help; they don't betray," Theodora said. "Where would your Ballets be but for the women?"

"Ah," he said cynically, "I couldn't make illusions without illusions, could I?"

"The Green trouble will end with this," she said.

"It is over now," he answered. "The horse there are rounding up some gangs of disturbers. The streets are pretty free of them now. Some of the horse have been pushed out to the West to summon the parties there. It is odd how The City has gone all Blue in half an hour; you'll not see a Green favour anywhere. I was talking to old Theophanes just now. You know old Theophanes, the man who teaches us oratory? He hasn't a very choice reputation outside the Sixth Ward: in fact, he smells. He's a great speaker, but a very unscrupulous sort of low politician. He led the cheers at the Meeting. He said just now that Tino and Symmachus would sweep all the Tribes at the election; that after this, Hypatius won't get a single vote. Tino will be Consul, with Symmachus for a sort of make-weight. Tino has come on a lot since this morning. Half the City is going to the Palace now

to cheer him. This morning, I would have said he had
no great chance of being alive this evening, and no
chance whatever of being Emperor after Justo. It was as
near as that. Now I would say he will be Co-Emperor
as soon as he is Consul; he'll be on the coins next month
and on the throne at Easter. Justo'll resign or retire.
He's no longer able for it. You mark what I say, this
day has made Tino. Now, if he has the sense to marry
Kallimachus' sister, who has the birth he lacks, and
all the social graces, as well as a good deal of beauty,
he will make friends with his bitterest foes and be a most
successful Basileus."

This was a new thought to Theodora and a very bitter
one. It was so likely to be brought about. It was true that
the Green lords loathed Justinian, and that their loathing was shared by their womenkind. Yet all of them
were politically minded, ever scheming to keep and in-
crease their wealth and power. Was Kallimachus likely
to hesitate to urge his sister to marry Justinian and so
fuse the parties? If he did not, what was to save him
from confiscation and proscription?

By the next day all The City knew of Blue triumph
everywhere. The northern spearmen had retreated without fighting, in sad disorder from want of food; the
western horse had surrendered at Kallimachus' order.
Theophrastus, one of their advisers and suppliers, had
taken poison; Philemon, the vivid little man, who had
said that the Greens viewed Justinian more with pity
than with anger, had betrayed every man and secret
known to him. There was no doubt that Justinian was
the most popular man in The City; the Green revolt had

melted away. When the Consular election was held it seemed strange to most of the Citizens that anyone had ever considered a Green candidate as a possibility.

Theodora went to the outside of the City Hall to hear the result of the voting and to see the Consuls-Elect appear before the people to take the Oaths of Office.

A great crowd had gathered there in spite of a bitterly cold wind. She heard the comments of the crowd. "Six Ward has voted Blue solid, a thing never known before." "Tino is in, of course." "They say he's going to marry the Lady Aglae, Kallimachus' sister." "Lord," a man answered, "I should think he'd think twice about marrying into that fellow's family."

The tellers came forward to call the votings of the Tribes. Justinian and Symmachus were declared to be Consuls for the year by unanimous voting. She saw them come forward amid a roar of cheering to take the Oaths of Office. Usually the defeated candidates appeared to congratulate their adversaries, but Hypatius was not there. "He knows better," a man said. "He'd be hung if he appeared here."

She knew that the Emperor was ill abed but she wondered why the Empress had not come. A woman near her said, "Why isn't the Empress here?" Another woman replied, "Why, she has gone to the Nuns of St. Cleomene's, to arrange the Feast for the poor on Christmas Day." At this point there came a sudden hush. "Look," a man said, "There's the Lady Aglae. God, if she hasn't got some nerve."

Theodora looked, for the Lady Aglae was Kallimachus' sister. She came forward onto the stage towards the

Consuls-Elect. She was very graceful; she had much beauty of bearing; very pretty gold hair and a clever face with regular features. She held some sprays of olive which she tendered to the two Consuls.

"May I come?" she asked in a clear ringing voice, with the assurance that everybody would be glad to see her and to hear her. "May I come from the defeated Party to congratulate the Victors and to tender them these olive branches?"

Symmachus, who was the nearer to her, took the olive branches from her and said, "So old a Father Noah as myself is glad to take the olive from so fair a dove."

Everybody laughed and Aglae bowed and withdrew, having left an excellent impression upon everybody.

"These fair girls," Theodora thought, "who show every blush and are so willowy, what are they at thirty?" She knew very well that at thirty they would have won all the prizes and long since retired to enjoy them. Birth, wealth, leisure and much careful training had made it possible for Aglae to win these triumphs.

The play was now over; Theodora turned out of the crowd and set off home. She had not gone very far when she heard cheering, and saw a closed carriage trotting by with an escort in front and rear of trotting lancers. She knew at once that this was the Empress driving home from St. Cleomene's. She was recognised by the crowd and cheered with much good will. "Good old Pheemy," the boys cried. Theodora saw her, sitting in the carriage with her Chaplain, looking ill, she thought, and huddling against the cold.

When she reached home she found that there was a

note for her from the Empress' Chaplain, asking her if she could possibly come to the Palace that evening before sunset. She set forth and was presently admitted to the little room, where the Empress sat, huddled over the fire. She was looking very ill. Theodora knelt and kissed the hands stretched to her. She never was in the presence of Euphemia without having all the tenderness in her nature stirred to its depths.

"Madam," she said, "how can I tell you my gladness for your Cause and your nephew's triumph."

The old woman stroked her hair and said, "My dear, I've wanted to speak to you ever since the Meeting." She coughed a little and huddled nearer to the fire and said,

"Would you rub my hands, dear? I took cold, I think, at that cold Church of the Sisters." She gave her hands to be chafed, then withdrew them gently and again caressed Theodora's hair. "This dark hair," she said, "is worth all gold hair twice over. I never did hold with gold hair. You know who I'm speaking of?"

"Yes," Theodora said, "the Lady Aglae."

"That is it," the old woman said. "They've been getting at Justo, I mean the Emperor, that if Tino were to marry this gold hair he could end all the trouble."

"I don't doubt," Theodora thought, "and save Kallimachus, who is a convicted traitor, and save all the western estates which may be confiscated."

"You see, dear," the old woman went on, "the Emperor and I have had a saying since we came here, 'Purple must as purple is.' We can't think of what we would like, the same as other people; we must look to the power. Being Emperor and Empress isn't all silk under-

wear, like what I used to think it would be. I've seen it
with Justo. He'd have had not half the trouble he's had
on the Throne if I'd been one of these girls who go
about to the horse-races. You see, these nobles, as they're
called, are all related. When a man gets wealth from
robbing the State one way or another, they get hold of
him by marrying him to one of them; then they all hang
in a gang and do you down. I've seen this thing close,
dear, and suffered from it. I was born a slave; that's why
I wear high necks, dear, for the collar-galls show still.
I'm called Basilissa all over the world, but these people
know that I'm not Basilissa; I'm the slave-girl, Pheemie,
who followed the Regiment; they all know that, and I
see their sneers, though they think I don't, or if I do it
won't matter. And I don't mind much, dear, for I've got
Justo, who is a soldier, and one of the best for cavalry;
the Army will always follow Justo. But I have to think
now of Tino. We want him to be Emperor after Justo.
He isn't a soldier; the Army won't follow him; he'll have
to be Emperor by the priests and lawyers and old praefects and that; he'll have to be linked to these old purple-
gills, who got both hands in the Treasury somehow, and
now go to the race-meetings with their butlers and that.
They're all in here on their knees about it. Dear, this
Gold Hair, she would bring in all the western lords on
our side, who've been fighting us for years. Justo and
I've talked of it, and he said, 'You see the Theodora girl
and just show her that it is Tino's chance to settle the
State for the next hundred years.' She's got what he
needs, relations all over the Empire, all with pots of
money from what their fathers got, and thousands of

retainers. With her, he'll have the props he needs. Being
Emperor isn't all going in first and that; it's lying awake
thinking how to keep first; and Tino isn't one to think
of those things. You see, dear, I talk to you as I'd talk to
my daughter. I liked you from the first, and I know
you've got sense and can see it when it's put. It would
be pleasant to me and Justo to have you in the Palace,
let alone the joy to Tino, but ruin to the hope of him
being Emperor later. It would never do, even, for him to
be with you on the quiet, in the ringless way; the priests
would object. We've got to consider these things, so it
comes to this, dear, we shan't ask you here again, and we
shall put a squeeze on Tino who'll see it as we do. But
there, dear, I've been harsh which I don't want to be.
This race-course girl, who knows the betting and never
did her own hair, she won't know about priests and law
like you would, but she'll be able to prop Tino in the
ways he'll have to be propped. And now, dear, I don't
feel too well. It was cold at those Nuns in their stone corridors; for of course I always go barefoot like they do
to the Service. I'm not as young as I was. But I've talked
it out with you and been as I would with a daughter, if
I'd ever had one. You'll feel bitter with me at first, but
you'll come to see it as we do. Emperors can't marry as
they please, nor do much that they want to. You've got
such pretty hands, dear. You'll not mind my running on,
for I can't stand much more tonight, and can't give my
mind to being answered. I thought it best to say it all to
you. His uncle, my husband, the Emperor, will have it
all out with Tino. I must say that you've been a good
one. Now the last Emperor but one, he had someone he

wished to be Emperor after him and there was a girl in the way there. He sent for her and gave her a pot of money to go to live at Athens for a bit. You know I think a lot too much of you to offer anything of that kind. God forbid I'd ever think a girl like you could be bought. But I'm weary now. I'll ask you to go now. I've said it all. Only put it out of your head that you're to be Tino's. To be Empress is not much sport, when these Praefectual women, what I call race-meeting women, come by. Still, I've put some of them in the ashes they tried to put me in. There's some of them now that were in with Nicanor; they're ashy enough now in the cheek that were snorty when last we met. Nicanor's in his wet grave with the fishes at him. Still there it is. Kiss my hand, dear."

She held out her hand over which she had laboured long with ivy leaves, lemon-juice and other blanchers in the hope of whitening and smoothing what many years of toil and roughness had tanned and toughened. Theodora took it. She loved this old woman, this ex-slave and camp-follower, who had now blasted her hopes. She reflected that here she was, having her dismissal; this was the end. She would remember this little room forever. It had a fire, a small picture of the Annunciation, and great hangings of blue on which women had wrought the figures of the Apostles bringing the Gospels out of Heaven to Constantine. Well, this was sentence. There could be no appeal; one could not plead with Empire. She took the Empress' hand, caught it suddenly to her heart and kissed it.

"There, there," the old woman said, "young things

get over it. They're not like us; we don't heal at our age."

She seemed pathetically old and broken suddenly. She plucked a bell-rope by the fireside; her three waiting-women from Sardica appeared. They were tall, splendid and silent women, slippered with felt, wearing the long white robes with blue edging worn by all the servants of the Court. One of them bore in each hand a long thick white wax candle darkly smoking; the others bore blue blankets and over-wraps, which they placed about the Empress' shoulders.

"I shall go straight to bed," the old Empress said. "I cannot go to Chapel tonight. I will do penance tomorrow. Tell the Chaplain, one of you."

She turned to Theodora, and said, "You are young and strong; pray that it will be made easy for you. And pray for me, who am in need of guidance. Why is there no fire here?"

"There is a fire, Madam," Theodora said, for indeed some short blocks of dried ship-timber were burning well, and the old woman had been huddled over them.

"I am cold," she said, " the Nuns' corridor was so cold. I feel frozen stiff. Get me away then; why do you wait?"

They left the room.

When she was left alone Theodora stood looking into the fire, weeping silently. Some of the wood burned with vivid green flames. She felt crushed and weak, not for herself, but for life which struggles so hard, and then like this old Pheemie is broken and helped off the stage. She heard footsteps presently passing swiftly to and fro in the corridors; something was amiss. She knew that she had stood by the fire a long time, waiting the summons to go. Always until then she had been summoned to her carriage from the Palace. She thought, "Perhaps I am not again to be fetched away but may now walk. At least they shall tell me so."

Presently she heard the Emperor's voice at the end of the passage, asking, "Is she still there, then?" A servant said, "Yes, Lord." The halting step of the Emperor came along the passage and into the room.

As he closed the door, she knelt to him.

"Ah, girl," he said, "I did not hear you were still here."

She saw that he was all shaken and quaking.

"Oh, Sir," she said, "is the Empress ill?"

He sat in the chair in which the Empress had sat and said, "She's had one of these strokes." He began to weep and at the same time to swear, "Dammy, dammy, dammy, my poor little Pheemie."

"Sir," Theodora said, "I love her too, may I go to her?"

"I wouldn't mind if it was me," he said; "I'd hoped to go before her, what with my wound."

"Let me come with you to her," Theodora said.

"We've been together all the time," he said, "ever since Squadron C. The doctor said she'd never stand another of these strokes, and now it's come."

She took his hand and kissed it and wept upon it. They were somehow drawn very close in that moment of misery.

"We may as well go," he said; "we'll do no good, though."

He stood up, with some difficulty, and said, "You'll have to help me, girl, my wound's worse now than it's ever been."

She put her arm about him to support him.

"Girl," he said, "I was at Pheemie all the morning to put you away, to let that Gold Hair have Tino, and end this mess. Pheemie didn't want to. Did she put you away?"

"Yes, Lord," Theodora whispered. The Emperor's tears ran down his cheeks. Justinian had come in while they were speaking.

"She's not going to be put away," he said. "Will you come now? We can be with her now. The room is cleared. Theodora is going to be my wife even if I lose the purple by it. But she will be my only claim to the purple. Come, Theodora, we must almost carry him."

It was announced the next day by Heralds, that the prayers of the public were asked to remember the Empress Euphemia, now sorely ill. A special Service of Intercession was held. Then Heralds proclaimed that Almighty God had thought fit to take to Himself their sovereign Lady and Basilissa, the Consort of their Ruler, and that all The City should mourn.

On the day appointed for the funeral, The City was in the gloom of purple and black, with bells tolling and all streets crowded with sightseers. The Empress had asked that she might be buried in the little Chapel of St. Artemidorus, off the old aisle of Santa Sophia, so to that white and perfect shrine her little shrunken shell was carried. The Guards lined the streets; the Officers of the House led the procession; then came the Sardican pipers, playing their famous lament:

"The deer is lost to the forest,
  The otter is gone from the brook,
  Away is the bird of our joy."

Then came all Squadron C, in their blue with black plaids tossed over their shoulders; then the women of Sardica, her servants; then upon a transport waggon of Squadron C came all that was mortal of Pheemie, and then three figures walking together, the Emperor, Justinian and Theodora, followed by Symmachus and the Municipality, the Praefects, the University, and the banners of the Provinces borne by the men of the Navy. The Emperor walked with difficulty, gritting his teeth against the pain and the grief, and sometimes groping for support to those who walked by him.

Sightseers asked, "Who is that woman in black?" Those who knew the gossip said, "That is Theodora. She's betwitched Tino somehow. She's one of these dancers; she's one of these clutchers; she's got her fangs into him. He's going to marry her. It is an infamy."

Theodora knew well what they were saying and would say. She was at peace. She knew that she was one of this Royal family, as much one as the strand of a rope is the rope and its strength. She had seen the dying Empress recognize her and bless her as Tino's affianced bride.

Soon they had laid the old Empress away before the

Altar of St. Artemidorus of Syme, and had moved to the
High Altar of the Great Church. Here, beside the Patriarch, the Emperor declared that from that moment his
nephew, the Prince Justinian, Consul-Elect, Commander
of the Armies, would be his associate upon the throne,
co-equalled, co-powered.

Justinian came forward and knelt before the Patriarch,
and swore upon the Gospels to uphold Faith, do Justice
and practice Charity.

When he had taken the Oaths, he rose and took Theodora's hand. "Before God and men," he said, "I pledge
my troth to the Lady Theodora."